Praise for *Pilgrims* by Garrison Keillor

"In *Pilgrims*, Keillor weaves the same magic of his radio shows and his live appearances: He describes our own hopes and disappointments in such a way that pain and pleasure are mingled in an instant, and it's impossible to keep from laughing." —*Santa Barbara Independent*

"Keillor's self-mocking humor is simply delightful." —*Dayton Daily News*

"Chaucerian . . . After reading *Pilgrims* you'll be left with a big smile in your heart and perhaps just a wee tear in your eye. What could be more vintage Garrison Keillor than that?" —bookreporter.com

Praise for the Lake Wobegon novels

"A literary cartographer would find it necessary to trace, in forceful blue lines, tributary streams running from Mark Twain and Sherwood Anderson to the Wobegonian river of stories and novels that has issued from Garrison Keillor for more than twenty years. Not that Keillor's waters are larger . . . but because of similarities in sensibilities and focus. [The Lake Wobegon stories] manage to rev up emotional torque as if from nowhere, evoking a sense of heartache or longing, or perhaps guffaws instead." —*Chicago Tribune*

"[Keillor's] novels are edgier, racier, and more satirical than his radio monologues. [*Liberty* is] a kind of literary vaudeville, fueled by words such as 'galoot' and 'Shnozzola' and Keillor's wondrously long, wandering sentences." —*USA Today*

"Keillor's genius lies in the fact that after you finish reading this, you don't despair. He makes a strong case for the innate decency of the ocarina player, pig-manure vendors and even an odious governor and would-be member of Congress as they sweatily pursue their political ambitions. This is parody, of course, but—not for the first time—the bizarre reality of our actual politics outshines any parody that can be imagined." —*The Washington Post*

"What is it about the works of Garrison Keillor that keeps readers coming back for more? Keillor offers a basic comfort, like ice cream. In his narratives, the things we hope are true about life are confirmed: Those who preach holier-than-thou homilies will fall on their face; the hardworking farmer and his hardworking wife will be rewarded, even if it's only in a smallish sort of way; and the kids of Lake Wobegon will grow up to be, if not what their parents dream of, at least decent human beings. By reminding us of those things that are just stupid (and silly, and full of Keillor's hilarious invention), we let go of them, laugh at ourselves and our foibles and return to the common sense and courtesy we imagine—we hope, we pray—underlies the human condition." —*Los Angeles Times*

"It's Keillor's delivery—a sort of hushed, Thoarzine-inflected irony—that makes him such a draw." —*The Seattle Times*

"*Pontoon* is smart, it's well-written. . . . Keillor's approach in this very enjoyable novel is to lay out, one after another, the enormous inventory of his small-town character's quirks. Only a virtuoso could carry off such a method." —*Daily News* (New York)

"The jokes and themes [in *Pontoon*] will be familiar to Keillor's radio fans. But the tone is edgier. Keillor makes humor look easy." —*USA Today*

"[A] delightful latest addition to the Lake Wobegon series . . . there's plenty of fun to be had with the well-timed deadpans and homespun wit." —*Publishers Weekly*

"Full of odd twists and crazy (but lovable) characters . . . Wild surprises abound, but behind the chaos is a stirring tale about being true to yourself on all of life's little journeys." —*Parade*

"This is no 'aw, shucks' story. It's a book . . . about absorbing what life hands us and living with excitement into old age." —*St. Paul Pioneer Press*

"A hyper-busy slice of small-town life of the sort that Keillor regularly exploits so hilariously and affectingly, and the moral of which may be that we'd all best be humble. Only comedian of horrors Christopher Moore, in his tales of Pine Cove, California, rivals Keillor as a provincial farceur." —*Booklist*

ABOUT THE AUTHOR

Garrison Keillor was born in Anoka, Minnesota, and graduated from the University of Minnesota, one more English major. He pitched for the Jack's Auto Repair softball team, did an early morning radio show for ten years, lived in Copenhagen for a time, and sang bass in the Hopeful Gospel Quartet. Also sang with the New York Philharmonic and the Boston Pops. He owns a bookstore in St. Paul and is the author of 77 *Love Sonnets*. He has done his one-man show in theaters coast to coast. In July 2009, he celebrated the thirty-fifth anniversary of *A Prairie Home Companion*. His daily "Writers Almanac" has been on the air since 1993. He lives in St. Paul and New York City.

GARRISON KEILLOR

Pilgrims

A LAKE WOBEGON ROMANCE

PENGUIN BOOKS

PENGUIN BOOKS

Published by the Penguin Group

Penguin Group (USA) Inc., 375 Hudson Street, New York, New York 10014, U.S.A.

Penguin Group (Canada), 90 Eglinton Avenue East, Suite 700, Toronto,
Ontario, Canada M4P 2Y3 (a division of Pearson Penguin Canada Inc.)

Penguin Books Ltd, 80 Strand, London WC2R 0RL, England

Penguin Ireland, 25 St Stephen's Green, Dublin 2, Ireland (a division of Penguin Books Ltd)

Penguin Group (Australia), 250 Camberwell Road, Camberwell,
Victoria 3124, Australia (a division of Pearson Australia Group Pty Ltd)

Penguin Books India Pvt Ltd, 11 Community Centre, Panchsheel Park, New Delhi – 110 017, India

Penguin Group (NZ), 67 Apollo Drive, Rosedale, North Shore 0632,
New Zealand (a division of Pearson New Zealand Ltd)

Penguin Books (South Africa) (Pty) Ltd, 24 Sturdee Avenue,
Rosebank, Johannesburg 2196, South Africa

Penguin Books Ltd, Registered Offices:
80 Strand, London WC2R 0RL, England

First published in the United States of America by Viking Penguin,
a member of Penguin Group (USA) Inc. 2009
Published in Penguin Books 2010

1   3   5   7   9   10   8   6   4   2

Copyright © Garrison Keillor, 2009
All rights reserved

PUBLISHER'S NOTE

This is a work of fiction. Names, characters, places, and incidents are either the product
of the author's imagination or are used fictitiously, and any resemblance to actual persons,
living or dead, business establishments, events, or locales is entirely coincidental.

THE LIBRARY OF CONGRESS HAS CATALOGED THE HARDCOVER EDITION AS FOLLOWS:

Keillor, Garrison.

Pilgrims : a Wobegon romance / by Garrison Keillor.

p.   cm.

ISBN 978-0-670-02109-3 (hc.)
ISBN 978-0-14-311785-8 (pbk.)

1. Lake Wobegon (Minn. : Imaginary place)—Fiction.   2. Americans—Italy—
Rome—Fiction.   3. Minnesota—Fiction.   4. Rome (Italy)—Fiction.   I. Title.

PS3561.E3755P56   2009
813'.54—dc22   2009024891

Printed in the United States of America
Set in Aldus with Commons
Designed by Daniel Lagin

PILGRIMS:
A WOBEGON ROMANCE

The Pilgrims

1. MARJORIE (MARGIE) KREBSBACH, English teacher
2. CARL KREBSBACH, carpenter
3. DARYL TOLLERUD, farmer
4. MARILYN TOLLERUD, conference facilitator
5. CLINT BUNSEN, co-owner, Bunsen Motors
6. IRENE BUNSEN, tomato grower
7. ELOISE KREBSBACH, mayor
8. WALLY KREUGER, barkeeper
9. EVELYN KREUGER, barkeeper's keeper
10. FATHER WILMER, priest
11. LYLE JANSKE, biology teacher (ret.)
12. GARY KEILLOR, radio show host

From our small town the group had come
To view the glory that was Rome
Wellspring of art and poetry
And so much of our curriculum,
Science and mathematics and more recently
Pizza whose richness our pilgrims knew
Quite well. Now of this company
Of twelve citizens, good and true,
Was one named Marjorie Krebsbach
Who had assembled the crew
(Though she was shy and slow to talk)
To carry out a mission: to place
A photograph upon a burial rock
And give to grief a proper face
Of a young man lost in the Great War
And say a prayer for God's abundant grace.
But something else she traveled for
And that was to warm her husband's heart
Which had turned cold. For more
Than three months they'd slept apart
And she intended, if the truth be told,
To reignite his passion and to start
A new romance out of the old,
Which some say is impossible.
But they have not read St. Matthew's gospel,
The promise of the resurrection—
Mortality may change direction.
And that was why she flew to Rome,
To win his heart and bring him home.

DA VINCI

⁓⊹⊱≺≻⊰⊹⁓

The first of the pilgrims through the International Arrivals portal at Leonardo da Vinci was Margie Krebsbach, face scrubbed, fresh, grinning, towing her husband Carl who looked stunned as if struck by a ball-peen hammer, and then the others came slouching and shuffling along, jet-lagged, brain-dead, and right away she spotted the thin, spiky-haired man in the blue blazer holding up a sign—LAKE WOBEGON—in one hand, high, and she let out a whoop and let go of Carl. "This is *so neat!*" she said, meaning the sign—the words "Lake Wobegon"—here!—in Italy!—Great God! "We have to take a picture." So she pulled out her little PikClik as the other pilgrims groaned. *Please. No photography, please. And no whooping. Please. No enthusiasm.* None of them had slept much on the flight from Minneapolis to Amsterdam thanks to a small child named Rose who wandered up and down the aisles pinching people with slimy fingers and then the flight to Rome had hit turbulence over the Alps, a death-envisioning experience (12 MINNESOTANS AMONG THOSE LOST IN PLANE CRASH; EN ROUTE TO ROME TO HONOR FALLEN WAR HERO, THEY PERISH IN FLAMES ON SNOW-CAPPED MATTERHORN) and

3

now they were hoping for a soft place to lie down for a day or two. Lyle looked as if he'd been held hostage aboard a fishing trawler, lying on a pile of deceased halibut. Wally and Evelyn appeared to be under the control of aliens. Clint and Irene looked as if they should not be allowed to operate motor vehicles. Daryl had a weird smile on his face, as if he'd come to Rome with a sackful of dough from the church-building fund. Father Wilmer looked very bleak, as if he had seen unspeakable things up close. Eloise looked as if she had just eaten a plateful of boiled thistles. Carl appeared heavily medicated, and in fact was. A double dose of Placidol. Mr. Keillor was lifting his feet, first one, then the other, left, right, left, right, and trying to remember the word (English) for what he had taken two of on the plane to help him sleep. They were all off-kilter except Margie, standing arm in arm with the man from Columbo Travel. She looked simply terrific. Never better. Big smile, hair in place, stylish in black warm-up pants and green satin jacket, a brown fedora on her head, classy new black horn-rimmed glasses. She'd bought the hat in the Amsterdam airport. An impulse. A hundred euros. What the hell. She was stoked. Pumped. "We're in Italy! Italy!" she cried. The spiky-haired man smiled wanly, having been born in Italy, descended from Italians. He wore gray slacks and a blue blazer with a gold crest on the pocket, COLUMBO TOURS. She wanted to hug him but he stepped away, so she hugged Carl instead. "We made it, sweetheart. Good job!" And to the porter pushing the cart of luggage behind: *"Avanti!"*

Carl had been afraid of flying since a trip to New York three years ago to see Carla after she had phoned home to ask if she was covered by their health insurance (no) and he sensed pregnancy and flew out to see her (she wasn't but she read to him from a book about girls who grow up with emotionally distant fathers who are unable to form lasting relationships, and she cried and cried) and he went to the airport feeling dark and gruesome and on the way home, the plane hit teeth-shaking turbulence over Lake Michigan. An overhead popped open and an enormous black bat flew out and Carl screamed and threw up his hands and broke its neck and it fell on him, dying, flapping its great leathery wings. He jumped out of his seat and the flight attendant yelled at him to sit down, dammit. And the woman whose bat it was, a noted Berkeley bat researcher seated next to him, took the corpse and screeched at him for fifteen minutes that bats are harmless and any ten-year-old child knows that and he had gone and killed a rare specimen from the upper Amazon and upset the balance of the ecosystem and pushed the Earth closer to extinction. "Killer," she hissed. "You. You're a killer." As a result, Carl hadn't flown until now, a ten-hour flight from Minneapolis-St. Paul to Amsterdam and a two-hour flight to Rome. He had been inert with terror the whole time, silent, stiff, eyes open, respirating, refusing food and drink. "I'm proud of you, sweetheart," she said. He did not seem to recognize her. "I'm your wife, Margie," she said. "The mother of your babies. Isn't this romantic? *Italy.*"

Mr. Columbo got to work organizing the bags and Margie beamed at her group. "A historic moment deserves a group picture!" cried Margie. "Come on, squeeze together like you know each other," she cried. She pointed to Mr. Keillor at the rear.

"Take a picture," she said. She thrust the camera at him. He didn't understand—he was accustomed to being the photo-graphee. "Take it!" she said. "The camera. Take the camera."

"What do you want?" he said.

"We want you to take our picture with the tour guy."

"Couldn't we—" And then it dawned on him. He was not part of the "we"—he was *him*, a big cheese in the radio world maybe but an outrider among his landsmen, an addendum, a curio, a cigar-store Indian. He took the camera from Margie, or almost did, and it clattered on the floor. She picked it up. "Are you okay?" she said. "I thought you had traveled overseas before."

He looked at the little silver camera. "Doesn't this have a timer so we can—"

"No," she said. "It doesn't. Just shoot."

And the eleven of them, five in front, six in back, squeezed in tight. "Tighter," she said. They squeezed some more. "Cheese," said Evelyn. "Ovaries," said Margie. Mr. Keillor pushed the but-ton and nothing happened. "Lens cap!" cried Eloise.

"My Uncle Will was the first one to get a Kodak box camera with a timer," Evelyn said. "He was so pleased with himself for figuring out how to use it. He took hundreds of self-portraits. Pictures of himself, you know. Him with his old Packard. Him at the jigsaw. Him mowing the grass. Him lying in bed with Miriam. Oh, that upset her! She thought he'd lost his marbles. But there they are in that little double bed and his eyes are closed and hers are open."

The word he was looking for was Dramamine: he'd taken one when the plane lifted off from Minneapolis and it hadn't kicked in. He was wedged into seat 33J because Irene Bunsen had bullied him into giving up his first-class seat to Lyle Janske who she said was in bad shape having gotten the bad news that he had Alzheimer's. "This may be his last trip as the Lyle we know," she said. "Let's let him have the shrimp cocktail and lamb chops on jasmine rice and Merlot and *you* have the box lunch."

Well, how could you argue with that? So the radio man wound up sandwiched between a large embittered man and his angry wife with a fretful child on her lap, a couple from Rapid City, South Dakota, and no, they did not want to change seats with him so they could sit together. She was going to Rome to take up a fellowship at the American Academy and he was going along to provide child care. The child had colic. Mr. Keillor took another pill over Newfoundland. The child slept for an hour and resumed screaming on the descent into Amsterdam—meanwhile the woman had recognized Mr. Keillor and chose that moment to tell him that she used to listen to his radio show. She emphasized the "used to" as if it were some odd aberration like being addicted to butterscotch. "I have one word of advice for you," she said. "Don't sing. Someone should've told you this years ago. You're not a singer. Don't sing." The pill kicked in as the plane pulled up to the gate in Amsterdam and he was awakened by the cleaning crew, tiny Indonesian women with backpack vacuums. He thought he had landed on another planet. All of the passengers and crew were gone. He had to jog through the terminal to catch the plane to Rome and it was not lost on him that nobody in his group had come looking for him. Nobody. He hurtled down the Jetway as the lady gate agent was about to swing the plane door shut and she muttered something in Dutch that sounded like *dummkopf*. He sat down next to Daryl who said, "We were all discussing whether you'd gained weight or not. It looks to me like you have. Have you?"

He had come on the trip because he thought he could get a book out of it. A little comic novel called *Veni Vidi Vickie* about a Minnesota divorcée who goes to Rome to find the meaning of life and falls in love with a tall, dark stranger who turns out to be from Minnesota. The stranger is in public radio and yet he is a comely man with terrific abdominals and (as she discovers one evening) a terrific dancer and fabulous lover, so together they climb the heights of ecstasy on a fine king-size mattress in a four-star hotel. The Chopin etude "Tristesse" is playing, children laugh and play in the courtyard below. They lie quietly in each other's arms and he says, "Life is insurmountable and yet we mount up again and again and ride, glorious and free, across the river and into the golden uplands, hoping against hope, longing for that for which there are no words." And she whispers, "Thanks for being so wonderful." Something like that. The next thing he knew, the plane had touched down in Rome. Daryl said, "What's it like, being famous? You enjoy strangers coming up to you and fawning over you? I wouldn't, but I suppose some people eat it right up." And then he was standing in the terminal with a camera in his hand. "Just take the lens cap off and point and shoot," said Eloise.

And so the first record of their pilgrimage to Italy was a picture, slightly out of focus, of the eleven of them, large white sleepy people from the northern prairie leaning against each other, exhausted, vertiginous, smirking at the lens-cap mishap and the word "ovaries," namely:

The anxious and earnest Carl Krebsbach, president of Krebs-bach Construction, husband of Margie, father of Carla, Carl Jr., and Cheryl, and now the owner by default of a half-finished three-bedroom chalet on a two-acre lot on Lake Wobegon, built for a wealthy Minneapolis investment banker named Ladder-man who is now in the midst of a bitter divorce on account of a dalliance with a 26-year-old receptionist whom he promised to take on a 21-day cruise to New Zealand.

Ruddy, genial Daryl Tollerud, partner with his old man in a six-hundred-acre hog-and-corn operation. Father of four. Farmer of the Year in 1988 and 1997. In 1974 he missed two free throws and cost Lake Wobegon the District 47 basketball trophy. Score tied, one second left on the clock, all he had to do was make one free throw. He didn't. St. Agnes won in sudden-death over-time. *St. Agnes!*

The gracious and kindly Marilyn Tollerud, wife of Daryl and owner/operator of Mid-Country Meetings & Conferences Inc., which organizes public events such as the recent two-day Revitalizing Rural Minnesota Through Diversity, fourteen hours of earnest Lutheran discourse about (1) the need to cel-ebrate who we are and (2) joyfully embrace those who are different.

The likable and capable Clint Bunsen, head mechanic at the Ford garage and former chair of the Fourth of July parade, now, after a flagrant love affair with the young Angelica (who marched as the Statue of Liberty), more or less reconciled with his wife. . . .

The plainspoken and observant Irene Bunsen, gardener, mother, Girl Scout leader and camper (against her will but someone must do it), perpetual grand champion of the Mist County Fair Tomato Sweepstakes, committed to Clint, "in for the penny, in for the pound."

The brave and beleaguered Eloise Krebsbach, four-term mayor of Lake Wobegon, mother of three, brokenhearted now, having been dumped by longtime lover and volunteer fireman Fred Peterson, after all she'd done for him, including getting him into AA, where he met someone younger and perkier.

The sagacious and steady Wally Kreuger, owner of the Side-track Tap, and long-ago batting champion (.324) for the Lake Wobegon Whippets, which you would not guess by looking at him. A pillar of the Legion and the Knights of the Plume Columnar, but also a bartender, sympathetic to man's failings.

The watchful and matronly Evelyn Kreuger, née Schoppenhorst, wife of Wally, cousin of Margie, famous for her Nutty Nougat Coconut Caramel Bars, and longtime president of Catholic Mothers for Decency.

The patient and soft-spoken Father Wilmer, pastor of Our Lady of Perpetual Responsibility, a voice for tolerance and mercy (which leads some to suspect he has dark secrets, perhaps a lover somewhere, a gambling addiction, a faith problem). In November he was seen entering a storefront in St. Cloud that houses a tanning salon, a women's crisis center, and a psychotherapist's office. Father has no tan whatsoever. Never did.

The laid-back and long-suffering Lyle Janske, newly retired biology teacher at Lake Wobegon High, married to Carl's sister Ardis. He thinks it is a hormone deficiency, not Alzheimer's, having researched it online, and is taking large gelatinous capsules purchased from a source in Costa Rica. Ardis couldn't come: she needed a break from Lyle.

"Okay!" cried Margie. "Your bags are in the van! Let's add 'em up and move 'em out! Let's go have fun!" And turned and marched out to the curb and they slouched along behind and onto the white van, a 12-seater, as Margie sang:

Fight, fight, Lake Wobegon!
Go, go, you Leopards.
Fake to the left and right,
And run past them—up the center!

It's the leader's job to be positive and she was the leader now. *She had never been a leader before in her entire life.* Fifty-three years old and she'd always trotted along like a good girl, helping the nuns, clapping the erasers, a very quiet good girl who got good grades, joined clubs, wrote poems, married, raised kids, never a leader, and when Carl's sister Eloise moved back to Lake Wobegon from Minneapolis, her with her booming voice and confident clear-cut sentences, and was elected mayor, Margie deferred to her, but now Eloise was cast down by the loss of the treacherous Fred, and the torch had been passed. Thrilling. Absolutely thrilling. Having spent decades tolerating dopes and bores and obeying braggarts and petty tyrants, to at last emerge from her cocoon as a Benevolent Leader of Her People on an Expedition to a Distant Land.

In the Amsterdam airport, she'd spotted a book called *How to Deal with Impossible People* and snapped it up. The first rule was "Always Be Confident." "Start every endeavor with a surplus of Positive Energy." "Be a Builder-Upper." "Do not anticipate failure." Which struck her as profound—the sort of wisdom you'd never learn in Lake Wobegon, a colony of doubters and backbiters. And then, moments later, she saw Eloise weeping afresh over Fred and sat down and patted her hand. And Eloise was holding a sheet of paper that a strange woman had handed her.

A WORD TO THE AMERICAN TRAVELLER

Rome remains a hotbed of terrorist activity in the Mediterranean, with daily car bombings, knee-cappings, abductions, assassinations, and random killings. Most events go unreported in the mainstream media, which derives a good deal of ad revenue from the tourism cartels.

If you must visit Rome, follow a few sensible guidelines.

1. Do not wear American clothing. Buy Italian clothing as soon as you arrive, to reduce the chance of your becoming the target of a political shooting or bomb explosion.
2. Do not speak English. Gesture with hand signals.
3. Do not flash large amounts of cash. If you must use an ATM machine, find one on an isolated street, or one that is in a recessed alcove.
4. If you feel you're being followed, go to a police station and be prepared to pay a fee (in cash) for protection.
5. Do not ride in cabs or on buses. Walk. Stay close to buildings. Never cross a street except in a throng.

6. Do not go out in the evening.

7. Avoid bathing, if possible. Strong body odor has been shown to be effective in warding off terrorist attacks.

8. Avoid tourist attractions, such as the Colosseum or St. Peter's or the Spanish Steps.

9. Avoid eye contact. Look at the ground. Smiling is not a good idea. Terrorists are offended by laughter and may lash out at people they perceive as lighthearted.

10. Do not drink coffee except in tiny cups. People with coffee mugs are presumed to be Americans. Drink tea, with milk.

Eloise thrust it at Margie. "Oh my God," she said, "we are in trouble now. See what you've gotten us into. A nun gave this to me. A nun."

"Listen," Margie said. "This is hogwash. Pure idiocy. We're perfectly safe." She tore the sheet into tiny pieces.

"You don't think we should talk this over?"

"Damn it to hell, Eloise. Just pull yourself together, willya? Get a grip."

Eloise was stunned. Margie never cursed—never ever. "You don't think we should—" Margie took hold of her shoulders and shook her. "Listen to me. Just grow up! I mean it! Get over it!"

Eloise nodded.

And right there was where Margie took command, pushing Eloise around, telling her to grow up. Anyway, the trip had been her idea from Day One. It was she who called them up in January and said, "Guess what? Carl and I are going to Rome. Want to go?" Where? Italy. Kind of expensive, isn't it? Hey, a person only lives once. *I've heard that. How much does it cost?* Less than you'd think. So she bought the plane tickets from a web site called Cheapskate.com and booked the hotel and phoned the pilgrims with regular helpful reminders (Passport. Cash card. Adapters for electric shavers.) and shepherded them onto the plane in Minneapolis (*What if someone else has taken our seat?*) and through Schiphol in Amsterdam (*Why do we have to wait so long at Passport Control when the Europeans go scooting on through?*) and into Rome (*Was it okay that I packed some Nut Goodies in my suitcase? What if they search my bag? I see the sign about not bringing food products into Italy—is Nut Goodie a food product? Should I tell the police or should I sneak into a restroom and flush it down the toilet?*). And she had dealt with Evelyn who sat there in Amsterdam holding a small cardboard box someone had given her.

Who was it?

"I don't know. He just asked me to take it on the plane for him."

Oh my God. Evelyn!

"What's wrong?"

So she grabbed the box and threw it into a stairwell. And she herded them away to a coffee bar where Marilyn had a meltdown while looking at a chicken salad sandwich and burst into tears and said, "Why didn't I bring Mother along? She would've loved to come. I never even thought to ask her. Oh my God. She was probably just waiting for me to say something and I never did. She's still hale and hearty, she could've come and enjoyed this. It might be *her last chance.* And I didn't even think to mention it. *It didn't even cross my mind!*" And she wept. "I am a bad person," she said. "God is going to punish me, I know it. I just hope he spares my kids." Oh, it was the old Midwestern ritual of brutal self-accusation—out of pure vanity people lashing into themselves—*how worthless I am!*—and thereby dragging sympathy and praise out of you—No, you are *not* a bad person, you are a *good* person, and no we don't hate you, not at all, we all *love* you. Indeed, we do. So she had comforted Marilyn and rounded up the sheep and moved them to the next plane and on the flight to Rome she had reminded Lyle why they were going to Rome—to put a picture on Gussie Norlander's grave—and at the Customs counter she said *Buon giorno* to the policeman who checked her passport and *Grazie* when he handed it back—and at the baggage carousel she had spotted a porter and tapped him on the shoulder and said "*Per favore, signore,*" and so well, with rolled *R*'s and all, that his face lit up and he poured out his heart to her in Italian and she simply raised her hand and said, "*Sono Americano*— I'd rather speak English. Thank you. *Grazie.*" And the man grinned and squeezed out some English. She handed him ten euros, he brought a cart for the bags. So cool. Eloise whispered, "Where did you learn that?" "In the movies," she said.

True. *Roman Holiday* starring Audrey Hepburn as a princess spinning around Rome on the back of a Vespa, her arms around Gregory Peck. Margie saw it in high school and Audrey became her patron saint whom she tried to emulate, her ballerina elegance, her bubbly demeanor, though bubbliness did not come naturally in Lake Wobegon. People tended to be dry. A woman who bubbled was considered ditzy. You were supposed to be a little dark. Treat yourself to dark scenarios about your kids, the schools, the elms, the future of the bluebird species. Any effervescence was a symptom of unreliability. If you bubbled, people didn't want their kids to ride in your car.

She took a deep breath and put on an Audrey smile and cried, "We are going to have *such fun* in Italy! Fun such as you cannot even imagine! Boy O boy O boy. This is one for the history books! C'mon, let's see some happy faces! Smile, darn ya! You people look like somebody peed on your sugar bread. Lighten up! We're on vacation! Seven glorious nights and six fun-filled days!" She poked Carl. "Right?" "Right," he said. She got in the shotgun seat in the big white van as Mr. Columbo loaded the bags in back. Enormous bags. The others had packed like refugees who might never see home again. For her: two carry-ons. Underwear, jeans and pullovers, one black dress, one pair of walking shoes. "If I need more, I can buy it there," she told Marilyn. "It's only a week." Marilyn admitted she had brought four sweaters *Four sweaters?* Four sweaters. Just in case.

Marilyn, Eloise, Evelyn sat in the second seat; Wally, Irene, Lyle, in the third; Carl, Daryl, Clint, Father, in the backseat. Mr. Keillor stood by the open door, waiting for someone to scooch over. "Jump in," said Margie. "Where?" he said. "Anywhere." The seat with the three ladies was full and so was the second, what with Irene parking her carry-on bag next to her. Father Wilmer said, "I'm afraid there's no leg room back here. It's tight for me and you have longer legs." Finally, Irene heaved a sigh and moved the carry-on bag onto her lap and Lyle swung his legs out to allow the radio host to squeeze in between him and Irene—"I have to sit on the outside on account of my knees," he said. So Mr. Keillor found himself wedged in tight, trapped, like a caged animal. He slipped his left arm around onto the seat back behind Irene—to make more room—and she said, "Don't." So he had to sit crooked, Lyle's elbow in his kidneys. When the van pulled away and bounced in a pothole, it sent shock waves up his spine. Just last Friday, a black limo had picked him up at LaGuardia and taken him to Town Hall for *A Prairie Home Companion,* where he shared a dressing room with Yo-Yo Ma who was gracious and treated him like Somebody, and now here he was back in the fourth grade among cruel bus mates. "We may need a bigger van," he muttered. "Some of us may need to lose weight," said Irene. She sighed a long articulate sigh. Which he remembered suddenly and very clearly from years ago.

They were juniors in high school. It was May. She and he, sitting on the iron rail by the side door to the gymnasium. Under an old wounded elm tree split by lightning and still alive. Sun pouring down, she in her white blouse and denim wrap skirt, a half circle of sweat under her arms. He, not daring to look at her:

"I was thinking about going to the Prom but I don't know. I might have other plans. It's hard to tell. Were you planning to go?"

"You mean, to the Prom?"

"Yes."

And then he realized that she did not want to go to the Prom with him nor anywhere else. She did not want to be sitting there beside him. There was magnetic repulsion going on. She was about to throw up her arms and scream, "Get this person away from me!"

"Oh, I'm sorry," he said. "I just realized, I can't go, I told some people I'd do something else. Sorry."

"That's okay," she said. She gave him a sidelong glance and in that glance he withered like a delicate shrub in a hard frost. Here he had almost asked her to the Prom, had opened the door to the possibility of his perhaps asking her, and then withdrawn this non-offer. Then she cried, "Hey! What took you so long!!" to some guys in a souped-up Model T pulling up and she ran and jumped in the backseat.

And now, years later, he was that kid all over again, seventeen years old and six three, 150 pounds, high-water pants, size thirteen shoes, horn-rimmed glasses slipped down on his nose, short hair shaved up high in back, pipsqueak arms, solemn voice that broke into adolescent duck quacks. Why had he come on this trip? Some dark lust for punishment had driven him to travel back to the Land of Pain.

And he was subsidizing the trip! Oh God. The ultimate irony! Fifty-seven thousand dollars he was paying!

You escape the cold steel bars of high school and go off to a happy life in radio broadcasting as the host of your own show and then, through weird circumstance, you donate money to pay for your old neighbors to visit Rome and you go along for the honor of the thing and they punish you for your good deed. What a dope! Dumbhead! *Stoopnagel!* You could've spent that money on a fourteen-day luxury cruise on the Baltic and instead you are jammed into a van with the Jealous & Resentful!

The van hurtled down a ramp to the freeway, hit another pot-hole, which drove a nail into Mr. Keillor's spine, and flew past construction sites, piles of concrete slabs and logs and gravel, and then a grove of palm trees and twelve-foot rosebushes. They drove through a little village, tangles of fencing and bungalows perched on hills, clinging to steep rocky slopes. It looked like California. Apartment buildings and every apartment with a balcony that overflowed with billows of flowering vines. Margie leaned forward and tried to commit it all to memory. She had expected Italy to be exotic, swarthy men sitting on wine barrels under arbors strumming mandolins, singing in plaintive tenor voices as big-hipped ladies swung their skirts and old nuns laughed and old men argued, hands in the air waving, but of course Italians go to offices too. They have dental appointments. They must go shop for toilet paper and put it on the roller. And then she saw a burst of bougainvillea growing out of an old de-crepit apartment building, five stories high. One enormous plant. And then gigantic wisteria plants that looked like they were eat-ing a three-story house. "Look," she said. And someone said, "What?" And then it was gone. A string of bicyclists crossed an overpass as they sped under and then Carl said, "How long until we get there?" Like a child on a car trip. "Fifteen minutes," said Mr. Columbo.

"What if our rooms aren't ready?" said Carl.

"Then we'll walk around and look at the sights," she said.

"Won't they be ready?" said Lyle in a pained voice. "Did we request for them to be ready?"

Mr. Columbo hit the brakes and took an exit off the freeway—

lento, adagio, thought Margie. "Scenic route, very historic," he said—and now they were speeding through vineyards, the slender gnarled trunks and canopy of intertwined vines webbed above. "Best wine in Italy comes from here. Ghirlandaio. Only two hundred barrels a year and they leave it in the wooden casks for five years and it costs a hundred euros a bottle and it is said to have special powers"—he glanced around, decorously—"to restore the *lib*-i-do." He pronounced it in a whisper.

"What about lipids?" said Daryl.

"Sign me up for a case," said Margie.

They came along a street of houses in pastel shades, coral, pink, pale yellow. A golden house with green shutters. He pulled over in front of a mud-colored building with pockmarked walls. "Artillery shells," he said. "Americans thought there were Germans inside and they blasted it with mortars and couldn't knock it down and then a child came running out waving a white bedsheet and they held their fire and then fifty or sixty more kids came out. And then two clowns in whiteface with big floppy shoes and little *ooga-ooga* horns on their belts. Luigi and Carlo. They were from a circus whose wagons had been destroyed by bombs and their trained dogs had run away and also a llama and an old spotted horse. The two of them got caught in the Allied tank assault and ran for shelter in the castle and found the cellar full of terrified schoolchildren. So they painted themselves up and got into costume and put on a show, whacking each other with the slapsticks. When they heard an incoming shell, Luigi bent over as if to let a great fart and when the shell hit, Carlo fell down and waved his arms to disperse the smell. It was very funny. They did some of their act for the Americans who suspected the clowns might be booby-trapped. They made them drop their trousers right there in front of the schoolchildren, which the clowns did, clowning around, their hands clasped over their privates, eyes rolling, heads bowed. And then a shot rang out. A German sniper on the roof. An American raised his rifle and blasted away and the sniper fell four stories to the pavement and landed with a big crunch and that was the end of the comedy and the war resumed."

The van drove on.

Mr. Columbo slowed down coming through a piazza and pointed off to the left—"There's the balcony Mussolini came out on when he spoke to the crowds"—and they looked up at the little balcony. "After the war, they went around and shot people they called collaborators, but hell, almost everybody collaborated. If you wanted a nice life, you went along with the Nazis. There weren't many heroes."

"Well, we came here to celebrate a hero," said Margie. "An American by the name of Gussie Norlander. He was from our town. He died in the liberation of Rome."

Mr. Columbo shrugged. "All dead men are heroes, and the rest of us are cowards."

They drove on across the Tiber, a shallow snot-green river, with stone walls and broad footpaths on either side, the dome of St. Peter's looming up.

"Will we have the opportunity to see the Vatican?" said Father Wilmer, changing the subject.

"I am at your service," said Mr. Columbo. "I am here for you. Whatever you want, I am here to provide."

"Assuming that is acceptable to Mr. Keillor," added Father. "I don't wish to dictate where we go. Probably he has seen it all many times." He turned to the author. "I heard you had been given a VIP tour of the Vatican once."

The author shifted uncomfortably in his seat. His legs were numb and his bladder was about to let go. He told Father Wilmer that at the Vatican, VIP stood for "Vastly Ignorant Protestants" and that his tour guide, Father Reginaldo, had an aversion to crowds and so the tour skipped the Sistine Chapel and the Michelangelo *Pietà* in favor of the Vatican kitchen and a warehouse where shards of statuary were glued back together.

"What's that I smell? Chicken?" said Daryl, and some of the pilgrims snickered.

In Minneapolis, Irene had read a story about chicken flu in Europe that caused nausea, loud whirring sounds in the eardrums, hallucinations, vomiting and diarrhea—as much as four gallons in one outburst—followed by shame and depression. She had passed the story around to the others, and while they pooh-poohed it—still, the thought of four gallons of poop suddenly blowing out of you was hard to get out of your mind. "What if it's true?" said Irene. "Better go easy on the chicken until we can test it out." And she and a few of the others agreed that Mr. Keillor could be the guinea pig. The man had a strong constitution. Let him chow down on some chicken and then keep an eye on him.

Irene had purchased what she believed to be a chicken sandwich at a food stand in the Rome airport and then noticed the label, *cervello*, brain. It was fried like an egg, between slices of bread. She unwrapped the tinfoil and looked at Mr. Keillor who was resting his eyes. "How about some breakfast?" she said. He looked at the sandwich. It was the first kind gesture anyone in the group had made toward him, it had been one insult after another—Clint Bunsen saying, "People keep telling me to read your books and somehow I never find the time." Lyle suggesting he see a doctor about nasal blockage. In the Minneapolis airport, Marilyn Tollerud going on and on and on about Mr. Keillor's radio rival Ira Glass, Ira Glass, Ira Glass, idol of urbane young women from coast-to-coast, and how much she enjoyed his writing, his mumbly style, and how she listened to podcasts of Ira over and over and over and over. Even Evelyn had let him have it: she said, "I heard you stopped drinking and I thought, Thank God." (This, from a woman who had tended bar at the Sidetrack Tap and seen men plastered, loaded, bombed, stewed, fried to the gills, falling down shit-faced. He had gotten drunk in the classic WASP style, quietly, alone, at home, late at night, straight whiskey in a glass, listening to Bach organ chorales, weepy, no trouble to anyone. . . . How did he come to be the goat here?)

The chicken sandwich looked good. "Thank you," he said to Irene. "That's very sweet of you." And he ate it, all of it, aware that everyone in the van was watching him. "Delicious," he said. "My grandma raised chickens and I used to catch them when she needed to slaughter a few. I don't know if I ever told you this story—I used a wire clothes hanger to catch them by the ankles—they could run really fast—it was a wire hanger that you unwind to make a long straight wire with a hook at the end—they'd run into the lilac bushes and I chased them—I was probably seven or eight at the time—my dad cut their heads off—anyway, this one time I remember . . ."

Margie listened to his convoluted tale as the van slowed in rush-hour traffic. How did this man ever come to be telling stories on the radio? Finally, thank goodness, the van pulled up in front of the Hotel Giorgina and she disembarked. Stood on the sidewalk. *Rome.* Sunny and warm. A brick-paved street, little Fiats and scooters parked. A broad yellowish concrete walk with marble curbs. Two women approached, arm in arm, in dark heavy coats, one of them walking a little brown dog in a red plaid sweater. Handsome well-put-together women who strode past, paying her no mind, inviting no comment from anybody.

Rome. And she thought back to January, when the idea of the trip to Rome sprang into her mind.

CELIBACY

The night Carl stopped sleeping with her was a Sunday night, very cold, a pinkish purplish golden sunset, and she was on the phone with Mom in Tampa who was fussed-up about Dad. Next door, the slow grind of a frozen engine that did not want to start. Carl was watching Gophers basketball on TV, then switched to a documentary about the Inuit, then a show in which people yelled at each other and the audience laughed uproariously, meanwhile Mother said Daddy was losing his grip on reality. He was 86 and had bought a new Buick and gotten the extended warranty. He was entering sweepstakes and contests left and right. He complained whenever the temperature dropped to the fifties. And he had got his undies in a bunch over Barack Obama who would be inaugurated in a couple weeks and then would legalize gay marriage and tax the pants off people—Daddy, who had never been exercised about politics before, jumping up from reading the newspaper and yelling, "When are people in this country going to wake up?" "Is he taking his lithium?" said Margie. Carl switched to a silver-maned preacher prowling in front of a blue-robed choir with Bible in hand and then a woman deep-frying a turkey and Margie told Mom to fix supper earlier and get Daddy to take a walk in the evening and work some of that anger off. "He won't listen to me," said Mother. On the TV a boy with a serious overbite and dead fish eyes sang "Sweet Dreams, Baby" to recorded accompaniment a half-step flat. And Carl said, "Well—I guess I'll cash in my chips," and rose from the sofa, switched off the TV, padded into the kitchen, ran a glass of water and took his Mycidol, his Lucatran, hawked and spat in the sink, and rummaged around in the kitchen for something and then on the credenza in the dining room. "Where are my reading glasses?" he said. She said, "On the hutch."

"It isn't a hutch," he said. "It's a buffet. Or a sideboard."

"Call it whatever you like, that's where your reading glasses are."

She could hear him get his glasses off the hutch and then go upstairs and down the hall to what used to be Carla's bedroom. She thought he'd gone in to check the radiator. She finished up with Mom, told her to hang in there, and let Boo and Mr. Mittens out to poop in the snow and turned on WLT for the forecast (overnight low of minus fourteen, partly cloudy tomorrow, chance of snow), then let the cats back in, turned out the lights, and went upstairs. Carl was in Carla's bed, lights out. She stood in the doorway for a meaningful moment. And said, "It's sort of cold in that bedroom, isn't it?" and he murmured something about, no, it was fine. It was an odd thing for him to do and she thought of pointing this out to him, but oh well, whatever. Maybe he was upset about her referring to a buffet as a hutch. Maybe went in there so she'd ask him what was wrong and then he could say, "Oh, nothing" and she'd say, "Well, it must be something," and then he'd tell her. Too much trouble. So she left him there in the four-poster bed with a white muslin canopy over it and a Martina Navratilova poster on the wall and girly things on the dresser (or credenza) and went to bed, dreamed she was in a boat, water lapping on the hull, men's voices on deck, rigging, and someone playing a trombone. Woke at six. Showered. Breakfast with Carl. And nothing was said about the night before and the next night he went down the hall and the next and suddenly it was a week later and he seemed to be camped there for the duration—his Civil War books stacked on the bedside table, his reading glasses, his white-noise machine that made ocean surf.

"Do you want me to clear Carla's stuff out of her room?" she said. No, he said, it was fine.

"Is something wrong?" He shook his head.

"What's on your mind these days?"

"What do you mean?"

"You seem worried or upset or something."

"I'm fine," he said. The mantra of Midwestern men. He could be fibrillating wildly and half-conscious, blood trickling down his chin, but if you asked him he'd say he was fine.

So every night she said good night—sometimes he responded, sometimes not—and she went off to bed and propped herself up on four pillows and took up *O Paradiso* which her Book Club was reading, Evelyn, Eloise, Irene, Marilyn, Arlene, and Judy, a memoir by a Minnesota farmwife whose dairy farmer husband's heart burst while shoveling manure. He had had a run-in with a cow who'd been switching him in the face with its tail, which it had freshly defecated on. Hit him, *splort*, and he just plain lost it.

Pure barn rage. A 1,500-pound Holstein and he took a swing at her. Didn't hurt the cow but it had a different attitude about milking after that and seemed to be sowing discord in the herd. It took a lot of the pleasure out of dairy farming, walking into the barn and feeling the resentment and those eyes following him as he walked down the narrow path between the rows of rumps and the tails lifting and great bursts of cowflop excreted his way. It gradually wore him down and one morning he collapsed. "I lifted up his head and held it on my lap as I called 911 on my cell phone and as I did, I was thinking, 'Earl is gone and you've got to get out of here, Joanne, and find your life.'" Two weeks after the funeral, she sold the farm, moved to Italy, and found the meaning of life. "I never knew what unabashed happiness was until I got to Rome and learned to live with gusto and express joy and grief, to dance with my arms in the air, to throw my head back and laugh, to frankly explore my own passions and desires. The me who lived on the prairie was not the real me inside, she was a woman wrapped in cellophane, an unopened Christmas gift."

Joanne had raised three children, shoveled snow, vaccinated hogs, explained algebra to her offspring, made Christmas, baked cakes, and stuck her right arm into a cow's hinder to straighten out her uterus. She had plowed and disked and cultivated, she had slaughtered chickens. Suddenly she's on the Via Veneto drinking espresso at midnight and talking about reincarnation to Francesca, a woman she met in art class, sketching naked men in charcoal, telling her about Minnesotans and how locked-up they are. How they find it useful to be pessimistic, knowing that eventually they'll be proven correct. How she, Joanne, has decided to live in the blessed present. Seize the moment. People back in Lundeen were scandalized that she had buried Earl and taken off like that. They expected her to mourn for a year at least, preferably two.

The book club was sharply divided over *O Paradiso*. Margie and Marilyn and Eloise thought that it was Joanne's life and good for her to show some spunk and go her own way. The older women thought, "What if everyone just did as they pleased? What about the children?" Reading *O Paradiso*, Margie felt like slipping across the hall with a glass of red wine and dropping her nightie on the floor, diving into bed, saying "Hi, isn't this what you were hoping for?"

What was his thinking there? Why had he chosen celibacy? *And Eve said unto Adam, "Why are you ignoring me? I am the only woman around." And Adam said, "Am I ignoring you?" Eve said, "You haven't made love to me in a long time." And he said, "If that's what you want, fine. It's up to you. You tell me. I'm not a mind reader. If you want to, that's okay by me." But he made no move in her direction.*

"It takes two to tango," she said. "We can make love or not, either way is fine. I am only pointing out that we haven't. I don't want you to make love out of a sense of obligation or pity."

He said, "Well, as long as you don't care, then let's not. I don't want you to do it on my account."

"Well, it's up to you," she said. "If you want it, fine. But if not, that's okay too. No pressure. " So they didn't do it. And so Eve died childless, and Adam lay in his old age and had a vision of great cities that would never come to be, grand inventions never to see the light of day, unwritten books, the vast unfulfill-

ment of God's promise, and he wished he had made love to his wife but it was too late.

Oh but it wasn't about sex, not really. It was about touch and proximity and the way she could ask him, if she wanted, to please rub her back and he would. She lay on her side, back to him, and he lay on his side facing her and with his good right hand kneaded her shoulders and neck and made gentle circular sweeps down her back to the base of her spine and caressed her buttocks and then back up and then, if she were lucky, he would scooch up close and fit his frame to hers, the whole length of her, spooned in tight, and she'd lift her head and he'd slip his left arm under it and his right arm around her belly and his face in her hair, breathing into it, and sometimes they fell asleep that way and woke up still commingled in the morning. That was what she missed. The spooning, the comminglement.

For one week, two weeks, it was a curiosity, and after two weeks it was a sorrowful situation, and she went to work trying to solve it. She wore a red blouse and red lipstick. (Which he didn't notice, she had to point it out to him. "I like it," he said.) She spritzed perfume on her neck, the bottle he gave her for Christmas, *Mystique.* She bought him a box of chocolates (it triggers seratonin in the brain) and she stood behind him caressing his shoulders (to stimulate oxytocin). She wore skimpy black underwear. She put on a Lulu Walls CD.

> *You don 't love me anymore*
> *You walk right past my door*

We're still married but what for?
You don't love me anymore.

(Lulu Walls was glamorous so it was hardly credible that any-one would walk past her door. That woman had to lock her door, she had men taptaptapping on her door morning, noon, and night.)

"Why are you sleeping in the guest room?" she asked him in early February. "I like to read late at night, I didn't want to disturb you," he said. Which was crazy, of course. He always had read in bed, sometimes until two or three, so engrossed in a book that he didn't hear when she talked to him. She'd say, "I am moving to Nepal and switching to Buddhism. I don't know—I've felt some-thing missing in my life and Buddhism seems like the thing for me so I am changing my name to Serene Wisdom, but you can just call me Whiz. Okay, pal?" And Carl says, "Okay," and his eyes do not leave the page.

"Did you hear me?"

"Yes."

"Oh, and I'm going to Nepal with a man I met at a Buddhist web site. His name is Joyful Anticipation."

One morning she followed Julie's advice on the *Rise and Shine* show on WLT and she locked the door and took off all her clothes and stood in bright light studying herself in the mirror, her creased belly, her bulbous breasts, her sloped shoulders and big hips, and felt bad. What a nothing she was. She wasn't fat, she wasn't a string bean, she was just sort of incredibly ordinary. One of the world's four billion brunettes. Five foot four, 122 pounds, glasses, big feet, big hands. No wonder he didn't care to undress her. Midwestern men go gaga over Asian girls or lanky Swedish models or freckle-faced Irish girls or dark Latinas with the swing in the hips, but the butcher's daughter, mother of three, teacher of English—not high on a guy's list. Every day a man sees hundreds of lovely young mammals peddling soda pop, automobiles, underwear, power tools, one tasty morsel after another and he comes home and finds a lumpish lady scrubbing the bathroom floor. Who wants to seduce the cleaning lady?

She sat down one morning and wrote him a note—*Sweetheart, you've left our bed without a word of explanation. Are you mad at me? Having an affair? Am I suddenly repellent to you? Do I snort and toss in my sleep? I love you. I miss you at night. You are a wonderful lover and the only man I ever loved and I can't bear sleeping without you and not knowing why. Please talk to me. Please. Your loving wife, Margie*—but it sounded so needy and pitiful. So she tore it up and wrote him another. *Did you ever lust after me? Did you ever feast your eyes on me? Did you ever feel an uncontrollable urge to rip my clothes off and throw me down and Have Me Right Then And There? And if so, how did you control that uncontrollable urge?* And she tore that one up. And that morning she wrote the first poem she'd written in years.

I sit and say nothing for fear
My words will turn to stone
And though they are sincere,
They will become a prison of their own.

Words do that. Words spoken in anger
Are inscribed in brass,
A loved one becomes a stranger,
The door blocked: Do Not Pass.
And so in hope we can transcend
This current bout of misery
I don't say anything, dear friend,
I'm waiting for what joys might be.
But I hope you know, my darling one.
I love you, after all is said and done.

She put it in her jewelry box. And then she decided they should go to Rome and find out how to live joyously.

REMEMBERING GUSSIE

It was a quiet week in Lake Wobegon, the moon a crescent in the early evening sky, the planets Jupiter and Venus side by side, and then (1) Carl stopped sleeping with her, (2) she took a phone call from a woman named Maria Gennaro in Rome about a World War II hero, August (Gussie) Norlander, (3) she called Gussie's brother Norbert Norlander in Tulsa, and (4) she saw a dead woman at the side of the highway, under a yellow tarp.

Four stories in five days.

It was a Monday at Lake Wobegon High School. She had come down to the office from her eleventh-grade English class, leaving them to work on the quiz on Cummings's "since feeling is first / who pays attention to the syntax of things / will never wholly kiss you; / wholly to be a fool while Spring is in the world / my blood approves." (*What do you think "syntax of things" refers to? Do you agree that "feeling is first"? Try to explain the phrase "wholly kiss you." Do you regret an instance in which you were a fool?*) She gave the class a little talk about passive aggression—how people can have very specific expectations how things should be done, and yet never tell you what they want. If you ask them, "Is this okay?" they just say, "Sure. Whatever." Though actually they hate what you've done, and think you're a fool, incompetent, possibly in Satan's employ. The only way you know this is that they never look you in the eye. *Say what you think*, she told her students. *I want to know how you really feel. So tell me.* They looked at her, suspicious, thinking it might be a trap. *I would rather know what you truly think than have you make up something to try to please me.* They weren't sure how to take that. They stared at the poem.

When she (Margie) thought of "wholly to be a fool," she thought of her niece Melody Krebsbach, Donny's girl, who ran away from home at 15 to be a model. She'd told her mother one morning over the oatmeal, "I've been thinking of leading a nomadic life." Hard to imagine a girl who loved her bed so much sleeping in ditches, but a week later she was gone. She was devastatingly beautiful, shockingly thin—tiny flat butt, legs like rake handles, a brassiere like two demitasse cups—one good fart would've blown her away—and a month later she was in *Vogue* ("The Urban Guerilla Look") as Mladia Majerkova and then the pendulum swung over to Bruised Fragility and then American Slut and she looked good in stiletto heels and python pants and orange blouses with no buttons, everything hanging out, but she was so skinny that her underwear fell down if she walked fast, unless she wore boy's briefs, which she couldn't do, and she got on powerful muscle relaxants laced with codeine, and was skidding toward addiction when a juvenile court judge—Melody was 16 at the time—put her into foster care with an Amish family near Lanesboro. Her Amish name was Modesty. She donned the brown woolen dress and white bonnet and learned to churn butter, which let her express anger in a useful way. No TV, no radio, no cell phone: it was all good for her. She gained fifty pounds and fell in love with an Amish boy and there she is today, the mother of six kids, built like a brick outhouse, churning butter, spinning wool, baking pies. *Kids*. So dramatic. It's got to be high-priced glamour or the life of a serf. No in-between.

Margie came down to the office to pick up her mail and also because she felt a little overwhelmed by what "wholly kiss you" might mean to her pupils and if one of them would pour out a story about sex in the backseat, kids sometimes bared their souls in English class. And then what are you supposed to do? Marilyn Tollerud's son Darren blurted out, in a paper on Frost's "The Road Not Taken," that he was gay. Was Margie supposed to send the boy to counseling? Tell his mother? She just gave him an A, wrote "Well-constructed—nice use of personal detail—very persuasive" at the top and patted his curly head. *Good luck, son. Welcome to the land of confusion. We saved a spot for you.*

The superintendent, Mr. Halvorson, was in a bad way that morning, having passed by the girls' toilet and heard young voices singing:

> Rah rah for Wobegon High
> I've got some crystal meth we can try.
> And a bag of mary jane—
> We can smoke it with cocaine.
> We won't go crazy, we won't OD.
> We'll go around in pure ecstasy
> Taking little pink pills
> And washing them down with beer.

Margie had heard the song long ago, but Mr. Halvorson had been insulated by his high office—he was horrified. "What am I supposed to think about this?" he cried.

"Think positive," she said. "Or give up. Your choice."

Doris the school secretary was trying to decipher the beer-stained receipts from the Friday night basketball game and Margie stood by her desk reading a circular from the Professional Organization of English Majors about the burgeoning interest in poetry—writing of poems up 28% among 18–25-year-olds when the phone beeped and Doris picked up: "Who?" And again, "*Who?*" She said "Hold on" and put her hand over the mouthpiece and rolled her eyes. "Some whacko says they're Italian." Margie picked up. "My name is Maria Gennaro, I'm here in New York," the woman said. "Excuse my English, it isn't that good. I'm from Rome. Italy. I'm in New York on my holiday and I called to find out where is Lake Wobegon. I do not find it on a map."

"Well, we're on some maps and not on others."

"How far is it to drive there?"

"Two or three days, I suppose. Depending."

"Oh." The woman was disappointed. "I was hoping I could make it in a day. I have a flight back home on Wednesday." Hard to imagine. An Italian woman disappointed that she couldn't come visit Lake Wobegon in the dead of winter.

"Do you have family here?"

"I do. Or I did. Do you know a family named Norlander?"

"Yes. But I don't think they live around here anymore."

"I am trying to locate them."

"So these are distant relatives?"

"I don't understand."

"Cousins?"

"No, my father. His name was August Norlander."

August Norlander was famous in Lake Wobegon for his heroic death in the liberation of Rome. At the Memorial Day services at the cemetery, someone always told the story about the farm-boy who enlisted in the army after the Japanese bombed Pearl Harbor and who went off to serve in North Africa under Eisenhower and then went ashore at Anzio. One of our own boys, only a few years removed from hoeing corn and playing football, and in the battle for Monte Cassino south of Rome, he met his end. And then someone read the official citation for the Medal of Honor:

Wearing a priest's vestments for camouflage, and a red skullcap, Cpl. Norlander walked up the hill ahead of his platoon and called out to the German machine-gun emplacement, "*In nomine Patris, et Filii, et Spiritus Sancti*" and then in German, "*Frieden. Der Friede Gottes*," and then swung what appeared to be a censer on a chain but which in fact was an explosive device and hurled it toward them as he reached under his chasuble for his Browning automatic, firing 167 rounds and throwing eleven hand grenades in addition to the ED, killing fourteen Germans and wounding twenty-one, as his vestments turned crimson from his own wounds, but he continued firing, even as he fell to the ground, until at last he was killed by a barrage of bullets. Out of respect for his heroism, the Germans raised a white flag of truce and permitted medical corpsmen to come and remove the body.

It was part of the ritual, along with the Gettysburg Address and "In Flanders Field" and "My country, tis of thee, sweet land of liberty"—the heroic sacrifice of August Norlander—and it posed certain questions to the inquiring mind: What is the morality of using religious garb for camouflage and calling out a benediction as one is preparing to blow up the very ones you are blessing? Is all fair in war? Young people pondered these things, but meanwhile August Norlander was a legendary figure, striding up a hill, prepared to die in the war against Naziism.

The football field was named for him. Norlander Field. A bronze plaque with his likeness was fastened to the gatepost next to the ticket booth. Wobegon players touched his nose as they trotted onto the field. Sometimes a coach would use August's story as an example of putting yourself on the line for the sake of one's teammates.

He had a daughter in Rome? This was not part of the August Norlander legend. The woman said, "I feel so sad that I have never seen my dad's hometown. And now I'm sixty-four and who knows if I ever will? I came to New York with my sister. Half sister. My dad died before I was born. My mom married another guy, an old friend, but she never forgot my dad. She was in love with him always and she still is. My mom is ninety-three. Her mind is gone except for a few things that are real to her and one of them is my dad. She sits and talks to him all day. I wanted to bring her back something from Lake Wobegon."

Snow was falling beyond the window. She could make out the steeple of Our Lady of Perpetual Responsibility in the white haze and the HOME-COOKED MEALS sign on the front of the Chatterbox and the red brake lights of cars. People leaned into the wind sweeping across the lake and lumbered past the skeletal trees and through the clouds of exhaust of cars warming up that never got warm and it just seemed miraculous to look out at winter and hear an Italian woman ask so warmly about Lake Wobegon, wanting to know more about you and where you live. An Italian woman sentimental about her Lake Wobegon roots. You don't get that sort of thing every day. Doris thought it was a complete hoax.

"Nonsense," she huffed, "tell her to peddle her papers elsewhere." Daily contact with adolescents had given Doris a suspicious nature. She guessed the Italian woman was out to get money and this would be the first in a series of phone calls aimed at extorting a check.

To Margie, the phone call seemed like a gift. August Norlander had left, a boy of eighteen, and gone to war and fathered a child in Rome who now wanted to find out where she came from. (Had she noticed some odd quirks in herself that might be hereditary? A tendency toward gloomy solitude? A craving for fried herring?) A Roman woman half Minnesotan. A sort of mermaid. Living at the bottom of the sea but curious to come flip-flopping ashore and see what pedestrian life is like. Well, so was Margie curious to get out of her own watery world. Teaching in the same high school she'd graduated from thirty-five years ago. Just like it said in the school hymn—

> Hail to thee, our Alma Mater,
> Would that we might longer dwell
> Here in thy hallowed hallways,
> But we bid farewell.
> Through life's dangerous lonely passages

Along the coasts of grief and fear,
In our hearts we'll e'er remember
How you loved and taught us here.

Well, she had skipped the voyage along the coasts and stayed in the hallowed hallways. Same scarred oak tables, same sweet polish on the maple floors, marble bust of Minerva in the niche by the library, and traces of lipstick from the annual St. Valentine's Day prank. THE REWARD OF A THING WELL DONE IS TO HAVE DONE IT. EMERSON in gold lettering by the gym—the place hadn't changed much except for the computers. Same bitter smell of disinfectant in the science lab where she memorized the planets in order—Mercury Venus Earth Mars Jupiter Saturn Uranus Neptune Pluto (*My Very Educated Mother Just Served Us Nine Pizzas*)—and here she was, thirty-five years later, two doors down, teaching the past perfect subjunctive. *If only I had done, if only we had gone, if only they had come.* She'd gone precisely nowhere. The inmate had become a warden. Kids she went to high school with now had ropy necks and liver spots and were planning their hip replacements, but she was stuck in her teenhood. She still trotted down to the Chatterbox Café for the chili and grilled cheese and noted the same dumb signs on the cash register, DANGER: DISGRUNTLED EMPLOYEE and DON'T ASK ME HOW I AM—I MIGHT TELL YOU and TIPS ARE GRATEFULLY ACCEPTED—CASH ONLY, NO IOU'S. The same faded prints of Mount Rushmore, the North Coast Limited, the Split Rock Lighthouse. The same smells of coffee, bacon, toast, chocolate malt, burnt beef. The dusty breadth of Main Street, the faded FOR RENT signs in the empty storefronts that once purveyed shoes, jewelry, and menswear. The old, fading small-town blues. And her old pal Darlene, forty pounds heavier, still waitressing after all these years, still saying *Oh for gosh sakes!* and *Who needs it?* and *What kinda deal is that?* or *That's a bad deal you got goin' there.* Or *What's the deal with him?*

Embarrassing to live in this time warp. Studies show: early praise promotes personal growth, it makes a big difference if your mother fussed over you. It gives you an expectation of success. But if she didn't, then defeat rises up at every turn. And Mother did not fuss over Marjorie, she looked at her and shook her head. You pay a big price for that, but nobody uses the term "poor self-esteem" because it's what everyone has. Calling people depressed is like calling them Causasian. Yes, and so what else is new? Trot into Skoglund's Five & Dime with its ancient aroma of paper and mucilage and Arnie Skoglund standing waxen-faced behind the glass case with the fountain pens nobody uses anymore and here is Mr. Faust your old history teacher who used to tell you you're gifted and here is your choir director Miss Falconer still crisp and pert as if about to lead the Girl's Sextet in "O Holy Night."

Embarrassing to be plodding along the same well-worn path as her parents, through the backyards of the lawn chairs, birdbaths, feeders, the old clothes poles, the old neighbors clinking the iced tea on the porches and missing the children who ran away from this dreamy life—the life of clunky antiques and photographs in gold frames. What a backwater it is. You can be within ten miles of here and ask people where Lake Wobegon is and they never heard of it. A clannish tribe that *does not care to be interesting.* In the Cities, people walk around with flashing lights in their hair, tattoos of snakes on their necks, wearing shirts made of poppies: for them, uniqueness is a full-time occupation. *Fine. Whatever you want.* And to the west is North Dakota where people go and are never seen again. (It is bigger than it appears on the map.) They drive west and I-94 peters out into gravel roads and then trackless open space occupied by nomadic tribes of Deer People. And here we are between the bright lights to the south and the vast emptiness to the west, a way station, where she had settled (it seemed) permanently. Married Carl, had three kids, and now she was right smack where she started, little Margie Schoppenhorst, Class of 1973. Class Poet.

And now the phone call from Miss Gennaro brought back to her the memory of her ardor for Audrey Hepburn on that Vespa behind Gregory Peck, buzzing through the ancient streets and around the stone-paved piazzas and the beautiful word *bellissimo* that stuck in her mind—she thought of it now and then in odd perfect moments, the morning after a snowstorm, when the rack of lamb came out of the oven *perfecto*, when she glimpsed weeping at a basketball game or a big snort of pleasure or an appreciative belch or a smart-ass retort. *Bellissimo.* The love of life. *La dolce vita.* Buoyant personalities, high-wattage conversations with big gestures, the spirit of carnival and dancing in the streets and the frank enjoyment of the flesh and adoration of the *bambino* but also respectful of geezers, and grinning at the incoming platter of spaghetti. And the land of lovers.

Amore.

That's what she wanted. Truly. Not to be like Darlene.

Darlene, aching for love and angry at men, and sliding toward her extremely late forties, despising her ex-husband, Arlen, and still missing him fifteen years later.

After Arlen decamped, Darlene had been very close to her dog, a border collie named Sonny, and people noticed that she was wearing a wig made from the dog's hair. It was an odd color for a woman, grayish blond, and nobody wanted to ask and eventually she told Margie that Sonny had been seeing a therapist for adoption anxiety—she'd gotten him when he was already a year old—and the wig was to help him bond to her. Sonny died in his sleep, in the driveway, run over by a garbage truck. Darlene took to her bed for two weeks. Nobody mentioned that, either.

"Oh for crying out loud, that's just unbelievable," Doris said after Margie said good-bye to the Gennaro woman. "You bought that, hook, line, and sinker. What's the deal with that anyway? Somebody better fill you in on the birds and the bees, kiddo."

So Margie looked up August Norlander's old obituary in the Lake Wobegon *Herald Star* ("LOCAL BOY LOST IN ITALIAN ACTION") and Googled his brother Norbert Norlander, an oilman in Tulsa, Oklahoma.

The call from Maria Gennaro led to Norbert in Tulsa and also sort of led to a trip to St. Cloud to buy an English-Italian dictionary and a *Michelin Guide to Rome*, and on her way home there were police cars and flashing blue lights on Highway 10 and in the southbound lane, a blue Toyota, its rear end smashed in brutally. And a yellow tarp spread on the shoulder. Margie pulled over to the shoulder. Eight men stood around the yellow tarp and lifted it and held it over the body of a woman in a bright red dress, face down on the ice and gravel, as a young man in a black jumpsuit bent over the body and snapped pictures. She lay with one leg twisted, neck bent. The eight men stood solemn, eyes on each other, not looking down. A light snow was falling. The young man touched the side of the woman's neck. And then they put the yellow tarp back down and a man in an orange hazard vest approached pushing a gurney and Margie pulled away, a witness to the death of Mary McGarry of Little Falls—there was a brief story on the evening news—who died when she braked hard to avoid a deer and her car was rear-ended by another car. Fifty-five, the mother of three, on her way to accept an award at a banquet for having been a foster mother to twenty-one children, pronounced dead at the scene. Her own good works responsible in a way for her death—going to accept an award, killed en route. A victim of her own charity. One minute she's driving and listening to the radio and then a beautiful animal leaps onto the road in a blind panic and the Foster Mother of the Year slams on her brakes, pure reflex, and is slammed from behind and her neck snaps and she is gone. In a burst of reflex and adrenaline, a terrified deer frozen in front of her speeding car, a *whomp* on the brakes, and then it's all over, and now the troubled children will need to find another pair of arms to hold them, Mrs. McGarry has caught a train to a star. Death does have dominion after all. Margie thought she glimpsed the driver who crashed into the woman. A young man in a red plaid jacket leaning against a police car, smoking a cigarette, being interrogated. Long black hair, cowboy boots. A mother bites the dirt, James Dean lives on.

She came home and after supper (chili burgers and cole slaw and rhubarb pie, a sparse conversation about the children, the usual), while Carl read the St. Paul paper, she got out a green garbage bag and grabbed the centerpiece in front of him, the turtle shell Carl Jr. painted in Boy Scouts ("Slow and steady wins the race") and threw it in the bag, and the plaster bison, mother and child. ("Bye, Mom." "Bye, Son.") He said nothing. She tossed Cheryl's poetry, three poems, printed in a little magazine, *Transcendent Upheavals*. She pulled magnets off the refrigerator—tomatoes, pelicans, orange-crate labels—and the plaque over the table (GOD BLESS MY MESSY HOUSE) and the Minnesota loon salt and pepper shakers. Into the bag. He stirred but did not speak. The Scrabble board on the counter. The jar of chicory. The expensive copper skillet, a gift from Carla, seldom used.

When he heard the skillet clank, he looked up and asked what she was doing.

"Cleaning out stuff we don't use anymore. Life is too short to accumulate junk. Who gave us this chicory anyway?"

He didn't know. "That's a pretty expensive skillet to just throw away."

"It's going to the Goodwill."

"Oh. Okay."

And then he said, "Who is Norbert Norlander?"

"What about him?"

"Saw his name written on a slip of paper on the counter."

Bingo. Now there is a way to get a man's attention. Let him sniff another man in the vicinity. Jealousy, the oldest aphrodisiac in the book. She took her sweet time answering. Poured a cup of coffee. "Norlander," she said. "Oh. Right. Him. Somebody called the school, looking for him."

"Where is he?"

"Tulsa."

"Oh," he said. "Friend of yours?"

"Not yet. We'll see what develops." And then she made a perfect exit. Flashed him an Audrey smile and sashayed on out through the door and into the snow and put the garbage bag in the backseat of her car. Snow falling and the air antiseptic clean, the *boomboomboom* of ice cracking in the cold, a clear sky and the constellations in place, Orion and the Dippers and the Great Antelope, Jupiter and Venus snuggled up next to the moon, light shining from the high bell tower of Our Lady of Perpetual Responsibility. *God grant you eternal rest, Foster Mother. God give you unending joy in His Holy Presence and the Presence of All His Saints*, she thought, though she had no clear idea that this would actually happen. It was only a thought.

That night she lay in bed, seeing herself lying on the cold roadside under a yellow tarp. A motorist stopped and asked a cop who it was and he said, "Some woman from Lake Wobegon."

"From where?"

"Little town not far from here."

"Never heard of it."

"Well, you're not missing much."

"What happened?"

"Deer."

"Oh." And he rolled up his window and drove on. Suicidal deer lurking in the ditches, exacting a terrible revenge for hunting season, waiting for good women to come along, women who have eaten venison sausage. You're listening to Mozart on the radio and suddenly antlers explode into your face and sharp hooves do a death dance on your torso.

Death is not far away. So why not travel to Rome and bring a rhubarb pie to a daughter of Lake Wobegon? Bring her a scrapbook of pictures of Main Street at Christmas, the grain elevator, the Catholic church. A bumper sticker (LAKE WOBEGON, GATEWAY TO CENTRAL MINNESOTA). A copy of the school hymn. ("Wobegon, I remember O so well how peacefully among the woods and fields you lie./ Wobegon, I close my eyes and I can see you just as clearly as in days gone by."

Life is short. Why wait for spring? Why lie cooped up in the nest, sick with cabin fever and four months of winter yet to go. Men sat in the Sidetrack Tap, lost in the mists of whiskey dreams, but not Margie. She wanted to go somewhere, see something different. Do it now. Soon she'd have to rescue her elderly parents in Tampa. Mother hated Florida. The heat, the vicious insects, the clamminess of air-conditioning, the snakes, the danger of gator attacks. She kept her equilibrium because every day, Monday through Friday, she tuned in to *Bright Horizons* on the Mutual Radio Network, the story of Broadway star Brenda Stanford and her search for fulfillment as a wife and mother in the sleepy village of Littleton, sponsored by Rainbow Motor Oil. Brenda had suffered extensively—unfaithful men, ungrateful children, greedy relatives, fatigue, boils, temporary blindness, and so forth—but her sunny resolve had never faltered. "Somehow I believe that this will all work out for the good eventually," she said, and indeed it did. Mother shared this belief although Daddy was pissing his pants and she suffered panic attacks that rendered her pale and breathless for hours. If the mailman rang the buzzer, Mom went to pieces. Meanwhile, Dad was wearing a button—ASK ME HOW I FEEL ABOUT OBAMA and below it, another button—TREASON. In their little cul-de-sac in Holiday Gardens, surrounded by retired Jewish schoolteachers from New Jersey, Mom and Dad were the only wingnuts on the block, and now they'd gotten a big black dog named Rush that Dad couldn't handle—he'd fallen twice and been dragged down the driveway. The dog went ballistic whenever he spotted a UPS man or anyone in uniform, and Mom, who was terrified of dogs, spent hours in her locked bedroom saying the rosary, and so Margie would have to fly down there, have a Come-to-Jesus talk, lay down the law, throw away old medications, put Rush up for adoption. A miserable, thankless job. But first, Rome. Pleasure before duty.

She made a list:

1. Find out all about August (Gussie) Norlander.
2. Check available flights to Rome.
3. Make an appointment with a doctor and get that lump in my left breast looked at. I do not want to die right now with all of this happening. A doctor in Little Falls or St. Cloud. Not the Lake Wobegon Clinic.

She had no faith in Dr. DeHaven whatsoever. The man couldn't tell a brain tumor from ordinary dandruff. Or a dilated displacement of the lower delphinium. He'd put you on Hydrofluoricaminosulfagalactic bioxychloridated lucite and try to shrink your cerebral hyacinth and a month later you'd be billed $45 for the removal of corns.

NARROW STREET

⌒⌒⌒◦⋯⋯◦⌒⌒⌒

The Hotel Giorgina was just off the Piazza del Popolo, five floors, a white tile building with aluminum trim and dying ficus trees in the front windows, the bust of a bosomy goddess in a niche beside the glass door.

Mr. Columbo opened the van door, set a step stool down, bowed—"*Signore, signori, benvenuto.*" The pilgrims clambered out and trooped into the lobby, towing their luggage. There was coffee in the air, and the yeasty smell of fresh baking. A sleepy old man in a faded brown bellhop outfit sat behind a high desk with a silver call bell on it, potted ferns on either side that appeared close to death. He looked at them with great impassive dignity as if he were the owner of the hotel but might, under certain special circumstances, carry bags up to a room. "*Buon giorno,*" said the desk clerk, a young man with long pomaded hair, behind a counter. "You must be the Krebsbach party." The room keys were there in a jumble in front of him, brass keys attached to wooden knobs. Eloise plopped down in a row of red and orange chintz-covered chairs with saggy bottoms, two love seats in the middle. "I could sleep for a week," she announced. A huge gilded mirror hung on the wall over marble-topped tables. The furniture had a *donated* look, as if the manager's grandma had sent over her living room before she went to the hospice. Evelyn sat next to Eloise and Irene took a seat too. Marilyn sat down and put her head on Irene's shoulder. The young desk clerk in his rumpled dark suit stood at the reception counter and smiled an official smile. A brass luggage carrier stood alongside the desk. Two small elevators and next to them a narrow stairway, and standing at the elevators, a man and woman with four suitcases, one the size of a refrigerator. "How are we going to get this into the elevator?" she said. "I told you not to bring it," he said. "What was I supposed to do? Not bring clothing?" she said. "Pack lighter next time," he said. "Maybe you should've gotten us a hotel with a normal elevator," she said.

Father Wilmer examined the stacks of newspapers on the marble table: *USA Today*, the *International Herald Tribune*, *Il Tempo*, and the *Frankfurter Allgemeine*. And a brochure for a tour of Rome, including a performance of *La Traviata* in English. "I feel just fine," he said to nobody in particular. "Not a bad flight at all. I got halfway through a biography of Chesterton."

Margie felt a twinge of panic—*What if the reservations didn't go through? What if I'm surrounded by angry people shouting in Italian?*—which she stifled. Mr. Columbo was loading the luggage onto a cart, Carl and Daryl overseeing the work.

Mr. Columbo was very sorry but he had to hurry away to a tour group from Germany to pick up at eleven and then a French group this afternoon. "You speak all those languages?" said Daryl. "Yes, of course," he said. "All my life." He spoke to the bellman who shrugged an elaborate shrug. "He says he must stay in the lobby and watch the door to keep gypsies away," said Mr. Columbo. "Can you manage on your own?" Margie nodded. "Certainly. Been doing it all our lives." He stood waiting and it dawned on her—*duh*—the tip. How much to give him? She fingered the bills in her pocket and pretended to count the bags in the mountain he had piled up, and pulled a bill out and it was a hundred euro note. She thrust it at him and he looked surprised. And then charmed. Grateful. He put his hand over his heart and bowed slightly, and with great delicacy lifted the hundred euros from her hand and tucked it into his pocket, bowed, and exited.

The couple with the refrigerator suitcase had wedged it into the elevator with four other suitcases on top, no room for passengers, so he pressed the button for the second floor and had her hold the elevator while he went up the stairs. "Don't forget that the second floor is actually the third floor," she said. "What are you talking about?" he said. "They don't count the first floor as the first floor. The second floor is the first floor," she said. "Why in the world would they do that?" he said. "Just go," she said. "I'm going," he said. "Well, we can't hold up the elevator forever," she said. He put his hands on his hips. "You think you can get up there faster, go ahead," he said. "Just go," she said. "I'm sick and tired of your noise," he said. She looked around at the pilgrims waiting in line behind her. "You're embarrassing me," she hissed. "Look who's talking," he said. "Just shut the hell up and go to the third floor and get the damn bags off the fucking elevator," she said. "We can talk about divorce later." He stomped up the stairs and she turned to Margie and smiled. "Where are you folks from?" she said.

"Minnesota."

The woman looked thoughtful. "It gets cold there, doesn't it?"

Margie nodded. "Where you from?"

"Boston. We just flew in. Leo's been working too hard. He's a clinical psychologist. I told him not to drink on the plane but they kept bringing the wine around and he kept saying yes." She looked at Margie with sorrowful eyes. "This was supposed to be a *happy* time," she said. "Our first vacation in fifteen years."

"It'll be fine. You wait and see." And then the angry ringing of a bell inside the elevator and the woman let the doors close and up it went. "He's usually much nicer than this," she said.

The Giorgina was an American enterprise, part of the Whitefish hotel chain—the big white fish mounted on a plaque behind the desk—but the beds, it turned out, were small and hard, meant for small peasant people used to sleeping on floors, not grown-up Americans. And the towels—Carl unfolded one, it was a linen dish towel, not a bath towel. He pointed this fact out to her. "Make it work," she said. He tried to open a shade. It wouldn't go up. "Christ," he said. He was like a big sullen teenager. Two nights before, he'd sat looking at a picture book from the library, *Rome, the Eternal City,* and rolling his eyes. "Get a load of this," he said, pointing to a church interior, a gilded altar with cherubs suspended overhead. To him, a carpenter, Rome was the capital of European decadence and bad taste. Too much marble, not enough pine. "Unbelievable," he said, pointing to golden cherubs peeing water into a fountain. "Where do people come up with this stuff?" Bosomy big-hipped signorinas and their greaseball Casanovas lounged on a street corner and checked their cell phones every couple of minutes. Mafiosi like buffalo in pinstripes. Chaos in the streets. Rivers of cars. Madmen for taxi drivers. A new government every couple of weeks. And now this—tiny towels.

Well, she could've put them in a four-star hotel with marble shower and towels as big as bedspreads. It would've suited her just fine. But Carl detested luxury. She remembered the summer they vacationed for five days at the Happy Bison Motel in Bismarck, North Dakota. A compromise: she wanted to go to San Francisco, he wanted to stay home. His cousin Jim was a bartender at the Happy Bison and he got them a 40 percent discount on rooms. It sat out in a field, looking like a nursing home or warehouse, surrounded by acres of asphalt, and their rooms were next to the lounge where The Hitchhikers played until 3:00 A.M. Semis went by at 100 m.p.h. all night and the air conditioner sounded like a power lathe. After that tribulation, she should've booked them into the Hotel Eden—something extravagant—but in deference to Carl she'd gone the two-star route. It was his own fault.

She stripped off her clothes *wop-bop-a-wop-bam-boom*, hoping he'd notice, but he was still sulking, turning the clock-radio dial, hearing gibberish, so she tiptoed into the bathroom (leaving the door ajar to tempt him) and figured out the three knobs in the shower—one was for temperature, one for volume, and one for pulsation—and she washed off the grime of travel and stood under the hot water hoping he'd join her, then gave up, dried herself, using a dish towel, making it work. He sat on the bed, head in his hands. He'd been stunned by the flight over, the Placidol, the two early-morning beers in Amsterdam, and then there was the towel problem, the bed deficiency, the ventilation problem. If you closed the window, the room was stuffy, and if you opened it, you heard horns honking—Italians expressing fury, disbelief, self-affirmation, alienation, social criticism—a nation of blowhards passing by. Naked, she bent down and fished the *All U Need 2 No* guidebook to Italy out of his suitcase and tossed it in his lap. "Read up on the ruins," she said, "and you and I can go look at some later."

"I am a ruin," he said. She pulled on jeans, a black T-shirt with gold-sequined MINNESOTA across the front, then thought better, took it off, put on a plain black blouse and a brown jacket. No bra. And her big wraparound Italian starlet sunglasses. She felt good. Three hours of sleep on the plane seemed to suit her quite well. Maybe she'd been oversleeping all these years.

He said, "You're not going to bed?"

No, she was going for a nice long walk around the town.

He begged her not to. As if she'd announced she was going to swim into the ocean and see how far she could get. "Aren't you beat?"

She was a little tired but she hadn't come to Rome to sleep. Why waste the time? We're in Italy. You and me. In Italy.

"Please don't. For my sake. Please."

"It's Italy, darling. It's a NATO country. They're Catholics, for God's sake. I have a cell phone." His jaw dropped. She pulled out her cell phone and pushed a number. It rang and then there was the recorded voice of Carla. "It's your mother," said Margie. "I've run away to Rome with my lover, Carlo. I may not come back. You can have all my pots and pans. *Arrivederci,* darling."

That seemed to astonish him. She—his wife, Marjorie Krebsbach, the English teacher—had figured out how to extend your cell phone coverage to include Europe.

"When will you come back?"

"In a couple hours."

He seemed so unsettled. Unlike the placid, capable man she was married to. He went in the bathroom and washed his face and lay down on the bed, looking so vacant, so forlorn, she thought maybe she should stay with him, be a good wife and comfort him in his distress.

Nyaa. He already has a mother and one is all you get. Go. Git. Do something for yourself for once.

"Bye."

"A nap might do you good," he said. She turned away, but when she got to the elevator she wondered what he meant by that. Was he inviting her to make love?

Well, then let him say so. He had waited three months to bring up the subject so let him put it in clear English. *Darling, I want to rip your clothes off and make crazed love to you.* That's not so hard, is it? He'd made love to her with sweet abandon back when he believed the world was coming to an end in 1999. At midnight on December 31, the world's computers would flicker and die and the electrical grid go dark and planes fall out of the sky, so he stockpiled batteries and gasoline (for a generator). He bought three hundred-pound bags of rice. And pasta. Pistols. And he made love to her that December sort of wildly, roughly, loudly, several times, and then January 1 dawned. Nothing had changed. The clocks had not stopped. The snowplow came clattering up the street. The old guys on the radio were telling the same old jokes. He sold the generator on eBay. They ate rice for the next two years. Lovemaking went back into low gear. But it was lovely while it lasted, the end of the world.

The elevator door opened and she peered around the corner into the lobby—she did not want to hang out with another pilgrim right now. She wanted to look as Italian as possible. She could buy a silk scarf, Italianize herself. Look aristocratic. Walk purposefully, no map in hand. No sluggish person next to her saying, "Well, look at *that*, wouldja. Wonder how old *that* is." She was a traitor, a turncoat (literally), abandoning her troops, but so what. Let them sleep. The coast was clear, the old bellman sat behind the bell desk, expressionless, and she scooted out the door and into the street.

She strode down the sidewalk, swinging her arms. A few motorbikes buzzed by, a tiny taxi. A matinee-idol cop stood at the curb and watched from under hooded eyes, hands clasped behind his back. A man in a tailored brown suit walked his dog. The man wore a white apron festooned with silver and gold badges and puffed on a cigarette. His longish black hair, nicely oiled, was swept back on the sides, a sculpted look. Three young women walked arm in arm past her, six high heels tapping on the paving stones, taking long strides. They looked absolutely *bellissima*. Tall and lean and dark, womanly, striding forward into life. Three Audreys heading off to sit in a *caffè* and regale each other with tales of the sad-assed world of offices and copiers and clueless managers in pinstripes.

She plunged into a stream of walkers heading across a main drag into a narrow, dark street. A herd of short people, Japanese, dressed as if for a wedding, chittering away, and three Arabic women in black burkas. (Eloise would be having a fit right now, waiting for the bomb to go off.) A man in pajama bottoms and a black T-shirt ("FRA DIAVOLO PIZZA") and sandals hustled along. A man with corn-silk hair, no shirt, a tweed jacket two sizes too small, whistling. A display of paintings for sale, cheap: ballerinas, St. Peter's at dusk, a still life of wine bottles, dogs sitting in an empty piazza. A falafel stand tended by a man with a badger face, a kerchief around his head, the radio playing funeral music. The happy jangle of voices around her. A man on the prowl, hands in his pockets, standing in a doorway, the glint of his eyes. He looked as if he might accost her, ask for money, try to sell her a stolen watch, pinch her butt. She whispered under her breath, as she passed, "Don't mess with me, buddy." And he didn't.

Oh my God. She felt great. Oh my God, the freedom. Overwhelming. Walking tall, going where you cared to go, stopping to stare, moving on. *Freedom.* Where had she been all her life?

Well, she'd been raising three children and keeping the ship on course through the storms, maintaining good hygiene and nutrition while standing guard on the scholastic, religious, dental, and moral fronts and keeping up a cheerful demeanor and suppressing outbursts of violence. Kids. They had the stamina of goats. Bouncing off the walls and yammering nonstop. Wore you out so you caught all the viruses they brought home, which they got over in twenty-four hours, and you were a zombie for two weeks. They crawled into bed with you at 2:00 A.M. and threw up. One of them only ate food that is white and another one loved to walk into the room and scream and another one needed to make Getting Dressed in the Morning into an Ibsen tragedy. At night, she was so exhausted that the thought of having sex was like the thought of running the high hurdles. No, she lay in bed thinking of all she must do the next day, organizing the cakewalk for the spring carnival and baking brownies for the bake sale and encouraging the bloom of individuality—Carla the queen bee and Carl Jr. the gifted misfit and Cheryl the comedian—and offering basic financial/transportation/shopping/counseling services, twenty years of steady interesting work, plus teaching eleventh graders the difference between "anxious" and "eager," and "nauseated" and "nauseous"—and you get the kids out of the house finally, the last one gone. You give a graduation party for her—nobody gives one for *you*, no party for graduating parents. (What do you graduate to? Nobody knows.) You must've learned *something* from parenting—and no, there's nothing. You know less about it than when you began. You learn about prayer. Which you do when there's nothing to be done. *It's up to You, God.* You wish you had prayed more and yelled less. You regret that you didn't laugh more, that you told them 2,000 times to pick up after themselves when 850 might have been enough. Parenthood was a huge stupefying parenthesis in your life and now you must pick up where you left off (which is where, exactly?) and meanwhile you've learned nothing about life except that you want more of it. The three little Krebsbachs were gone and all the advice she'd dispensed to them didn't seem so useful to her. *Be careful of free offers. Get up early and do what you need to do before you have time to worry about it. The way to do hard things is to do them. Trouble is easy to avoid so long as you stay away from it.* Good cautionary advice but she had lost her caution in the course of teaching it to her children. She was hoping for free offers. And to find trouble.

She strode onward, map in her pocket, no fear of getting lost.

If she got lost, not a problem. She was well lost already. Nobody here knew her, nobody expected her to smile and say hello to them. Nobody was going to stop her and ask how is Carl, is Carla pregnant yet, did Cheryl get the job? Nobody would ask why she couldn't come to the spring choral concert and hear "Shenandoah" for the thirty-seventh time. Nobody would look at her and think, "Back in high school we all thought she was going to go places. Wonder what happened?" Nobody would think, "Gee, I liked that outfit she was wearing yesterday better. And those old brown oxfords have seen better days." She walked steadily on, crossing busy streets against the light, darting between slow-moving walkers, and when she heard a snatch of English, she turned her head away and quickened her step. She was Marjorie Parmigiano and she was en route to a lunch date with Enrico. She ducked into a shop, snatched a six-foot scarf off a shelf, bright green, paid up, tossed it around her neck, marched on. She had a feeling she was being followed but she didn't care. This was the way to travel. Solo. Nobody to make small talk with. Like it says on the sign in buses: PLEASE DO NOT ENGAGE DRIVER IN UNNECESSARY CONVERSATION. And there is so much of that in the world, people announcing the obvious. In Lake Wobegon, a man stopping another on Main Street: "So you're in town too, then." "Ja, I thought I'd come to town. Why not." Two men announcing their presence. Dumb. No, a person should travel alone so as to skip that stuff and fully absorb the carnival around you, be the silent invisible observer following the path as it opens up through the rolling crowd, finding the gaps, pushing through, your ears, nose, eyes, skin, tongue fully engaged.

Little cars buzzed by, little boxes on wheels, only room for the driver and a friend and a bag of groceries. A closet on wheels. Around the corner came a procession of twelve men in black carrying red parasols and chanting something in Latin or Italian that sounded like a credo but might have been a cheer for a school team except they were in their thirties and forties. Priests? Soccer players? They wore no priestly collar and they smelled of powerful cologne. They pushed past her and nobody else paid them heed and so neither did she. She stopped to look at posters (NO AL NUCLEARE) with ominous yellow barrels. A man pushed a cart along the street, selling Italian flags, postcards, plastic Popes, bottled water, little Pinocchios, Blessed Virgin Mary napkins and paper plates, rosaries and crucifixes, and orange pop. She bought a can and popped it open. Less fizz than in America and it tasted of real oranges. She passed a *farmacia* and a shop selling black scarves and mantillas. An interesting cul-de-sac where the street simply came to a stop and a passageway began. A handsome naked man stood in a recess in one wall, his stone chest and flat abdomen, his stone penis and scrotum, a cloak draped over his left arm. He could've wrapped it around him but chose not to.

He reminded her of Daryl Hansen, that goofy kid who went to Chicago and changed his name to Darren Anton, joined the Lindsay Longet Dance Experience, became gay. When the Longet company came to the State Theater in Minneapolis, the Hansens were there in the front row, Mr. and Mrs. and some aunts and cousins, about twelve of them, and they got to see their boy in a dance called "Diagonal Incarnation #7" in which he appeared to be naked but the Hansens said nothing about that when they went backstage afterward and neither did Darren. They only talked about the weather (cold) and the new dog (dachshund) and their vacation plans (Black Hills). He said he missed home. They said the dancers all seemed so talented.

Just beyond the statue, two old men sat on plastic chairs facing each other, a chessboard across their knees, the black queen gone, the white bishops sniping at the king. Above them, a sign POPO-LARI LIBERALI and a gargoyle stuck out its tongue and hissed at passersby. She stopped to admire an old apartment house, five stories, tile roof with about twenty little chimneys and flower pots, and the most wonderful rough golden yellow finish to the stucco, chipped, worn, mottled, streaked—in Lake Wobegon, they would've repainted it pronto but here it stood as is—the rough texture made it look like a Van Gogh painting of a building. A great work of art sitting and pretending to be an ordinary building. She turned left into a narrow street. One lane of parked cars, one of traffic, two narrow sidewalks. Four- and five-story buildings jammed together on either side, the top floors catching the sunlight, the lower ones in perpetual shadow. The long arm of a construction crane over it. The graffiti on the wall was beautiful, indecipherable, like the signatures of statesmen on a treaty ending a war.

And then she remembered her cell phone—with European service—and she dialed Maria Gennaro's number. It rang a strange burry ring and Maria answered. "Where are you?" she cried, and when Margie told her—Via del Pellegrino—Maria said, "You're not far from my house. Sit down and have a coffee. I'm there in five minutes."

MEETING MARIA

he sat down in the Spagnolo Giardini and ordered espresso. The very first espresso of her life. Her first morning in Rome and she felt like a native. "*Nativo. Natale. Indigeno. Locale. Naturale*," said the dictionary. Learning the language was going to be a cinch. (*Facile. Ordinario.*) No sweat. (*Senza sudare.*) A piece of cake. (*Un pezzo di torta.*) The coffee came in a demitasse. She put a spoonful of sugar in and drank it, a bitter syrup, and signaled for another. And a croissant. And before the second coffee came, a tall woman stood grinning in front of her. She wore a black shirt and slacks, green wool jacket, brown oxfords, and carried an enormous umbrella and a canvas shoulder bag. Margie stood up and Maria took her hand. She doffed her red woolen cap and kissed Margie twice on each cheek, left cheek *smack smack* and right cheek *smack smack*. And held her close and tight and then at arm's length and laughed. A handsome head on a long neck, her black hair streaked with gray and parted in the middle and pulled back in a silver clip. She had the long Norlander nose and she had Gussie's sweet smile. "Now at last I have a sister," she said and hugged Margie again. And held on.

Margie got tears in her eyes. It had been so long since anyone had found her so interesting. Nobody in Lake Wobegon hugged her like this.

Maria sat down and said a few words in Italian to the waiter and said to Margie, "I have waited for this moment for sixty years." She set the shoulder bag on her lap and opened it and took out five photographs: a blond kid with a big grin and several teeth blacked out, painted freckles, holding a pitchfork; the same kid in the third row of an old Lake Wobegon Leonards football team, a leather helmet under his arm, looking a little tentative; same kid holding up a cornstalk and tassel; him in a Whippets uniform, holding his bat up high, looking determined; a formal portrait of him in steel-rim glasses, a checked sport coat, white shirt with open collar, unsmiling.

"My papa," she said. "I never knew him. He died before I was born, in the liberation of my city. I grew up with my mother's memory of him and a feeling of terrible loss. I was a sad little girl. I felt that life could never be as good as it could've been if Papa had lived. God cheated me. And so Lake Wobegon was my El Dorado. My *paradiso*. I was going to visit there when I was twenty-one and then my mother got sick. I planned to go before I turned forty and then suddenly I was forty. Lake Wobegon was where everybody was full of love and sunshine and told jokes and poured syrup over their cakes and danced the hopping dance. Big fish the size of trucks leaping from the water. Paul Bunyan and his blue cow. Cold winters. So cold that words freeze in the air and in the spring they melt on the ground and people sweep them up into baskets. Big farms and tractors, enormous pumpkins that people carve doors and windows in and live inside. Big tomatoes. Thousands of lakes. Birds who make a wild warbling sound like a woman crying."

"They're called loons."

"And they're real?"

"Yes, of course." And Margie leaned forward, opened her mouth, tilted her head back, and made the high-pitched gurgley yodelly wail of the loon. The waiter approached, as if ready to apply the Heimlich maneuver.

"Beautiful," said Maria.

And she pulled out a slip of paper. "I wrote down questions," she said.

What is the population of Lake Wobegon now, and what was it in 1941 when Papa left home? *About the same, two thousand.* Why do they call it "Wobegon"? Doesn't that mean "sad and bedraggled"? *Yes, but it's also an Ojibway word that means "the place where we waited in the rain for you for two days and two nights."* And what about the dogs who play baseball? Mother told me about that. And does the snow get to be three and four meters deep? And do people stand on the ice and fish and are farmers not allowed to marry? *We have a baseball team called the Whippets, but they're men. Old guys. Not very good. I don't think the snow gets that deep. People do go out on the ice and fish, yes. But farmers marry. Except the Norwegian bachelor farmers.*

"The day I called you from New York, I was at my friend Ellie's apartment on West End Avenue, looking out the kitchen window at the Hudson River and trying to imagine what you looked like. Where you were. I had thought about that phone call ever since I was a kid, picking up a phone and calling Papa's people, and I used to imagine they'd speak to me (in Italian, of course) and tell me everything was going to be okay, not to worry. It was like having an imaginary best friend. When I dropped out of university, when I got pregnant and then lost the baby, when a man I had loved killed himself by jumping off a bridge, I imagined people from Lake Wobegon telling me to settle down, be patient, the world is full of beautiful things, open your heart, in time you will be okay, and remember: it could be worse. That was Papa's motto, Mama told me. 'It could be worse.' So when I called you, it was such a thrill. I'd told Ellie about Lake Wobegon, the fairy tale of my childhood, and she said, 'Just pick up a phone and call.' I said, 'I can't. They'd think I was crazy.' She said, 'Call up the high school. They talk to crazy people all the time.' So that's what I did."

Margie ordered a third espresso and a basket of rolls with cheese. Such a revelation—landing in Rome and finding this magical stranger. She had thought about Maria so often since their first conversation almost three months ago, imagined the two of them becoming friends—Oh God, she needed friends, all she had were relatives and neighbors and people from church—and now suddenly here she was. Maria looked her in the eye and told about herself: She was sixty-four years old, she had worked in a big real estate office and was now retired, she had survived breast cancer, she was planning trips to Egypt and India, she had three boyfriends, maybe four, whom she saw now and then on weekends. Mario and Roberto who were married, Gianni who was not, and Benny who she believed was not but she couldn't be sure. A man could be wonderful for two or three days and after that, you started to find out things you didn't want to know. Much nicer to have several in rotation. Less danger of being dumped. "They're always so happy to see me," she said. "Even Mario, who I've been with since his previous marriage." She saw no advantage to having a child, none whatsoever, and so she didn't. A simple rational choice. "Children are all stink and noise and if something bad happens to them, you feel horrible for the rest of your life."

"Are you Catholic?" said Margie.

"I am and I'm not. I love the church, it's like my Papa, I'm sorry he died but life goes on, right? How about you?"

Well, where to start? "I'm a teacher. I'm fifty-three. I teach high school. Carl and I have three kids. We've been married since I got out of high school."

"Is he the only man you've known?"

Yes, he was. The only one.

"Is he good in bed?"

Margie looked down into her coffee. "We're sort of having problems. We haven't made love since after Christmas."

"Then he's found someone else."

Margie shook her head. "He's too busy."

"No man is too busy. Your husband is out on the town."

"There is no town to be out on."

"You're naive."

"I live in a little town where secrets don't stay secrets for long. Women down at the Bon Marché Beauty Salon tell stories. I would have heard something by now. Really."

Margie explained that Carl was a dogged worker, the go-to carpenter and handyman of town—he got a dozen calls a day from people with problems and he'd say, "Okay, give me a few minutes to get some tools together and I'll be right over." Fuse burnt out, door stuck, window busted, toilet plugged, plaster falling—they called Carl and he went and half the time he didn't even charge them for it. So where would he find the time to arrange secret meetings in motels?

"A man wants what he can't have. He has one woman, he wants more. The heart longs for the impossible and it doesn't ever stop, even when it's broken, it keeps on wanting. Does he drive a truck?"

"An old camper. He keeps tools in the camper part."

"He's slipping it into her on top of the tool chest. He's mounting some lady whose shelves he just nailed to the wall. Ask him about it. Men are scared. You surprise them with a direct question and they'll either confess or they'll lie so badly you can see it leaking out of their ears. Do you talk about sex?"

My God, no. Never. She would rather walk naked through the streets than sit and have that sort of conversation. It just was what it was, sex, and certainly they'd never ever talked about it, who did? Nobody she knew. Never argued much, never had much in the way of bad feelings. He was a carpenter, the town handyman, a soft-spoken man, faithful, reverent, clean, brave, and she didn't know how to ask him, "Why don't you want to mess around with me?"

Maria pulled out a pack of smokes, offered one to Margie, took one for herself. "I started again," she said. "After the breast cancer. What the hell. What have I got to lose? I'm not going to worry about dying. Done that already.

"Of course, maybe I'm more realistic about men because I was created by a guy fooling around. I've been thinking about my dad so much. I live in a little street in Trastevere below the Janiculum Hill and I go for walks in the evening and I feel like he's there and he's restless about something. He wants to get his story straightened out. You're the first person I've told all of this. I know you have a kind heart."

"To think that August Norlander begat a child in Italy is sort of mind-boggling."

"So people in Lake Wobegon know about my papa?"

"They named the football field for him. His name is on a brass plaque in the front entrance of the high school. It says LOST IN SERVICE, which the VFW thinks is defeatist, so they raised a stink and now they're raising money for a new one called THE GREATEST GIFT. He's right there. And we mention him at the Memorial Day service at the cemetery every May. And they read out loud that story about him charging up the hill in the priest's robes and blowing up the German machine-gun nest, swinging an explosive on a chain."

"Yeah, well—it never happened. Take my word for it."

It wasn't a complete surprise to Margie. She had always questioned the priestly garb story—too G.I. Joe–like, and when she got the call in January and accepted that Our Local Hero had made a baby one fine night in 1944, it opened the door to new information. And then Norbert had sent her a few of Gussie's letters. She had reread them on the plane over, one written during the battle for the Benedictine Abbey at Monte Cassino in which Gussie described the range of snow-topped mountains around it, the ferocity of the Allied bombing, the night sky lit up with cascades of detonations. He had been marching with his platoon along a dirt road through the ruins of a village, and they stopped for smokes, and lay inside a garden wall and lit up, and one man found a battered Victrola in the house and cranked it up and a little orchestra played "Bye Bye Blackbird" and Gussie got up and danced a jig and that was when the brigadier spotted him and took him into custody as his aide-de-camp. The brigadier was on foot, having been de-Jeeped by a pair of colonels, and was lost and dejected and his feet were wet, and there was Gussie jigging in the mud, a big grin on his face, and the brigadier said, "Corporal, you've been reassigned to my outfit. Go and find me a vehicle." Margie did not think the young man dancing to "Bye Bye Blackbird" would charge a German machine-gun nest, swinging an explosive on a chain.

Maria said, "The truth is that Papa never killed anybody. He told Mama that. He was with the brigadier who was a dedicated coward and Papa stuck with him, and then he went AWOL the night before the liberation of Rome and came into the city by bus, arriving before the American army, and snuck into a hotel where my mother was waiting for him. He slept with her and left in the early morning hours, a little hungover, I suppose, and slipped on some ice in the street and hit his head and died in a hospital a week later. She had him buried with Keats and Shelley in the Protestant Cemetery. I'll take you there."

NORBERT

The day after Maria phoned in January, Margie called Norbert Norlander to tell him about his Italian niece. His housekeeper answered. 'He's not here," she said. "He's suffered a setback." She gave Margie another number, the Angels of Mercy nursing home on Immaculata Drive. His bedside phone. His voice was growly, like he was turning a crank and grinding peanuts. Probably he'd worked outdoors with heavy machinery and had to shout a lot. "Where'd you get my name?" he said. He got weepy when she mentioned August.

"Jesus God in Heaven, I was all packed up to fly to Rome the week before Christmas. I was going to go over and put his picture on his gravestone. I promised Mother thirty years ago I'd do that and dang it, I just kept putting it off. I was running myself ragged, drilling oil wells down here and going through a divorce and dealing with bladder cancer. Anyway, Gussie's in a military cemetery outside Rome. He was an aide to a Brigadier Somebody, a one-star general, and he was having a great time in Italy, he was hotfooting it around and avoiding heroism and he was in love with an Italian gal he met during the Anzio landing. She came out in a rowboat with a lantern and guided them in."

"Gennaro?"

"That's it. How'd you know?"

"Her daughter called me yesterday."

"Oh. Her. The communist. I cut off contact with her. She's just trying to get money out of this. Don't kid yourself. I'm on to her game. She just wants to get an Italian court to declare paternity and come over here and collect money for child support, take my home, my car. You don't want to mess with her. Talked to her once and she gave me an earful about Vietnam. To hell with her. Anyway, Mom died in '78 and in the hospital she made me promise her on a Bible to go to Rome and find his grave and put Gussie's picture on his gravestone. Mom was a sort of mystic. Being married to my dad, she had to be a mystic—how else was she going to know what was on his mind? She was taking laundry off the line one day and lightning struck the pole and, *bang*, it gave her mystical visions. Gussie appeared to Mom in some of these visions and some days he was happy, some days he just sat with his head in his hands. She baked chocolate-chip cookies for him but he had no appetite. He said things like 'It wasn't like you think it was.' She said, 'How was it, Gussie?' He said, 'Not like you think it was. But it's all over, it doesn't matter,' he said. And then he'd moan. That made her cry and he'd say, 'Ma, they all died and it didn't matter. Nobody cared. It didn't change a single thing. The world goes on. They just went up the road and died in the mud and the filth and then life went on and it didn't matter. The Germans didn't want Italy and neither did we. It was all for show. A big opera except they shot the orchestra. What was the point of it?' She spent her last days talking to him. And after she died, by God she started dropping in on me and saying, 'Why haven't you done what you said you'd do? Honor your brother.' In Mom's family, they always put a picture of the dead person on the gravestone, as a sign of respect. The picture said you were *somebody*. Not just a lump of dirt. You lived, you laughed, you danced the polka. The army inscription is all cut and dried, name, your outfit, date of death, that's all you get, and she wanted him to be *somebody*. She said to me, 'Norby, he's lying there like a piece of garbage.' I said, 'Ma, you can't bring back the dead.' She said, 'No, but we don't have to treat him like trash.'

"She'd saved up money to go to Italy and by the time she had the fare, she was in a wheelchair so the money sat in the bank and then in her will she designated it for the purpose of putting his picture on the gravestone. Ma was a bulldog. Let me tell you. Once she got an idea she stuck with it.

"I promised her I'd go to Rome and put it on his gravestone. And that gave her peace at the end. So finally I was all set to fly to Rome and then I met a woman online and she talked me into going dancing with her and we were doing a mambo and I got dizzy and slipped and tore my knee to shreds and they operated on it and it's still not right and now they're taking me off painkillers. I'm in rough shape. Oh ducky, I wish to hell I could find someone to do this for me."

"You want me to go to Rome? I can go."

He was in pain. He sounded like someone was sitting on his

chest. He said, "I never met you, never knew any Krebsbachs when we lived there. I'm sure you come from good people though."

"Actually, I am a Schoppenhorst," she said. "Krebsbach is my husband's family. My dad was the butcher. On Main Street, next to Skoglund's. It's gone now. But I'd be happy to do it." She was afraid he might croak right now and then what?

"It would be such an enormous favor." His voice broke. He was about to get on the bus to heaven. A nurse came in his room and he put his hand over the phone. Muffled voices. He came back to the phone. He sounded groggy. Maybe they'd shot him up with Percocet.

"A guy always assumes he has more time, you know? And I think maybe mine has run out. So there's no point in being coy about it. If you'd do this for me, I'd be in your debt forever. If you said no, I wouldn't blame you at all. You don't know me from a bale of hay. If you'd go to Rome and find my brother's grave and put his picture on it, if you would do that for me"—he took a deep steadying breath—"I could be at peace with my mother. I don't know about God, but Mother, yes."

She didn't exactly say yes—she said, "I'll do it if I can get some people to come with me"—but he wept. "That is a huge load off my mind," he sobbed. "You have no idea. I've thought about this every day for the past ten years."

And then he dropped the other shoe.

"Ma left the travel money in treasury bonds and now it's $150,000 so if you want to go and take some people with you, there's money for that."

She was about to say that she couldn't possibly accept money from him to go to Italy. And then she swallowed those words and said, "Well, let me think about it."

After they said good-bye, she wanted to ask him straight out:

Why did Gussie attack the German machine-gun nest? Was his unit pinned down?

What else do you know about the Gennaro woman? She sounded very nice to me. Tell me the truth.

Do you have children? Are you rich? Are you a Republican?

Do you have any nice memories of Lake Wobegon? Were people nice to you?

It dawned on her that night that fate had chosen her to lead a trip to Rome, she who had never so much as led a trip to Melrose or Sauk Centre. There are things that will not be done unless you do them yourself. And she went into training for it. A brisk walk in the morning, fifteen minutes out and turn around and come home. More fruit. Cinnamon tablets and fish oil and vitamin E. Dandelion tea. She had won a great prize, the good faith of the Norlanders, who would handsomely provide for a group of Wobegonians to travel to Italy for the purpose of plastering a picture of their dead son on his tombstone. This much was clear. But how many travelers could fly over and back for $150,000? Maybe a dozen. Who should go? And who does not get to go?

Now there is the question.

No, no, no. *You do not have to take twelve people on this trip. It does not take twelve people to stick a picture on a gravestone. You and Carl can do this, the two of you. Fly first class and stay in a five-star hotel. Why not?*

WHY NOT

1. It would be selfish and sinful.
2. People would be angry and not speak to you and you'd have to move to Minneapolis.
3. Bad karma. Something bad would happen. Carla would be robbed by a thug. Carl Jr. would lose his job and go on food stamps and get fat, as poor people so often do, and take temporary work as a subject in cruel experiments.

WHY

1. It would not be selfish or sinful. It was your idea to call Norbert Norlander and he offered you $150,000 to go to Rome. He didn't say you had to take along ten other people.
2. So what if they do get angry? Their problem. And if they're so small-minded, maybe I want to move to Minneapolis anyway.
3. Superstition. Not part of Christianity at all. Grow up.

And then she thought, "No. This is a story. You are only a character in it. You're not the author. You don't have to justify a beautiful stroke of good luck. Accept it. Smile and say thank you. You have endured long stretches of tedium and your share of sudden hard blows. You love a man for his good humor and good heart and marry him, try to do the right thing, make a nice home with music playing and the smell of baking, bring your kids up to work hard and tell the truth, and you go through the miserable arguments ('You don't care about me and the kids. You don't care what we want or how we feel. We're just baggage to you') and you survive those and then you have to survive the worst blows, the miseries of your kids."

Their daughter Carla was the brainy one who was supposed to go to college and become a scientist and instead she fell in love with Jack the guitarist and followed him to New York where she lived in various states of illusion for three years—Budding Actress, Soon-to-Be Singer, Author of Memoir—moving from sublet to sublet in far upper Manhattan. When Carl flew out to rescue her, she was staying with an ex-boyfriend and his girlfriend, sleeping on their couch, to save money for singing lessons. She was dressed all in black with a red shawl, dark red lipstick and fingernails, and her hair seemed to be styled at random, in the dark. He asked how she was. Fine. Good.

"I came out to make sure you're not sick."

"I'm not," she said.

"Are you pregnant?"

"No," she said, "I'm not."

"You're sure?"

"Yes, I took a test yesterday. I'm not."

Okay. Good. But a large chasm opened up at his feet, and he flew home in a slight panic, which made the bat episode even worse. A month later, Carla met Bradley, fresh out of chiropractic school, and melted right into marriage to him, and now was trying to have his baby, which she believed would save the marriage from the dead weight of Brad's anxiety. He had to avoid chocolate, loud noise, and direct sunlight, and needed to have a child for a sense of "completion," whatever that meant.

A long story. *Ai yi yi.*

Carl Jr. had quit a good job with Northwest Airlines—"It's getting in the way of my life," he said—to be a songwriter and barista in Seattle, content to make four hundred lattes a day and write songs about uncertainty and indifference. He had tried to find himself in Minneapolis and now he was trying to find himself in Seattle. He was sort of tracking himself across the country.

He attended Wisconsin Wesleyan for one year, the year that puncturing holes in each other's bodies was the vogue on campus. It was a coed dorm and there was a lot of sex going on and beer flowed freely and they used a leather punch to install new metal in each other. He got an eyebrow ring, a nose plug, a neck ring, and an odd bacterial infection that went on for three years. Something usually found only in owls.

Margie was pretty sure he was gay. He lived with three roommates, two of whom were definitely gay, and he never mentioned girls in a romantic way. No girlfriend. And he dressed gaily and fussed over his apartment. Unlike regular men. You went there and expected to see empty beer bottles on the floor and pizza boxes and underpants with skid marks but instead it was immaculate and had vases with dried weeds in them and lamps with tassels and a black-and-white striped throw over the sofa.

And Cheryl, the spunky one in the family, gone to Minneapolis to be a free spirit and enroll in a community college (Dance Workshop; Introduction to Film; Human Sexuality; and a composition course, Keeping a Personal Journal), and that lasted for a year and now she worked at the cosmetics counter at Wal-Mart and was finding out that life is real (though her Facebook page showed 865 "friends," most of whom she had never met). She wore tiny blue rectangular glasses. She never cooked. She sang in a vegan punk band, Dead Babies:

> If you eat meat, why not drink blood?
> Pick up roadkill out of the mud.
> Nice fresh weasel crushed by a diesel.
> And if it's rotten, serve it au gratin.

A whole catalogue of trouble. And now Carl didn't want to sleep with her anymore. As Carla used to say: UNFAIR.

But now comes $150,000 walking through the door on its hind legs, hand outstretched, and *Hello Stranger*. She might have to lie and tell Carl she won the money in a contest. Name the Lake Home, Fly to Rome—"Honey! Wowser! Look at this! I won! I won! O boyoboyoboyoboy. They chose my entry, 'Lake Haven' and now we can go to Rome, you and me, darling."

And then Mr. Keillor stepped in and made his generous gift to the August Norlander Memorial Expedition.

MR. KEILLOR SPEAKS

Mr. Keillor was coming to address the Thanatopsis Women's Club at their February luncheon at the Sons of Knute Lodge ("My Life in Broadcasting"), rescheduled from September when, if the truth be told, he'd gotten a better offer (he said it was the flu but the next day he was doing Larry King. LK: "Your last book, *Spittoon*—I laughed so hard, I practically busted my hernia." GK: "Thanks. It was a joy to write.") and Judy Ingqvist asked Margie to introduce him.

"He needs no introduction. Everybody knows him too well already," she told Judy.

"Everybody deserves an introduction. Just don't mention his marriages and he's very sensitive about his age. And his looks. Butter him up a little and pop him in the oven."

"Why me?"

"Because you're our writer, Margie."

She rolled her eyes. "Oh please—"

"I love that poem of yours. Don't be so modest. It's good."

"That poem" was a sonnet Margie had written too many

years before. Good grief. And now her old friends' daughters had it read at their weddings.

> To those who are in love, each day is a gift
> And this is why we embark on marriage
> To see the beloved every day and our hearts lift
> And we sit together on a bench amid the foliage.
> Dear you nesting comfortably at my left side,
> Your head on my shoulder against my cheek,
> Arms around each other in the fragrant eventide,
> And we whisper in the dark and then we do not speak.
> Your body and mine fit so comfortably. I put
> My hand against the side of your beautiful head
> And we sit peacefully merged from head to foot,
> Wrapped in one thought that doesn't need to be said.
> Once we walked home and you kissed me at my door.
> This is the day we say good-bye no more.

Margie winced everytime she heard it. So girlish and naive, written when she was eighteen and still dating Larry whom she didn't like, but she wrote the poem and when it appeared in the *Literary Leaf*, people congratulated *Larry* for God's sake. Assuming he and Margie were engaged. God help us. "I didn't know you felt that way," he said. "I don't," she replied. It was humiliating. To be known for a thing you'd done so many years ago. Like some old souse in the Sidetrack still thought of as a star quarterback though it had been a thousand bottles of whiskey ago. She had borne three children—three epidurals, three epi-siotomies, three kids breast-fed and toilet trained, three leaky boats launched—and now her biological clock had stopped and her life expectancy clock had begun. She was fifty-three. Twelve years to retirement, twenty-seven years to octogenarianhood. But here in "the Little Town That Time Forgot" she still was the brainy girl with her nose in a book who wrote sonnets.

So she would have to introduce Mr. Keillor. —"It doesn't have to be long. Just make him feel at home."

"Well, the truth is that I'm not such a big fan of his work," she said. "I've tried to read it and just can't get into it."

"Just rattle off his awards and tell people his radio show has four million listeners and let it go at that."

Four million people, tuning in to hear Mr. Keillor's quiet monotone murmuring on about the weather and gardening and how he once threw a tomato at his sister. Unbelievable. How empty people's lives must be. But of course on any given day there are millions in nursing homes, unable to reach the OFF knob—millions more in correctional institutions where a cruel warden might force entire cell blocks to endure two hours of folksy chuckles. She'd heard his radio show a few times, while running errands on Saturday, twisted the radio dial and there he was, murmuring away, telling stories about a gloomy small town she didn't recognize at all, full of righteous yokels addicted to tuna hot dish.

Oh well.

She dressed up for the occasion, snazzy black pants, pale yellow blouse, and low-heeled pumps, applied some blush and rose lipstick. Then her big down parka. A bitterly cold day and her car wouldn't start and she was about to set out on foot the four blocks to the Sons of Knute when her father-in-law, Florian, drove by and insisted on helping, an old man laboriously attaching a pair of jumper cables to her battery step by painful step, shimmery snow falling as if inside a snow globe, billows of steam from chimneys, and then she had to invite him in to warm up with a cup of coffee, and he sat and complained about Myrtle and how she wanted to go to Florida in February and if she wanted to go so bad, why couldn't she go, dammit, why did she have to drag him along with her? "So what's going on with you?" he said. And she told him she had some travel plans of her own. Rome. In April.

"Oh my gosh, Myrtle's going to have a fit if she doesn't get to go with you," he said.

Oh God. No way. Not her shrieking mother-in-law. Her voice could strip wallpaper. "She can't come. You have to be in good shape. We'll be climbing mountains."

"She's been climbing all over me for fifty-two years. You bet she's in shape!"

It was bitterly cold, so the Sons of Knute cloakroom felt crowded because everybody was twice as big with their big down parkas on, a parade of dirigibles with moon boots and chopper mittens.

Thanatopsis met in the Knutes' ceremonial room, horned helmets and musty animal skins and Norwegian banners hanging on the walls, framed photos of former Grand Oyas, some stuff in Norwegian, a painting of King Haakon standing in the middle of Main Street (as if!) looking like a man with a migraine. Judy had sprayed the room with lilac mist to mitigate the odor of cigarette smoke. Sixteen round tables, blue tablecloths, a copy of Mr. Keillor's *Love Sonnets* at each place, the room packed with women, Sister Arvonne chattering about the inauguration of Obama and how thrilled she was to have a president who can open his mouth and talk, and Myrtle Krebsbach in her jet black wig, her cackling laugh like sharp hammer blows, Eloise hollering at somebody across the room. The Catholics were loud, the Lutherans soft-spoken as a rule. (Except for her, Margie.)

And now Judy Ingqvist was at the lectern, twenty feet away, opening the meeting, tall, dignified, blond, while Eloise was still flapping around the room, whooping, winking, poking, wearing a corsage the size of a toaster. Fascinating to watch her. Wobegonians tended to be polite, leery of giving offense, so they are easy prey for a loud, pushy person like Eloise. "I don't believe it!" she screeched, and whacked Mary Magendanz on the shoulder. "He said *what*? What a crusty old booger he is! Well, we'll clean his clock for him. We'll take him down a notch or two." The old boys who used to run the town were utterly dumbfounded by Eloise. She blew into town, went to a council meeting two days later, stood up and spoke, and she never stopped. The old boys were only interested in roads, roads, roads, and dead opposed to zoning or libraries or historic preservation, they were all about road grading and dumping gravel and filling potholes and God forbid we should spend money on a public tennis court, what do we need with that? Eloise came in and rousted those old boys and made them cry in their beer. She blew them out of the water. Val Tollefson had asked Bud to haul dead brush out of his (Val's) yard with the municipal truck and Eloise hung him out to dry. Misuse of public funds, plain and simple. She depantsed him in public and the old boys quietly folded their hands and let her walk over him. The power of surprise attack. Meanwhile, Myrtle was talking about pancreatic cancer, and the guest speaker for the day,

Mr. Keillor, sat at the head table, smiling in a non-directional way. He wore a black suit a size too small, a white shirt, and a bright red tie with coffee stains. She noticed a green leaf on his cheek, so she walked up and said hello. "Good to see you," she said and pointed to her cheek. "You've got a piece of salad or something on your face." He brushed it away. He looked peeved. A person should be grateful to have facial food pointed out to them, but not him. Oh well. She wondered how he felt when he returned to his old hometown. Did he regret his career of self-display—did he understand that the self he paraded was not the one everyone in Lake Wobegon remembered? To them, he was a small dark cloud of a man given to sarcasm and ridicule, a man of false humility covering enormous self-regard, but on the radio, he was jovial and winsome, Pal to the People, Celebrator of Home & Family & Heartland & Hard Work. He was an ace at the classic American game of playing dumb. An educated man pretending to be a simple peasant, the oldest dodge in the books, the secret of demagogues and flimflam men since time immemorial. Somehow he'd achieved fame of a sort, but at home he was strictly a nonentity. Lake Wobegon High was a small school but many people in the class of 1960 didn't remember him at all. Years later, when he became famous, they saw his picture in the paper and thought, *Who? Where was he? In some state facility for troubled youth and got his diploma in summer school? Was he in our school?*

She glanced at the sheet his publicist had sent, which mentioned New York, Los Angeles, San Francisco, cities he'd performed in, colleges that gave him honorary doctorates, magazines who had published the *drip-drip-drip* of his pen. The career did not line up somehow with the spooky teenager he was at LWHS who would walk up to girls and say, "Do you think that life is real or is it only a dream and if so am I in your dream or are you in mine and if you suddenly woke up would I disappear or would I go into somebody else's?" Seeing him, waiting for his moment to shine, she had an urge to counsel him. ("Take a year off. Two years. Find out who you are. Get reacquainted with your friends. Plant a garden. Find some hobbies.") And then she felt a burst of resolve. *Go up there and steal his thunder. Blow this dude away. Show him he is dealing with serious people, not flibbertigibbets.*

She stood, gripped the lectern, and her carefully memorized introduction ("It's my honor to introduce a man who literally needs no introduction . . .") went up in smoke, poof, and she was left speechless—a sudden sideswipe of the brain that left her afloat in emptiness like a hawk on an updraft from which she saw them with terrible hawklike clarity. Myrtle turning away to dredge up a Kleenex out of her coat pocket. Eloise staring forward, her mind a million miles away. Judy Ingqvist smiling the professional encouraging smile of a pastor's wife. Margie's sister Elaine examining her cell phone. Cindy Hedlund on the verge of an enormous yawn. Arlene Bunsen squinting, her finger exploring a small red pustule under her eye. Irene Bunsen, hands folded so she could look down at her watch. Marilyn Tollerud looking as if she were on the verge of flight, Dorothy sitting placid and content and Darlene next to her brooding over her lonely life. And then Margie let go of the lectern and she said, "Before I introduce today's speaker, I want to talk about something very close to my heart." And stopped. And the room was utterly still.

"Sixty-some years ago a fine young man named August Norlander left Lake Wobegon and joined the U.S. Army and went off to North Africa and then to Italy in the winter of '43. Many of you know the story of how he charged a German machine-gun nest single-handed and lost his life and thereby saved his battalion from getting wiped out. As it says in Scripture, 'No greater love hath a man than he will lay down his life for his friends.' He grew up among us, on a farm just north of here, he enjoyed a happy childhood, rode his bike on our roads, played football for the Leonards, was in the senior class play, and then on a fall day in 1942, he got on a bus and never came back. His old mother grieved for him and it was her fondest dream to go to Rome where Gussie is buried and place a picture of him on his tombstone. As you know, that is an old German custom, and a way of honoring the dead and showing that we remember them. She couldn't make it to Rome, so she asked her son Norbert to do it, and now he's too old to go, and so, in April, Carl and I are going to Rome to finally honor August Norlander as his mother wished. And I hope that some of you will want to come with."

And people started to clap, and then some of the women jumped to their feet, and Mr. Keillor rose to his feet and clapped, which startled Margie and she stepped modestly away from the podium just as Eloise came galloping up to the front to grab a leadership role. People were standing and applauding, and she stepped up as if the applause were for her!

"Count me in!" she cried. "If you don't mind traveling with your sister-in-law, I'm with you, count me in!" And Myrtle hollered, "I'm with you!" And there were other shouts from women to count them in. Margie held up her hands for silence. "Thank you for your support. And now here is our main speaker, Mr. Gary Keillor."

Mr. Keillor hesitated. He had been expecting something fuller and richer. He smiled at her as if to encourage her to go on and tell about his books, his radio show, and so forth. Whispers of "Italy" rippled through the room like rain on a roof. He looked uneasy but then he always had: the man was born furtive. He lumbered to the podium as the room buzzed like summer cicadas crying *ItalyItalyItalyItalyItalyItalyRomeItalyItalyItaly*. He stood smiling his odd half smile and listened to the birdsong around the room *ItalyItalyItalyItalyItalyItaly* and he said what an honor it was to be there talking to the women of Lake Wobegon and how women were the most important people in his life and everything good he had done in his life was done in hopes of the approval of women and that he was personally thrilled by the introduction—how about a big hand for Margie Krebsbach? (APPLAUSE)—and how August Norlander deserved to be remembered and how he couldn't help but be reminded of Memorial Day services up at the cemetery where the bugler sat in the old oak tree to play "Taps" and the VFW honor guard fired a rifle salute and how he, as a Boy Scout, had stood and recited:

> In Flanders Fields the poppies blow
> Between the crosses row on row,
> That mark our place; and in the sky
> The larks, still bravely singing, fly
> Scarce heard amid the guns below.

And just then came a crash from the kitchen, as if the refrigerator had fallen over—he jumped back, but recovered, and bravely continued:

The boy stood on the burning wreck,
My Captain lying on the deck,
And O the bleeding drops of red—
"Shoot, if you must, this old gray head,
But curfew must not ring tonight!"
Cannons to the left and right
And theirs not to reason why
Under the wide and starry sky,
Under the spreading chestnut tree—
"One if by land and two if by sea!"
So gather ye rosebuds while ye may,
For today may be our dying day
And when the summons comes to go
Rejoin the ones we used to know,
May we with our forefathers say,
As they ascended yon mountainside,
"Excelsior!" and the maiden cried,
"Turn back!" and the youth replied
That he would not til he had tried,
He had miles to go before he slept
And promises that must be kept
And thoughts that lie too deep for tears.
Oh yes, too deep for tears. Too deep.
Just like those brave men who sleep
In Flanders Fields.

The audience sat in silence. *Was that how the poem went?*
He held out his arms and said that he had been gone from their
midst for too long, that he was always refreshed by their com-

pany, and that he wanted to say right here and now that if the good people of Lake Wobegon organized a trip to Rome to honor our war dead, he intended to go with them.

Or that was what he meant to say. *I want to be a part of your trip to Rome.* Or *I just want to say—let's all go to Rome.*

But what he actually said was: "I want to pay for everyone who wants to go to Rome."

Pay. He offered to pay. It was like striking a match to dry tinder.

"Let me just clarify—" he said, but already the women were rising to their feet. Another standing ovation. They stood, old classmates, neighbors, babysitters, red-faced, cheering, pounding their mitts, pumping their fists. He stepped away, his face flushed, and Eloise Krebsbach yelled into the mike, "Isn't he something? Let's hear it for Gary Keillor. I speak for everyone in Lake Wobegon, Mr. Keillor, when I say, 'All is forgiven!'" A pained look on his face and a big laugh from the crowd. And she led them in a cheer, *hip-hip-HOORAY hip-hip-HOORAY.* Eloise threw her arms around him and said, "You can come speak at Thanatopsis anytime!" and he murmured something about having to check with his accountant, and of course it would need to be a registered nonprofit with an educational purpose. "Oh we can come up with an educational purpose," she said. "We'll call it the Norlander Memorial Fund. I'll have it registered tomorrow. We'll file the papers."

He didn't have his checkbook on him, he said. "You can write a promissory note out on a blank piece of paper," she said. "Works just as good." He demurred. He checked his cell phone for the time. He had to run. "We'll talk," he said, as he put on his coat.

"We trust you," she said, following him outside, into the wintery blast, the sky darkening in late afternoon. "But how about a phone number?" He handed her a business card.

GARY E. KEILLOR
Radio Host & Creative Consultant

Available for Public Speaking
Graduations, Motivational Award Dinners, Memorials

1. "The Road Not Taken". 15 min.
2. "God, I'm Hungry!" 20 min.
3. "The Life Well-Lived" 10 min.

OTHERS AVAILABLE ON REQUEST.

RATES VARIABLE, 10% DISCOUNT FOR FIRST-TIMERS.

"What do we want him for?" said Irene. "He just wants to latch onto this and get some publicity for himself."

"He offered to pay for whoever wants to go."

"Ha. Fat chance." The room was emptying, the word "Italy" still on people's tongues. Margie and Eloise were the last ones left.

"Sorry I got carried away," said Eloise. "Should've kept my big yap shut."

"It'll be an adventure, whatever it is," said Margie.

"Can I still come with?"

"Of course. But don't invite any more people."

THE ALLIED CAMPAIGN

That was the night Margie was fully intending to tell Carl about the Norlander bequest of $150,000, but now with the hoo-ha about Keillor's offer, she didn't need to. It could remain her own secret. What a beautiful secret. The money could sit in the bank accruing interest, awaiting some fine purpose, a trip around the world, maybe. She wanted to tell him. As soon as she got things figured out. Really she did. But it wasn't the right time. It was her money after all.

"So you're serious about going to Rome," he said. "I heard about what you said at the luncheon. Eloise is all up in flames about it. Calling people left and right. You're going to have a planeload. I'll bet you'll get three hundred people now." She put an arm around his shoulder and said, "If there were three thousand people, I wouldn't notice, so long as you came with me. This is for me and you. That's the only reason I want to go. I love you and I think we need to do something nice for ourselves."

Carl looked away. He didn't always respond well to pure feeling, especially loving sentiments, and that was why she so seldom expressed them.

"I dunno," he said. "It's expensive."

"You can't let your life be ruled by a stupid bat," she said.

"It's not that," he said. "It's the Ladderman house. That jerk is going to default on the whole thing and leave me holding a quarter million dollars of half-built house that nobody wants, least of all me. I trusted the guy and now I've got to pay. Ignorance comes with a high price. And then there's Cheryl. . . ."

He'd dropped in on Cheryl in Minneapolis and there amid the squalor was a stack of pamphlets about something called the Church of the Unified Mind. And there was a ring in her lower lip. Hard to ignore. She looked like a walleye who'd broken the line. And there was a boy named Andrew, with a wispy beard, his pants hanging low like he had a load in there, and when Carl asked him what he was up to, the kid shrugged and said, "Hey. Whatever." Cheryl was Daddy's girl. He never had the fights with her that Margie did. It killed him that she was sleeping with a loser.

Margie had been jousting with Cheryl since forever ("You're not going to wear that to the Prom. Get real. Hello? Sweetheart, the secret of attraction is mystery. You don't put it out there like fruit on a plate and have boys standing around staring at your rib cage." *"Okay then, I'll wear a burka to Prom. I won't dance with anybody, I'll sit behind a screen. Will that make you happy?"* "Honey, if you want, I can make something for you out of cheesecloth, Saran wrap, and some fishing line." Etcetera, etcetera.) but Carl was new to the game so he was shocked by little things like a no-good boyfriend. And then he saw the lurid tattoo that covered her entire left shoulder including her armpit! When she raised her arm, a cougar snarled at you from a cave.

Margie had dealt with the tattoo at Christmas (*Darling, that is permanent. Maybe it's cool now, but ten years from now, I don't think so. I had an uncle Harry who had a big tattoo on his belly of an American eagle holding Adolf Hitler in its talons. It blurred over time until it came to look like two chickens doing something dirty. Uncle Harry was a very nice man, but if he took off his shirt, people felt sorry for him. A word to the wise.*) and Carl found it nearly unbearable. His little girl, disfigured.

He came home from Minneapolis, his eyes red, holding a fifth of Scotch in a paper bag. He'd bought it down there and he'd been nipping at it en route. He said that he now knew that he knew less about life than the average ten-year-old. It was just too overwhelming. He was thinking about pulling up stakes, selling the house, making a new life out West. His old navy buddy Earl had offered him a partnership in his cabinet shop in Santa Rosa, north of San Francisco, on a hill looking out at the Pacific Ocean. Lots of work, good money, beautiful climate.

"So I don't think I can go to Rome," he said.

"It's the bat," she said. He shook his head. But she'd heard him one night cry out in his sleep across the hall, "Take her down, Jack. Secure the overheads." And woke up dripping sweat.

"Come with me to Rome, darling," she said.

"Well, let me think about it," he said. Which was his way of saying yes.

Dear Carl. He would need a powerful sedative. You could get this stuff online now, shipped out of Antigua air express in plain brown packages. Placidô worked beautifully. It was good for the heebie-jeebies, the jimjams, the fantods, and much more. Calmed you right down. You didn't want to look at the brochure that came with it, listing the possible complications—

angina, baldness, colitis, convulsions, collapsed lungs, diarrhea, eruptions, fatigue, fainting, facial tics, fibrillations, gastritis, hearing loss, indigestion, jumpiness, kleptomania, lethargy, mumps, neurosis, open sores, pinkeye, quaking, redness, shingles, tension, upset stomach, varicose veins, whooping cough, eczema, yellow jaundice, and zenophobia.

She ordered 180 tablets for $310. The pills would dissolve nicely in coffee. Give the man a tall latte and his troubles would be over.

She bought him a new billfold for the trip. His old one was moldy and torn and the bucking bronco was worn off.

And two days later by express mail, a manila envelope arrived, postmarked Tulsa, with N. NORLANDER in big black letters scrawled by an old man on heavy medication, and inside a note to her in his almost unreadable hand.

Dear Margie (if I may),

Ever since you said you'd go to Rome for me, a total stranger, and fulfil my promise to my late Mother I have been crying like a baby for sheer gratitude. I thank you. You are bringing me Peace of Mind, such as I have not known since Mother passed away. I'm sure she is smiling down from Heaven.

My brother August (Gussie) was a true original and had he not died tragically in the bloom of youth I do believe he might've gone on to do great things, maybe in the movies. Don't laugh. He had a way about him that reminded me of Gary Cooper if you remember him. I'll bet you those wops thought he was from New York or California, not a hayseed from Minnesota. They probably took him for a playboy. Everywhere he wanted to go, he was in like Flynn. He came out of basic training a plain old PFC and within three months he'd become an Army combat librarian, a nice piece of work, dispensing reading material to the boys in foxholes. Then he attached himself to this Brigadier and made himself indispensable, stealing whiskey for him, spying, covering for his sorry butt. He wrote me the whole story. He was no fool, my brother. I thought you should know more about him, so have photocopied letters.

There are more, if you want more. Gussie had a lot to say.

Cordially, in your debt,
Norbert

Paper-clipped to it were six letters in faint typescript on yellowish onionskin paper, letters from Gussie in Italy, 1943–44. She carried them gingerly into the living room and settled down in the deep green easy chair and began to read.

12/31/1943
Dear Lille Bror,

Well, we are making our way slowly toward Rome, shooting at the Germans and trying to keep the Italians from stealing our shoes. You have to chain your Jeep to a lamppost and even so they'll siphon the gas and strip it of tires and spare parts and leave you the skeleton, all in about thirty minutes. Italians don't want us here and I don't blame them. The Germans liked to get drunk and walk arm in arm down the street singing their old college songs whereas Americans split up and go off in search of Italian girls. So they steal our transport to protect their women. The only Americans who get drunk are the married guys. Single men buy some wine and cigarettes and go around hoping to share it with someone. But not me. I'm a Minnesota boy and very careful about the opposite sex so I stay in my billet and read. They just delivered a trunkful of donated books including ten volumes of Mark Twain so here I sit, bombers overhead, reading Innocents Abroad.

I am a driver for Brigadier Alan G. Parker who is, like me, a civilized fellow with no heroic urges whatsoever. He lives in a Palazzo and his office is the size of a basketball court, high ceilings, drapes, gilded plasterwork and he sits at an enormous desk and thinks about psychological warfare, mostly about how to avoid it. My job is to defend his Jeep, procure whiskey, and keep an eye out for any newspaper reporters or Generals in the vicinity. He lives very well and so do I, and I felt guilty about that but I got over it. I am a lucky guy. I was sent here to kill people and have not done it yet. Our boys are in bloody fighting around Cassino, north of here, but my Brigadier doesn't go to the Front and so neither do I. Call me a slacker and a foot-dragger, but I am not the only one. The army is full of studious bureaucrats with fruit salad for brains who busy themselves with great matters and study maps and file enormous reports and it's a good way to keep warm and out of harm's way. Intelligence is the place for a slacker: these guys stay so secret they don't know where they are themselves. The Germans have their Goebbels and we have ours and meanwhile life and death go on. Men I bunked with aboard the Richards are on the front line where you kill the enemy or make him run or he does something similar to you. A brutal business. A buddy of mine came back from the front wounded. He'd tripped and sprained his ankle. "I got a kraut," he said. "He was sitting under a tree talking on a telephone and I walked up behind him and he turned and I shot him in the face." I asked him why he didn't take the man prisoner. "Why would I do that?" The day after I landed at Anzio, a lieutenant stuck his face in my tent and hollered, "On the line! Pronto!" and I did not pick up my rifle and go. I am a coward. I could've been court-martialled for insubordination but it was overlooked. I ambled toward the rear and busied myself counting trucks as they came by and writing the numbers down on a piece of paper. I am nothing but a coward. A pacifist in uniform. A mouse hiding in the corn. At any moment I could feel German talons in my shoulders and go flying through the air, but I will do what I can to avoid it. I am a coward. They name football teams for killers, the Lions, the Bears, the Warriors, except in Minnesota where we're the Gophers, and that's what I am, a terrified rodent, hoping to survive.

A sleetstorm outside and olive leaves blowing around, and I go around on foot to reconnoiter and witness the suffering of soldiers trying to fix tents that got blown down, men freezing, cursing, and I ignore them and return to the Palazzo and my snug little room and the fine Armagnac in the Brigadier's larder. A little glass of it gives a taste of nobility, which there is none of in war whatsoever. Last week three men died, run over by their own trucks, stumbling drunk through the night, and every day somebody misreads the coordinates and American shells fall on American foxholes. More than you will ever know have died from diarrhea. They list them as "battle-related" but really it was diarrhea. Many purple hearts were men shitting themselves to death. Dying shitless.

You ask if I still believe in God, no, I do not and now I think I never did. Nor do I think Americans are any better than Germans. What I do believe in is the beauty and dignity of the individual and I find dignity in cowardice.

And now I must think of something to write to the folks.

Dear Lille Bror,

Well I found myself an Italian girlfriend as you suggested I do but I don't know if I will get to make time with her since all the Generals are rushing to get to Rome and have their pictures taken parading down the Via Appia, they don't care about the Germans so long as they get their big mugs in the paper looking rugged and battle-scarred. I hope that General Kendall of the 88th runs over a land mine and gets aerated sky-high, it would serve him right. His boys are known to shoot at anybody for any reason whatsoever.

Her name is Maria Gennaro and she was a ballet dancer, tall and dark-haired, strong legs and a big rump. She danced in Paris and Venice and signed up for the anti-fascist underground whereupon she slipped in the bathtub and that was the end of dancing. Now she's attached to us as a translator. She promises to take me to St. Peter's and show me when to kneel and when to stand. She knows four languages well and parts of some others. Mainly she helps us keep the partisans from executing the fascists they find. War brings out the worst in people if they aren't supervised closely. And in the midst of murder and piggishness, I met this lovely and sensible woman. I took her to lunch which meant I had to go AWOL which is easy to do, you just pretend to be lost, and if the MPs accost you, you say, "I can't find my unit." We went to a hotel for lunch and the food was good and we talked about morale. She said, "Morale is the ability to believe something that you know isn't true, namely immortality. The Polacks were sent to attack Cassino and their morale was fabulous and so they got annihilated. They were confident they would walk over the Germans and as a result they took the worst losses. We Italians don't believe in morale. We love life too much." She considers me dashing, if you can imagine. She wants to know about cowboys so I tell her some things. I've known her three weeks and she has said about a hundred times, "You are so handsome!" I guess she thinks I am handsome. So at lunch I was thinking we could get a hotel room but how would I know if she wanted to or not. I am new to this, you know. She touched my arm when we left the café and said thank you, if that is some sort of signal. She said to me, "When we get to Rome, I could find you an apartment with a garden." She seemed to imply that she would be there, too. I kissed her good-bye on the cheek and she didn't slap me, so I've got that going for me. She is twenty-eight. I gave her a carton of Chesterfields for the nuns. She lives in a convent near Anzio though I don't believe she's taken the vows herself. I worry about her with all these sex-starved Yanks around. I gave her a .45 pistol and a smoke flare. It may take more than a bullet to stop these guys.

Well, I must go now and win the war.

Your brother,
Gussie

The next morning, she called Norbert and he asked her if she meant it when she said she'd go to Rome for him. "Yes, I told you I would and I will." "My lawyer thinks I am crazy to send $150,000 to someone I never even met," he said. "But it's Mother's money, not mine. And she died in the peace of knowing I would keep my word to her. She knew that her boy's grave would be properly marked." And Norbert started to cry. "I'm sorry," he said. "You'd think a man could talk about this and not blubber, wouldn't you. I mean it was sixty years ago. Jesus." He gave his nose a honk. "He was just a great kid. A great great kid. He got all the bad luck, I got all the good." He told her he had once performed in the circus, shooting a lighted cigarette out of the mouth of a lady acrobat as she swung on a trapeze and him with his back to her, aiming the rifle over his shoulder, a small rearview mirror attached to his glassses, and later in the show he was wrapped in chains, wrists handcuffed, ankles strapped, and thrown in a tank full of piranhas that went into a feeding frenzy when he dropped in. And then it came out that the rifle shot blanks and the lighted cigarette had a small explosive device in the tip and there were no piranhas, just ordinary minnows and the frothy water was caused by the carbonated crystals in his pants. "A mob was waiting in the dark as we took down the tent that Sunday night, and I had to be smuggled out in a crate marked DANGEROUS SNAKES with two big pythons who were busy swallowing rats. When you escape lynching, everything that happens afterward is a Bonus. I've had a good life. No regrets. Just this one. I never fixed up my brother's grave. I'm counting on you, kid."

FENDING OFF THE MOB

Mr. Keillor went off on a long lecture tour of the West and Eloise was unable to reach him for two weeks, so all the commotion he'd aroused fell on Margie. Eloise had other projects on her plate now—a community concert series, a bike trail around the lake, a plan to consolidate Lake Wobegon schools with the Millet schools, the making of a Lake Wobegon web site, a plan to turn the old depot into a historical museum—every week some brilliant new idea burst forth to occupy her for a few days and then dwindled into the shadows as she got caught up in something new. The trip to Rome was now in Eloise's rearview mirror. Her last word on the subject was that it might make a good story on CNN if Margie would organize a parade to kick it off. A parade in March? No way, said Margie. Too cold. Eloise was telling all Rome applicants to call Margie. The day after Thanatopsis she got sixty-seven calls—*thank God for voice mail*—one message after another: "Margie, it's Ronnie, Ronnie Schaefer. How're you doing? Listen, I heard that you're planning this trip to Rome in April and Lonnie and I talked about it and we'd like to come with if you still have openings. Give me a call, would you?" One after another. And fifty-six the next day. People walked up to her in the middle of Sunday morning Mass as the choir sang an irritating song called "I've Got the Joy Joy Joy Joy Down in My Heart"—Carl wanted to go to the Contemporary service now, it began an hour later. She stood there clapping along because if you didn't clap and smile people thought you were an atheist or had PMS, so she clapped unhappily, and people thrust notes in her hands, saying *Put us down for Rome. Marlene & Ken* and *There are ten Luegers on the list for Rome, not eight as Jon told you on Wednesday. Ten (10). Please call if you have any questions.*

There would've been more calls except that people in Lake Wobegon knew Mr. Keillor's penchant for making up things and so his offer of a Free Ride to Rome was not given as much credence as if, say, Gary Eichten, popular WLT newscaster and host of *Eichten at the Mike,* had said it. Nonetheless, Margie got tired of telling people that Mr. Keillor was very busy and to hold your horses and not get your hopes up. Darlene asked her six times in two days, "When will I hear about Rome?" and Margie told her that there was a strict quota on non-Catholics traveling to Rome and they were required to carry a rosary. Not required that they actually use it, just have it in their possession.

"Well, I'll be damned," said Darlene.

Margie skipped lunch at the Chatterbox for three days. She drove to Little Falls to do her grocery shopping. She turned the phone off and pulled the shades.

Judy Ingqvist called to say that she and David couldn't come since the trip to Rome fell the week before Palm Sunday—D-Day was March 25—so that wouldn't work for them.

"I'm sorry," said Margie. But she wasn't sorry at all. David Ingqvist was a pill. Anytime you tried to make pleasant conversation with him, he had to tell you how horrified he was by George W. Bush. Margie was a Democrat, so was Carl, but enough is enough. Obama was in office, so let's move on. But it wasn't W who got the pastor's goat so much as his brother Michael. Four years younger, an All-American tackle at Concordia—or he would've been, but he got nailed for steroids and dropped out, turned to pro wrestling as the Messenger of Death, doing nasty pile drivers and spinal twists, then came to Jesus by parachuting into a Billy Graham rally at Daytona Speedway that made the front page of the *New York Times*. Went to Wheaton and took over a tiny geriatric church in Denver and grew it from 75 members to 14,000 in three years by communicating to people that God Is Not an Angry God, He Is a Happy God. You couldn't mention Michael to David, nor even mention Colorado. He would get silent and leave the room.

Marilyn said that she and Daryl would love to come. Or she would love to, and he was agreeable. "He doesn't want to do anything with me anymore. I don't know why. He'll go to a basketball game with anybody who wants to go but if I want to do something, he finds some excuse not to."

Eloise called to ask if it would be okay to bring Fred.

"Absolutely not."

"Please. I'm afraid he's going to leave me."

"No. Too much drama."

"He quit drinking. Honest. He went to Hazelden after that nonsense in Sauk Centre and he's dry now. But I think he went into treatment just to get away from me and meet some needy young woman and I believe he's met her."

"The rule is Spouses Only. Fred is not a spouse. He's a louse."

Eloise started to cry. "He's all I have in this world. Hazelden was so good for him and then he met her and now she's convinced him that he needs to go on his life journey with her. How can he do that to me? *How can he throw me over after all I've done for him?*"

The next day, as Margie was getting home from school, Eloise drove up. She was a mess. Bloated, red-eyed from crying, her long hair tangled up in back, her linen pants a mass of wrinkles. Margie offered her coffee. Eloise asked for vodka. No ice.

"I was the one who got him into AA, for God's sake. Ten years he and I were together. Every Saturday night I made supper for him. I listened to his troubles. He has a genetic intolerance of winter and a compulsive fireplace obsession. He poured out his heart to me. I went to bed with him. I held him until he went to sleep. That time he went crazy at the Fireman's Cookout in St. Cloud with a fire hose between his legs and he shot water at people and knocked them down, I was the one who got him out of jail and into couples counseling. We discovered there are three kinds of relationships—conflict-avoidance, validating, and volatile—and that ours was number three. That took six weeks and cost me $800. Then one very cold night he fell off the wagon and went to Sauk Centre and pissed on a policeman. I rescued him again. Shoveled him into Hazelden for six weeks and paid half the freight and now he goes off with this tootsie who stands up in AA and tells a long story about what brought her there and he feels sorry for her and now he's *sleeping* with her. It absolutely breaks my heart." And Eloise fell into Margie's arms and it sort of broke Margie's heart too. As bossy as Eloise was, nonetheless she had propped that man up and treated him with tender kindness and then he dropped her like a used Kleenex and took up with someone twenty-one years younger.

"I must be some kind of horrible person. That he couldn't wait to get away from me."

"You're not a horrible person. He is."

"I must be. People hate me."

"Nobody hates you."

"Yes, they do. I am just a bad person. I'm loud and controlling and I do nothing but make people miserable. My kids tell me that all the time. And they're right."

Eloise said she wished she could kill herself. She finished the vodka. "Don't go getting into trouble now," Margie said, and two minutes later, Eloise backed out of the driveway across the front lawn and destroyed two small spruces and a rosebush. Margie called Father Wilmer. "Eloise is in need of some help. I wonder if you could go over and talk to her."

"About what?"

"Fred dumped her. You know about Fred. "

"I do," Father said, with a sigh.

"Now she's gone to pieces and gotten drunk and she's driving around like a crazy person. Somebody needs to tell her to quit being mayor and move to Minneapolis where she can find a man who will be decent to her."

He murmured something about how much good Eloise does

and maybe we should all rally around her and give her more support. "She doesn't need support. Support won't cut it. She needs
intervention. Speak to her, Father. That's your job."

Father said he would pray for her. Certainly. He would pray for
her daily. "Is the trip to Rome on?" he said.

"If Eloise hangs herself with a coat hanger, the trip to Rome
is not on."

He said he would head over now and talk to her.

It was crazy, all the excitement about Mr. Keillor sending
them to Rome and Margie having to deal with them all—visions
of a 747 full of moochers and freeloaders, the loungers and wide-
rides, the Sidetrack crowd, the investors in lottery tickets, and
her the Shepherd of the Lurchers & Losers, trying to move them
on and off buses and through crowded sites in a foreign city—
great God, the thought of it. How to kill this ASAP?

ATTENZIONE

Thank you for your interest in our trip to Rome and thanks
to Mr. Keillor for his generosity. All expenses paid! The opportunity of a lifetime! If you wish to participate, be advised
that you must first (1) pass a test in basic Italian, (2) make a
declaration of faith (*dichiarazione di fede*), (3) name the Seven
Deadly Sins (*Sette Peccati Capitali*) and check off which ones
apply to you and supply details. And remember—Rome is the
seat of the Roman Catholic Church and all visitors to the
Eternal City, both Catholic and non-, must carry rosaries on
their person at all times. Rules regarding adultery are very
strict and if you have commited such a sin in the past ten (10)

years, you should let us know ASAP. Thank you (*Grazie*).
Additional information (in Italian only) from http://www
.portaleimmigrazione.it or http://www.poliziadistato.it/pds/
ps/immigrazione/soggiorno.htm.

She wrote up the notice and then decided not to send it out.
Most people would recognize it as a fake, but some, blinded by
greed, would not, and she did not care to hear their confessions.
She wrote up another:

Dear Rome-bound Traveler,

This is to inform you that two persons in our party are allergic to meat and alcohol and as a result, the entire trip must
be meat- and alcohol-free. No consumption of meat or alcohol will be tolerated. Thank you for your understanding.

That might do the trick. The thought of teetotaling vegetari-
anism would pretty well kill off interest, she thought. But why
not deal with the problem at its source—she got the Great Bene-
factor's address and sent him a note:

Mr. Keillor:

It was terribly generous of you to offer to fly everybody to
Rome, and I salute you for that, but I think we need to look
at this realistically. Flying three hundred people from Lake
Wobegon to Rome for a week is going to cost you more than
you are able to pay, I am quite sure, or even a hundred—I

mean, you're talking about a million dollars, right? Judging by the sales of your most recent books, I doubt that you have that much cash to spend. And even if you could afford to send fifty people to Rome, I think you can imagine the hard feelings it would cause when some people get to go and others don't. It will be brother against brother, children against parents. Marriages will break up. There may be bloodshed. Surely you, America's Favorite Storyteller and the Chronicler of Small-Town America, can understand this. People here are not as charitable as you may imagine. Perhaps they were nicer sixty years ago when you were young, but not anymore. How will you select the lucky winners? Will you give free trips to the Fifty Neediest People in Town? Hold a lottery and allocate half the prizes to Lutherans and half to Catholics? Hold an essay contest and ask people to write five hundred words on "Pasta, Pizza, and Puccini"? Guess the number of rigatoni shells in the Ford pickup truck?

No matter how you award the prizes, there will be rejects—and the more prizes you give out, the worse the rejects will feel—and the day you return to your beloved hometown to visit your poor old mother, you'll find a mob of angry people carrying torches who will chase you across the corn stubble late at night and you'll have to take shelter in the blind man's cottage and he'll try to be nice to you but eventually he'll say, "Why didn't you take me on that trip to Rome? I had a dream that I went to Rome and the Pope touched my eyes and I could see again. Guess that's not going to happen now." And he'll pull out a gun and shoot you. Or try to. Imagine being chased through a cottage by an armed blind man.

So I suggest that we make an announcement here and now that there was a misunderstanding and you are going to donate some money to the Shining Star Scholarship Fund instead and you will pay expenses for the twelve persons already signed up. How does that sound?

Sincerely,
Marjorie Krebsbach
11th grade English teacher
Lake Wobegon High School

P.S. I meant to tell you that I think that *Happy to Be Here* is, by far, your best book. It's funny and very stylishly written. You ought to go back to writing that sort of thing.

And that's what happened. Mr. Keillor's accountant, Mr. Ross, called from Minneapolis to say that what with Mr. Keillor's difficulties with the IRS over the claim of a three-week vacation on Antigua as a business expense—research for a screenplay—there wouldn't be money to cover an open invitation, but yes, $60,000 to cover expenses for the original twelve passengers, that would be okay, provided he could pay half now and half at the completion of the trip. "Fine," said Margie. And she put a story in the *Herald Star*.

News has reached us that Mr. Gary Keillor, the radio show host and author of *Happy to Be Here*, will be flying to Rome on March 25 with eleven Lake Wobegon residents to honor World War II hero August Norlander (LWHS, '40). Keillor, who was honored by the Thanatopsians at last week's luncheon, also clarified an offhand remark made at the luncheon which some misunderstood as an offer to pay passage to Rome for anyone who wished to go. The offer, in fact, was to contribute money to the Sons of Knute Shining Star Scholarship Fund. "We are extremely touched by Mr. Keillor's generosity," announced S.O.K. Grand Oya W. Lance Pedersen, "and I know that the boys and girls of Lake Wobegon are, too. Many more people will profit from his generosity than would have from a week's trip to Rome. I am glad that that was a slip of the proverbial tongue. I always knew his heart was in the right place, working for educational opportunity for our young people."

She didn't dare expect Norbert to actually send the money. In her world, depending on men to do the right thing was a risky business—many birthdays would've gone unobserved if one expected men to remember them—but he remembered, or some woman who worked for him remembered, and the check arrived by registered mail at the post office on Wednesday and Mr. Bauser was quite excited. Registered letters didn't come all that often. At first, he suspected legal proceedings, perhaps a settlement of a lawsuit for sexual harassment. He could see through the little cellophane window that a check lay inside. "Guess your ship came in, huh?" he said. He peered through the bars, his moustache twitching, as she signed for the letter. "Norlander," he said. "That's your rich uncle?" She smiled. "I knew a Norlander," he said. "Norbert Norlander. He was my older brother's best friend. Left here in 1950 and went to Texas and went into the oil business."

"I had no idea," she said.

"Word is that you folks're going on a little trip?"

"A person can always hope."

He smiled a small sour smile. "Must've known him pretty well if he sends you a check."

"I did him some favors and he insisted on paying," said Margie. "He's a sweet old man. Eighty-eight or something."

And he looked at her with eyes narrowed, thinking *Phone Sex*. A rich old Norskie in Tulsa, Oklahoma, had paid Margie to sit and whisper suggestive scenarios to him sitting naked in his wheelchair.

Fine. Let him think that. She didn't care. She stepped outside and heard booming sounds from the lake—the ice cracking on a warm day—and drove in to St. Cloud to deposit the cashier's check at a bank called Associated Federal in a storefront in the Granite City shopping mall. She'd never set foot in the place, nobody knew her there.

She had picked it out of the yellow pages and called on the phone and a woman said, "Thank you for calling Associated Federal. Need a new shower? Want to redo an old kitchen or add on a bedroom? Home improvement loans are quick and easy at Associated Federal. Just talk to one of our loan associates today. To check your account balance, press 1. To speak to a loan officer, press 2. To ask about our payroll saving plan and 401(k), press 3. To speak to an investment advisor, press 4. For employment-related questions, press 5. For all other matters, press 0." She pressed zero.

Another recorded voice: "If you know your party's extension, you may dial it now." A long pause. And then a young man said, "Hello?" He seemed confused about the idea of opening a savings account. He put her on hold. A piano played something that sounded like "What a Friend We Have in Jesus." And then an older man came on. He apologized. "We're a new branch," he said. "Still unpacking the boxes. How can I help?" She wasn't sure she should deposit a hundred fifty grand with people who didn't seem to be set up to accept savings, but she made an appointment to come see him. His name was Stanley W. Larson. He enrolled her in the Family of Depositors and presented her with an Associated Federal thermal coffee mug and a rubber gripper to help open tight lids. And a ballpoint pen and plastic pocket protector. She hid the deposit slip in her underwear drawer, and then thought, *What if she were killed on the highway like Mrs. McGarry?* So she wrote on a Post-it note, *This is my legacy to my children, $50k apiece. Spend it. Love, Mom,* and stuck it to the slip.

TINY TOWELS

Late their first afternoon in Rome, the pilgrims who had crawled into the sack awoke in a stupor and migrated to the lobby and parked themselves on the saggy seats under the dying ferns and awaited guidance. Daryl had found a brochure for a nighttime tour of Rome, starting at the Janiculum Hill, then "Grand View of the Entire City," the Trevi Fountain, Campidoglio, the Forum, and winding up at a nightclub called Nero's Palace featuring Apollo and the Exotica Slave Dancers. The picture showed bare-breasted women in chains and tiny loincloths. "You want to go see naked women dance?" said Margie. "Buy a DVD. Save your money." Daryl thought that maybe he did. He never had and he didn't mind admitting that he would like to do this. He looked her straight in the eye. "You have a problem with that?" "None at all," she said. "What do you want us to do if you're arrested?"

He said he had four hundred euros on him so he'd be able to pay off anybody who needed paying off. But the thought of arrest quieted him down and he put the brochure back on the stack.

"I do not have Alzheimer's, by the way," said Lyle loudly, to anyone who was listening. "I know you think I do and it's not what you think. I bumped my head. It could happen to anyone. I was getting something out of a cabinet, I stood up and banged my head on a cupboard door."

On the plane, he had said it happened when his car got stuck in the driveway when he was in a big rush to get to a meeting of the Organization of Retired Teachers in St. Cloud where a slender young gymnast named Tiffany was to demonstrate the use of the exercise ball for good abs and core, and he dashed into the house for a bag of sand, dropping the car keys in the snow, but didn't notice, so after getting the sand, he looked all over the house for the keys. Ardis had taken the extra set with her by mistake. And then he couldn't find his checkbook. He was in a towering rage, cursing, and in his rage, he beat his head against the wall.

Margie said it didn't matter, he was having fun in Rome and that's what counts. "Who's hungry?"

Clint was irked at the lack of room service. He just wanted an egg sandwich. "Any little café or pizza place has it. Ask for panini." But panini is a grilled sandwich. He didn't want his sandwich grilled. "Try something new!" she said.

Wally had ventured out earlier and located a McDonald's and suggested they head there. "Go ahead," she said. "Leave me out of it." "I just want to see if theirs tastes the same," he said.

"You're in Italy," she said. "McDonald's is for Italian teenagers. It's cool for them. It's not cool for you. I am going to an Italian restaurant to have risotto and anybody who wishes can join me."

"Who made you the boss?" said Daryl.

"Where is Mr. Keillor? Did he go find himself a snazzier hotel?" said Irene.

Mr. Keillor, at that moment, was in his room, in bed, watching soccer on TV, hoping it would ease him toward sleep. He wished the pilgrims would invite him to join them in whatever they were doing—dinner, a show, drinks on the balcony. He imagined them cruising up the Via Veneto, sitting in one of those street-corner cafés enclosed in glass, and him standing in a dark doorway, watching them. He envied people who asked for what they wanted. *Let's go out for dinner.* Such a simple thing, but he never could do that. The fear of rejection. (Go out to dinner? With you? You must be out of your mind.) He wanted people to offer him what he wanted and force it on him over his helpless protestations.

O please adorable man let me go swimming with you at the granite quarry in our underwear—or less.

O no no no, sweet Irene, you are too beautiful and I could never withstand the carnal temptation.

O please adorable man, it's dark and nobody will see us and we shall face temptation together, I will hold you in my arms to give you strength.

Well, all right. Just this once. If you insist.

Lack of social skills: that was what made him a writer. Nothing to do with talent whatsoever. He had spent the afternoon dozing and writing and filled sixteen pages of yellow legal pad with a chapter of *Veni, Vidi, Vickie* and then read it over and it seemed to him that he had dozed off around page four and the story had gotten away from him. There were things there that he didn't remember writing, a girl in a slinky dress climbing over a wall, a boat sinking on a reef while a man in the forward cabin watches the Sugar Bowl on a huge flat-screen TV, and not much about Rome.

And there beside him on the bed was a copy of *Sunset Trails,* the monthly magazine of the Elderly Lutheran Citizens Association—Irene had handed it to him on the van. "There's a poem in here that made me think of you," she said. He *knew* he should've chucked it in the trash. He *knew* it. But he opened it up to the Poetry Corner on page five.

> Loveliest of trees, the maple now
> Is turning yellow on the bough.
> In our yard and in the park
> It's luminescent in the dark.
> Now of my three score years and ten,
> Sixty-six won't come again.
> Subtract from seventy years that sum
> It only leaves me four to come.
> And since to look at things sublime,
> Four years is not a lot of time
> I give up ideologies
> And great long books and symphonies
> And trying to learn Portuguese
> And simply walk and look at trees.

It depressed the pants off him. Ordinarily he could forget that he was sixty-six, so long as he stayed away from mirrors, but here it was—*four years to go, Old-Timer! Almost made it to the barn, Gramps.*

Margie went upstairs and called Norbert in Tulsa and told him the Lake Wobegon contingent was in Rome, safe and sound, and would visit Gussie's grave in a day or so. "I envy you," he said.

"They told me today they may have to take my leg." A mishap with the mambo, a busted knee, a staph infection, it had been one thing after another.

He started telling her about the last time he saw Gussie, an October afternoon, 1942, the corn crop was in, and the pigs had gone to market, and Gussie announced he was going into the army.

"When?" Mother said.

"Tomorrow morning."

"What's the rush?"

"Why wait?"

"He had gone off on his own and enlisted without a word to anybody and he was to report in Minneapolis the next day. My dad said something like 'Be sure to take good socks because army socks are thin, you know.' Mother sat there crying and then she asked Dad if he wouldn't please say a prayer and he said, 'I forgot all of them.' So we didn't. Dad came from a little island off the coast of Norway and he was still an island man. In his own mind, we were on a big rock pounded by ocean waves and leaving home was a foregone conclusion. We went to bed and Gussie said to me in the dark, 'I'm never coming back. You know that.' Well, I did. He wasn't like us at all. He had his head in a book every chance he got. I'd wake up at night and there he was, by the window, reading by the yardlight. The next morning we ate our corn flakes and Dad says, 'Well, that's one less mouth to feed,' his idea of a joke, and Mother asked Gussie if he could shoot at another man, and Gussie said, 'If he was going to shoot me, I could.' And then we said good-bye. He kissed Mother—to shock her, I think—he'd never done that before—we're Norwegian, you know—and tossed his duffel bag in the trunk of the neighbor's sedan whose son was enlisting too, slapped me on the back, got in the passenger side, and away he went, with a big grin on his face. He hated milking cows, he hated winter, and he wasn't all that fond of Dad. He knew there was a better way to live somewhere. He wrote us letters from Kansas and then from North Africa and Italy. He wrote me dozens of letters. He was killed in June 1944, in the city of Rome. Mother and Dad got his personal effects in a package which they never opened and I opened it a couple years ago and it was a lot of books and jazz records and a picture of a woman he knew there."

"Miss Gennaro."

"I don't care to discuss it, frankly. I don't think those Italians were worth all the trouble we went to."

She said good-bye and went back to the lobby and the pilgrims were still sitting exactly where she'd left them. No consensus had formed around the McDonald's concept or the Italian plan, and now Father Wilmer said maybe he would head off to find a church and attend Mass. "Anybody else?" he said, hopefully. Nobody rose to follow him. "Well, maybe I'll have supper with you all and go to Mass in the morning," he said.

"What are you up for?" said Carl, who was half asleep. She took his arm, and it was limp, as if he'd suffered a stroke. Jet lag: a nap only makes it worse—bright light and a long walk are the answer. She whispered, "A roll in the hay is what I'm up for."

"Huh?" he said.

Daryl had seen a restaurant called Earl's Court that he thought looked good, so they stood mulling this over. "It serves English cuisine," he said. "Thus the name."

"There are plenty of nice Italian places around," said Margie. "That's where we are. Italy. Why not eat Italian? I saw one called Il Convivio about six blocks from here." Actually, it was more like a mile, but once they'd walked six blocks, a mile wasn't much further.

"This one is close," he said.

"I'm up for a little hike," she said. "Who else?"

"Well, who wants to go somewhere nearby?" he said, looking around for votes.

Nobody cared to express an opinion. They sat there by the dying ferns, sheep waiting to be led up the ramp and onto the truck. Finally, Carl said he would vote for nearby. Marilyn said that sounded good to her. Father Wilmer said it made no difference to him. Ditto Eloise. Ditto Lyle. "Let's go get a quick supper and tomorrow we can hike all over looking for Italian food," said Daryl, not looking at Margie.

A revolt. She should have squashed it right away and said, "I made reservations at Il Convivio." And that would've been the end of it. A failure of leadership. And democracy had reared its ugly head. People, given their head, choosing the exact wrong thing. She wanted to say: Trust me and let's go have an authentic Italian experience. Il Convivio: a cheerful little place with old waiters carrying trays of linguini and Chianti and if it's crowded, we'll find another one. She'd seen Earl's Court and it was a bar, dark and loud, but Daryl had gotten his back up. So she accepted defeat and followed them down to Earl's with its dark green wood and brass lamps and floral carpeting, the fake frescoes, and a pock-faced man at a little electric piano noodling at some tunes that, might, at one time, have been Elton John songs. She recognized "Benny and the Jets," but played as a lament for the dead. A tall silent suicidal woman led them to a table opposite the long bar. In the murk, there appeared to be three other customers, an old doddering couple in tweedy clothes and a fat lady at the bar, all of them good and liquored up. The suicidal woman passed out plastic drink menus three feet long and Daryl said, "You serve food here?" She pointed to the bottom of the menu: Hamburger, Cheese Toast, Spaghetti with tomato and basil, Caesar Salad, Soup du Jour.

Evelyn, a little giddy from exhaustion, sang:

> On top of spaghetti,
> all covered with cheese,
> I lost my poor meatball,
> when somebody sneezed . . .
> And then a big pigeon
> Flew over my soup.
> Then suddenly turned
> And flew back to the coop.

"She had a little brandy at the hotel," said Wally.

It was a miserable way to start a trip, Margie thought, but Daryl tried to make the best of it, ordered a Singapore Sling for himself and a Rusty Nail for Marilyn, a hamburger and a salad, and then, between the salad and the hamburger, he walked up to the front of the room to the pianist, whispered something, plopped a bill in the glass jar on the piano, and launched into song.

> *You are my inspiration*
> *My sunshine too*
> *We could start a whole new nation*
> *Just me and you.*
> *All my life I'd be smilin',*
> *Just two of us on a little island—*
> *What you say? Let's leave today.*

Carl had a vodka fizz, thinking it might wake him up. She pointed out that alcohol is not a stimulant. "It works differently on different people," he said. "Have a drink," he said. She didn't want one. She wanted to keep her mind clear.

"What's wrong?" said Daryl. "Have some fun. That's what we're here for." He was flying high on the thrill of having bested her. He said, "I'll order you a Grey Goose vodka straight up on the ice. We'll just set it right there. You drink it if you'd like. It's up to you. No pressure. Okay?" She did *not* want to give him the satisfaction of seeing her down in the dumps, defeated. "This is a fabulous place, Daryl. You have excellent taste," she said. "I'll bet the hamburgers here are out of this world." He looked at her, a little confused.

"You really think so?"

"It's perfect. You chose right."

Her approval confused him. He looked around at this dim little swamp and its mournful occupants and retreated into silence. The combination of jet lag and alcohol was a pitiful thing to observe. Even Father Wilmer, nursing a whiskey sour, had a sloppy way about him, his eyes full of vague feelings, murmuring inanities about a trip here in 1985 and someone named Harry or Larry, how remarkable it was to be back. "Unbelievable," he said. "Just unbelievable."

What's unbelievable about it? We live on one planet, called Earth. The Wright brothers invented the airplane and it's improved quite a bit since then. You get in and a couple of pilots fly you across the Atlantic. Which Lindbergh crossed in 1927. He was from Little Falls, Minnesota. He got up speed, pulled back on the stick, and up in the air he went. Same today. What's the big deal?

And now Wally, feeling boosted by a Manhattan, started telling stories about drinking. How Mr. Berge, three sheets to the wind, had mistaken his wife for a waitress. How Ronnie Kreuger found an article that said nutrients found in beer can prevent affectional deficit disorder and he showed that clipping to people until the paper fell apart. How Barbara Peterson, high on Kahlúa and crème de cacao, had sent her mother's body off to be cremated and deposited inside a green bowling ball . . . and those Lutheran ministers, twenty-four of them, schnockered on French champagne when they almost capsized Wally's twenty-two-foot pontoon boat. "By George, they wrecked the steering on that boat and do you think those yahoos sent me money to repair it? No, I guess not." Father Wilmer said it just goes to show there's no such thing as collective guilt—conscience is an individual matter. Daryl said, no, it only showed that Lutherans are cheap.

Father Wilmer said he used to have an old lady parishioner, ninety-two and a shut-in until she found other shut-ins, one of whom could drive. She owned an Oldsmobile and her name was Dotty. She was only eighty-five. She couldn't get her license renewed because her eyesight was so poor, so she stuck to the back roads. Which she happened to know very well, so poor eyesight wasn't a detriment. You'd see them on Fridays or Sundays, four old ladies in a pink Olds, their heads barely visible above the dashboard, going eighty, eighty-five miles an hour on gravel roads. Dotty had a rule. Never go faster than your age.

Wally asked what this had to do with drinking.

"Dotty didn't drink, but the other three did. To calm themselves down. They went tearing around for a couple of years and then they all died. It was Christmas Eve and they were at Dotty's house for eggnog and planning to go to eleven o'clock Mass. Dotty started the car to warm it up, but she forgot to open the garage door. I guess she was a little tipsy. They were sitting in her apartment, which was in the basement of her daughter's house. She was off at a party at her former husband's. She came home around 1:00 A.M. and found four dead old ladies in the basement, next to the garage. A choir was singing on the TV and the bubble lights were bubbling on the tree and it was quite peaceful. Agnes—she was the one who came to my church—she didn't want to be a burden to anybody, and in the end, she wasn't. We just picked her up and put her in the ground and pushed the dirt over her and that was that."

Daryl raised his glass. "Here's to Agnes," he said. "And all she stands for."

"They went as fast as they could for as long as they could, and they died sitting still," said Father Wilmer, wiping a speck from his eye.

Irene said she couldn't understand why men are so fascinated by stories about drinking and couldn't we please change the subject? "To what?" said Daryl. She didn't care. "Anything," she said. "It isn't possible to talk about anything," he said. "Only about something. Drinking is something."

Clint remembered when the Lake Wobegon Lutheran softball team played a bunch of drunken heathens from St. Ann's Episcopal Church who kept a case of Chardonnay chilled in the dugout and whose pitcher wore a martini shaker in a holster on his belt. By the fifth inning, they were staggering around cross-eyed and slurring their words, and yet the game was close. The Episcopalians lunged and flailed at the ball and hit doubles and triples, and the Lutherans took nice level swings and hit easy pop-ups to the third baseman. It was 9–9 in the bottom of the ninth, two outs, St. Ann's had two men on base, and their pitcher, blind drunk and talking to himself, stroked a long fly ball to Pastor Ingqvist in right field. The good man stood, crouching, glove at the ready, in perfect position, and the ball bounced off the heel of his glove, and the winning run came lurching home and the heathen shrieked and hugged and poured gin on each other and raised their shirts and bumped bellies as the Lutherans packed up their stuff and headed for the parking lots. The pitcher said to Pastor Ingqvist, "Good game," and Pastor Ingqvist told him to go fuck himself. People couldn't believe they had heard him say it, so nobody said anything, but Clint heard him. And that's what he said. Pastor quit the team at that point and never played again.

Carl said, "Reminds me of the tornado that smashed up the Ingebretsons' farm and their beautiful lawn and garden and flattened the house they'd just fixed up, and the old bachelor farmer across the road who sits drinking brandy all day, his dump wasn't touched, not a beer bottle was broken."

"I used to find broken beer bottles in my driveway," said Eloise. "Fred. He was an angry drunk. Angry at himself but he turned it on me. Anger was what made him hook up with a piece of trash. There's a lot of anger in love sometimes. Oh gosh, life is complicated. Have you ever been in love, Father?"

Father Wilmer looked startled.

"I remember that poor man from Millet who was so grieved at his father's death that he chained himself to the iron ring on the lid of the old tomb next to his dad's grave," said Father. "They had to bring in a special acetylene torch from St. Cloud to burn through the chain, which was some unusual alloy, and meanwhile the constables Gary and LeRoy had to sit and converse with the man. His name was Bill, he was drunk, delusional, but all in all, not a bad person, and as they waited for the welder to come, they asked him what his dad did for a living. 'Dad is dead,' he said. 'I know but what did he do before he died?' said Gary. 'Right before he died, he clutched at his chest and said he wished he hadn't given up whiskey six years before, if he'd known he was going to die anyway, he'd've kept right on, and he fell over dead.'"

"Could we talk about something else?" said Margie.

"Sure," said Daryl. "Go right ahead." And he launched into the story of Magendanz whose wife accused him of going ice fishing so he could drink whiskey—"Of course, she was right. That's the problem with women. They're always right"—and that's what he was doing in his fish house, getting deep into his cups, and that was why he had the shotgun loaded and aimed at the hole in the ice, waiting for the old lunker walleye Pete who had run away with his favorite lure, a Lazy Ike. He had his finger on the trigger when a pickup backed into the ice house and catapulted him out the door and the shotgun blew a hole in the side of the Rasmussen fish house where Mr. Rasmussen at the moment was changing from his insulated pants into his jeans and a few pellets of buckshot burned his bare butt and he exploded out the door and in one swift instant (1) lost control of his sphincter and (2) stepped into a hole in the ice with his left leg up to his thigh. For some reason, he did not break his leg, but he was good and stuck and his family's jewels were chilling on the ice with him there in an awkward position similar to a cheerleader doing the splits, except he is fifty-seven and the splits are no longer possible for him, nonetheless there he was. Until the fish bit his left big toe. And he came screaming out of there. "And doggone it if the fish wasn't hanging on. A decent-size walleye."

"What a lie that is," said Margie.

"The plain and simple truth. Ask anybody."

"You can't ask anybody, you can only ask somebody. And I'm telling you that somebody told you a big fib." She stood up and put on her jacket. "I'm not hungry," she said. "I'll see you all later." Daryl looked at her and said, "You don't like it here?" "It's perfect," she said, "but I've got to walk off some energy. Have a big time." Eloise asked her where she was going. "When you're in Italy, you want to see Italy," she said. It was against the rule—you should stay with the group; she had told her children that a hundred times—but she had to get up and get out and when she passed the sad piano player and the suicidal woman and got out the door and felt the fresh damp air on her face, she felt 100 percent better. So happy to escape from Earl's and breathe actual air.

She called up Norbert to tell him about how things were going in Rome. He said something about a cousin flying to San Francisco, and when she mentioned Gussie, he said, "How'd you know about that?"

"You told me. This is Margie. Remember?"

"Margie who?"

"Margie Krebsbach from Lake Wobegon."

"We left there a long time ago. I was twenty-five. My folks went to Iowa and I kept going down to Texas. I'm in Tulsa now."

"I know. And I am in Rome. I'm going to decorate Gussie's grave."

He growled. "Only Margie I know is my daughter Margie. She went to Rome a long time ago. She already took care of that. Mother wanted me to go but I couldn't so she went. He was my brother, Gussie. He died in Rome. He was a good man." And he hung up. Poor man had gone around the bend, Margie thought, but she'd call him back in the morning.

A woman was cleaning the gutter, sweeping the garbage along with a broom, dumping it into a sort of rickshaw she pulled along. Margie had been brought up to never, never, never, drop trash in the street, but others had not been, the world was their wastebasket, and some of them lived in Rome. The street cleaner wore a white shirt and black vest with orange safety stripes on it, black slacks. She made a great show of effort as she nudged the trash along, as if concentrating on each orange peel, each crumpled receipt, each plastic water bottle. Italians put on a good show of importance and bustle, but when you looked closely, you could see that nobody was doing much. The city police hung around in twos and fours, chattering away in their smart blue serge uniforms—belts, brass buttons, epaulets, white patent-leather helmets—but they didn't seem to be on the alert for wrongdoers whatsoever. Except for the storekeepers, nobody seemed to be doing much at all in Rome, just hanging out, enjoying the sunshine.

An old iron drinking fountain stood on the corner, water running. Four nuns and two priests stood next to it, all in full regalia, who appeared to be lost. They looked up one street and then down the other, muttering to each other in some raspy language. A plaque marked the home of Casanova. A black family nearby was speaking French, even the children. Impressive. Up the street, in the distance was (she guessed) the dome of St. Peter's. She hiked toward it, moving through a cluster of old men in old blue suits, white shirts, tufts of chest hair, standing toe to toe shouting and waving their hands. Small cars buzzed past and gorgeous dark women on scooters. Lights blazed in tiny shops selling silver ornaments, women's blouses, copiers. A vegetable stand, wooden crates piled high at either end. A lamp shop with a great confusion of lamps standing on the sidewalk, desk lamps, standing lamps, chandeliers.

Dear God in Heaven, she thought, *please make it right between Carl and me, but if it can't be right, let me know. I don't want to spend the next six years torturing ourselves over it. I know that promises were made. I know that. He promised he would love me always and I don't know that that's the case anymore. Sometimes these things can't be helped. You can't get blood from a turnip. So I'm just saying what I mean, which, if you are omniscient, which I hope you are, you already know, and I'm only saying that I know it, too. Amen.*

The four nuns turned on their heels, and the priests followed them. *Viva Italia! Just like in the movies!* Somewhere there was Audrey Hepburn on the back of the Vespa, her arms around the newspaper reporter, flying around Rome.

ROMAN HOLIDAY

She'd seen *Roman Holiday* twice, once at the Paramount in St. Cloud with her high school boyfriend Larry and then years later on TV with Carl, who fell asleep midway through, but years later he gave her the DVD for her birthday. It startled her, the sheer rightness of it. How did he know? A lucky guess? Had she called him Gregory in her sleep? Audrey is a real princess who wants to break out of the cordon of security and protocol around her and experience Real Life, and Gregory Peck takes her for a ride on his Vespa, intending to betray her confidence by writing an exposé for his newspaper. His sidekick Eddie Albert follows at a distance, snapping pictures. But Gregory falls in love, and how could he not? She is Audrey Hepburn, after all. He falls hard and she falls in love with him. And when he returns her to her life of privilege, they say a broken-hearted farewell. And the next day he proceeds through the official receiving line, bows, kisses her hand, and presents her with the story he wrote, which will never see the light of day. He gives her back her privacy, her right to be an individual. The true token of love.

That was the part that impressed Margie every time she saw it. Had Gregory asked her to marry him and had she abdicated her crown and followed him to Chicago or Dallas and borne his babies and ironed his shirts and made his meat loaf while he wrote editorials at the *Gazette*—wrong ending! The sign of his love was to give her the freedom to be herself, a princess, and not pretend that True Love is going to make up for everything.

Larry thought Audrey Hepburn seemed "stuck-up" and that the movie wasn't realistic at all, and that was the end of Larry. He had been a boyfriend of convenience and now he became baggage. Afterward, in the car, when he slipped his hand up her blouse, she took his hand out and said, "I don't feel like it tonight."

"What's wrong?" he cried. He'd been really counting on holding her bare breast in his hand. He had caressed the brassiere itself a week before and this was the logical next step.

"Maybe I'm stuck-up," she said. "I just don't feel like it. I don't think you and I are meant to be—"

He begged her to please, please let him show her his love. He breathed Wrigley's Juicy Fruit on her as he explained that for so long he'd been selfish and unable to express love, and then she had shown him what love means, and now he simply wanted to share that love with her because love that is shared with another will grow and grow and eliminate war and bigotry and oppression, and this is how we can change this world—through love, love, love.

"You just want to grab my boobs and you want me to stick my hand in your pants." She said this as nicely as possible as she placed her hand on the door handle.

"Just one. Just for five seconds."

"No, Larry."

He was stunned. Tears ran down his acne-scarred cheeks and he wiped his eyes and mumbled something about what if he died in a car crash tomorrow and she had to live for the rest of her life with the knowledge of having denied him the chance to show his love for her.

"Better drive carefully."

He moaned, he groaned, he banged his head on the steering wheel. "This is not the last time a woman is going to say no to you, Larry, so you'd better get used to it," she said. Oh that was cruel. And yet it excited her to let him have it. "I'm sorry," she said, "I like you as a friend but I don't love you. And besides, you want to settle down here and I don't. I want to see the world." She opened the car door. "I want to see the world with you," he whispered. Tears glittered in his eyes and he took a swipe at his nose. She could never love a boy who cried like that when he didn't get his way. After she got out of the car and said good-bye and walked into the house, Larry waited for her to change her mind—sat there for an hour before he drove away.

He called her a month later, penitent, pleading, Johnny Mathis singing in the background, and she had to tell him, "Larry, all those reasons I didn't like you before—they haven't changed just because you're drunk."

It was a movie that shook her to her core. *There can be love without possession. You can love someone who is free of your control. You can even love those who defy your control, your enemies.* (She mentioned this to Father Wilmer once: "If loving your enemies is ultimate Christian love, then isn't submissive married love an inferior love?" He didn't think so but he had other parishioners waiting to talk to him, who weren't going to try to snag him on theological issues.)

As it turned out, Larry joined the army, which sent him to Germany where he married a Dutch woman and joined her dad's company and made his fortune building resorts in Sumatra and eventually settled in Brussels, and Margie married Carl and settled down two blocks from her childhood home—ah, the ironies of life. And Larry came back to speak at graduation in 1997, blue pinstripe suit, shoes with tassels, face sandblasted and tanned, hair glistening, and he talked about how Lake Wobegon had taught him to march to his own drummer and light a candle rather than curse the darkness, and there she sat six rows away and didn't bother to walk up afterward and say hi, and anyway he seemed to be in a hurry to leave. He lived an airborne life, zooming across national boundaries, and she was just little Margie Schoppenhorst, the shy, studious girl who won the spelling bee on "eleemosynary"—meaning "benevolent" or "charitable"— and kicked the butt of former champion Charlotte Tollefson and was very eleemosynary to her. She rose in the world, edited the *Literary Leaf* and was Class Poet, and expected to rise up with eagle wings and soar off to worlds unknown.

People said, "So what are you going to do now, Margie?" and she said, "Well, I was thinking of going to college in Chicago, but I don't know now." She didn't go away to college because it panicked her to see herself failing miserably and coming home in disgrace and facing the relatives. Poor little Margie: *It was just too much for her.* So she told people she was "putting it off" for a year. That she "wasn't ready." With her college money, she bought a car. She got a job candling eggs. About the same time, she began to feel a feverish hunger to have children. She had her eye on Carl, had for years, she liked the cut of him, a hardworking easygoing man, but decisive—he once got bored with fishing and dove from the boat and swam to shore, leaving his three brothers behind. He once bought a silk shirt with lilacs on it and because the guys at the garage gave him a hard time about it, he made a point to wear it whenever he went to fill up with gas. He did not believe in God (he confessed this to her one Christmas Eve) but he went to church, confident that someday his faith would return. So she went to work at the egg warehouse, candling eggs, and then she married Carl. They made a nice couple. She fell in love with him when she was driving by a construction site on McKinley Street the week after high school graduation and heard hammering and the rhythm of it sounded like someone knocking on the door to her soul.

It was July, a steamy day, a scorcher, and he stood on the scaffolding, stripped to the waist, hammering nails into joists, and the rhythm was seductive. She was on her way to work at the egg warehouse, and she slowed down at the sound of the *whamma-whamma-whamma-wham*, four beats, and a pause while he pulled a new nail out from between his teeth, and *whamma-whamma-whamma-wham*, and she took her foot off the gas and the car drifted over into a slough of mud from the water hose running to the cement mixer and got mired in mud up to the hubcaps and stopped. The hammering stopped. He watched her for a minute as she gunned the engine and spun the wheels and mud flew and she knew he was watching her and she gunned it harder. And then he crossed the road and said, "Move over," and she did, and he got behind the wheel and rocked the car back and forth, back and forth, back and forth, back and forth, back and forth, back and forth, back and forth, back and forth, and got it up and out of the trench. "You okay?" he said. She nodded. She was dripping sweat.

He was four years older, he'd been in the navy, and then instead of joining Krebsbach Chevrolet, he went to Minneapolis and learned carpentry. But he was dating Anne Marie Meister, who'd moved to Minneapolis the same time Carl went to carpenter school.

Margie went to the egg warehouse and sat in the dimness, lifting eggs off the conveyor and holding them up to the candle, looking for blood specks, cracks, and thought about him and the car rocking back and forth.

She and Carl, who had finished carpentry school, dated that summer. They went to a dance, a movie, a couple of awkward dinners, before they discovered that what they both liked was to lie side by side in the grass in the cemetery and read books and also kiss and touch in the careful way that young people necked back in those days. They were married two months later.

Two nights before the wedding, they sat on his parents' porch and he told her about Anne Marie, whom he'd gotten pregnant, the year before. Her dad was the mayor and he sold life insurance. Carl decided to leave town and packed a knapsack and set out to hitchhike to California but the first car that pulled over to give him a ride was Mayor Meister. He told Carl that he'd have to do the right thing and marry Anne Marie, and Carl said he'd think about it, and just then Mayor Meister got terrible angina pains. He told Carl to get the nitro tablets out of the glove compartment. But there were none there. "Please help me," said the dying man, and fell into Carl's arms and died. The nitro tablets were in his pocket. He explained all of this to Anne Marie later but she blamed him for her dad's death.

Anne Marie was good and depressed. She went to see *Breakfast at Tiffany's* at the Belle Rive Theater in Minneapolis and sat in the dark, crying, and got up to go to the women's john and went through a door marked NO ADMITTANCE, STAFF ONLY and there sat a scrawny young man named Chick who was running the projector and she asked him to put his arms around her, which he did, and they started necking, and then they were naked, and the next day he went with her to the courthouse. The baby was born and they named her Tiffany. Anne Marie told Carl the whole story out of pure meanness and when he asked to see his daughter, she just laughed and said, "Fat chance."

Carl was crying as he told her this—so many forks in the road where he might've gone the wrong way and missed out on finding the Margie of his life. What if Mr. Meister hadn't found him on the highway, what if he hadn't died and thus made Carl a murderer, what if he'd never come back to Lake Wobegon from the navy? What if, what if, what if. He said that he would love her for the rest of his life and be true to her. She believed him. And then the fire siren blew. He was a volunteer fireman. He jumped up and said, "Come with," so she did. They raced down the hill to the firehouse.

The truck had left already, they could see flashing red lights at Our Lady of Perpetual Responsibility. Sixteen firemen there and Father Emil and Sister Arvonne and a flock of Canada geese, highly agitated, honking. A crowd was gathering. There were two geese inside the church, said Sister, and when she'd gone in to help them, they attacked her. The front doors were open wide.

People suggested that they get brooms or put out corn or ring the church bells. People love a crisis. The crowd grew. There was great excitement. People went home for their cameras. A show was about to begin. Men vs. Geese. And then Carl raised his arms for silence and told everyone to go home. "We can't get the geese out of the church with all this hullabaloo. Everybody, please, go home. Otherwise, we may injure one of these beautiful birds. And why? For your amusement? Please. Take a picture and go home."

The firetruck was driven back to the firehouse. People drifted away, reluctantly, not wanting to miss the action, but Carl coaxed them to leave, until he and Margie sat under a tree, just the two of them, on the warm September night, waiting for the geese to come out. The dozen or so geese on the lawn hunkered down, waiting for their colleagues, muttering to themselves. And then the two geese came out the front doors, their hips moving in an elegant sensuous rocking motion, and there was a rush of wings, geese dashing across the grass and taking off. The two of them walked into church. It was empty. They checked in the confessionals, up in the loft, nothing. The Blessed Virgin stood, head bowed, her hands reaching out to grasp their hands, and they stood in that deep and profound silence and that was when she first felt married to him. No small thing. To her, marriage was linked to that silence, and to the rush of wings, and to the excitation of the onlookers, and the mystery of their vigil that night.

She felt a saintly dedication to marriage back in those days and read religious manuals on the subject that said the purpose of this Holy Union was to produce offspring and to enjoy companionship, and as such it was ordained by God and sanctified by His church, a Holy Sacrament, Jesus working through the couple to bestow grace on the world. The indissoluble bond of marriage is between the man, the woman, and the Lord Jesus Christ, and each plays a part in keeping the sacred vows of fidelity and honor and obedience.

She believed this with a pure heart and her faith made her a radiant bride. Everybody said so. Their parents saw them together and wept for joy. "You are perfect for each other," Myrtle said. And it was lovely to be a couple and walk hand in hand at twilight and be greeted with smiles and hellos. A boost in status. So she never went away to college as she had planned—the catalogues of St. Mary's, Loyola, the College of St. Catherine sat on her bookshelf. She earned her B.S. by piecework, much later, after the kids were in high school, at the online University of Western Dakota, and graduated at the age of forty-eight, no party, no gifts, no photographs—she simply got her degree as a PDF file and downloaded it and printed it on heavy paper, framed it, and that was that. Mr. Halvorson hired her cheap—$16,000 a year, well below the bottom of the pay scale—and of course she said, "Gee, thanks," having been brought up to, and now she taught Shakespeare and Whitman and Ole Rolvaag to a whole roomful of Carls with a few Margies here and there. No more the poet, except for the occasional verse, on request:

The marriage of Florian and Myrtle
Now crosses the 50-year hurdle.
Let the rabbit dash
And flutter and flash,
I've got my dough on the turtle.

"Oh that's so nice," said Myrtle. And that was the story of Marjorie. She was such a nice person. She did nice things for people. *A failure as an individual, she became half of a couple.* Mother told her, the day she married Carl, "Life is what it is. People want to make it into a carnival and it just isn't. You have to take the good along with the bad. When you have a fight, don't go to bed angry. Kiss and make up and tomorrow will be better." Mother taught her to get crusted eggs off the bottom of a frying pan by heating soapy water in it, and she was right about that, but now Margie thought that there was something to be said for carnival going. So many miserable people sitting in offices doing meaningless work and pretending to like it and gradually getting stupider and stupider, defeated by the sheer boredom of their lives. Trapped by complicated apparatus—home, family, community— designed to make you happy happy happy but instead it's a prison. You have no real friends. People who know you and love you treat you like dirt and strangers treat you pretty darned well. Her sister Linda went to Costa Rica for a week and danced on the beach in a crowd of men and women who spoke no English and had the time of her life. They were so much nicer than the ones she went to school with. That's the bitter fact of life. Half of all marriages end in divorce. Two thirds of all second marriages. Three fourths of all third marriages! Evidently, experience is not a good teacher.

Well, so what? She still had ambitions, however remote. She was bigger in the hips, and had a broader nose than Audrey's, but did have the narrow shoulders and small breasts, and dark hair cut in a pixie. Didn't have the voice—had a Minnesota voice and said, "Oh for cryin' out loud" and "What kind of a deal is that?" and "Okay then, bye now," but she felt a certain Audreyness down deep. That indefinable *bellissima* quality. Everyone had some of that in them. She had two love letters from her father to her mother, summer, 1944, addressed to "My dearest Sweetheart" which he was not the type to say, nor "You overwhelm me with joyful desire" nor "I am enchanted by your picture and counting the hours until I hold you once again in my arms" which were in the letters too, and also "You are the only one for me, the great treasure of my days, the happiness that I never dared hope would be mine." In real life, Daddy was sarcastic, quick to anger, tight with money, and never mentioned enchantment, but it was still in his heart somewhere, whatever led him to write, "How lovely to be with you last night on the porch and to kiss you over and over and let my hand rest near your heart." Though he'd become a sour man mesmerized by wrestlers on TV screeching, baring their teeth like chimpanzees, swinging folding chairs, nonetheless he had some romantic in him. After all, he had cried when he walked her up the aisle.

She imagined that he sat on the porch with Mother and took a piece of wood and carved himself a little puppet whom he named Marjorie because he was lonely and wanted a daughter who would love him but he was a rough man who yanked the strings and made her dance when she didn't feel like it and so she never became a real girl because she had no genuine feelings of her own until she saw the movie *Roman Holiday* and here she was in Rome, the fount of true feeling, where, she felt, either she would win Carl back or she would leave him forever.

Why spend years agonizing over it?

Why can't you figure out in seven days how you feel about someone?

WINDFALL

Norbert Norlander died a few hours after she had phoned him from near the Spanish Steps and his lawyer called her with the news. The phone chirped as she was taking a shower at 9:30 A.M. Late night in Oklahoma. She stood naked, dripping, by the bathroom sink, looking at herself in the mirror. The lawyer was polite, professional. She told Margie that the old man had simply lain down in bed that night and never awoke. "It was very peaceful."

"Just the way he would've wanted to go."

"Indeed. So—let me get to the point. In his most recent will, Norbert claims you are his daughter and his kids would like to clarify that."

All she could think was *What a sweetie pie that gruff old Norwegian was.* In his gratitude, he had adopted her. She thought he had gone bonkers in the last phone conversation she'd had with him, but no.

"Is that so? Are you his daughter? His kids don't remember him saying anything about this."

"Well, his kids don't have anything to do with it. I don't remember him talking about them either."

"Do you have any proof?"

"Proof? I think the fact that he sent me $150,000 to go to Rome says something about how he felt."

"That was from his mother's estate, but never mind." The lawyer inhaled slowly. "Look. The kids don't want some long dragged-out court case. They just want to settle this. They're willing to offer $250,000 for this whole thing to just go away."

And a door opened in her mind's eye, a door to the bright blue sky with a few white clouds drifting in it. "I think a half million would be better."

The lawyer inhaled again. "I can offer you as much as three hundred fifty. I recommend you take it. I think that when you stop to think about attorney's fees and the years it would take for this to go through the courts—"

Margie said she thought $350,000 would be just fine. She gave the lawyer the address of Associated Federal in Minnesota. And hung up. She sat down on the toilet. Hard to grasp. Too hard. A woman named Maria called her from New York in January and one thing led to another, and she did a good deed for an old man, and now this. Poor old guy. You read stories like this, she thought—a lonely tycoon leaves a million dollars to a woman who gave him back rubs, or a kind neighbor who mowed his yard, or the pizza delivery boy.

So where were his kids when he lay dying? Skiing in Aspen? They couldn't be all that devoted if they didn't know how bad he wanted Gussie's grave decorated. Probably they'd refused to go to Rome. They didn't even know he was all banged up in a nursing home and fixing to check out. So phooey on them. She'd take the money. Damned right she would.

She came down to breakfast and heard Evelyn ripping into some rich guy in a story in *USA Today* who had lost half his fortune to Bernie Madoff and now had to sell his homes in Kennebunkport, Santa Fe, and Bainbridge Island. "Well, boo hoo. Poor little you. Tell us about it. People are homeless and starving to death and you want to live in six different places at once. Let me tell you something. Argentina is not weeping for you and neither am I. Just get over yourself and suck it up and find something useful to do other than invest in junk bonds and ride around in boats drinking gin martinis. This is life, honey buns. It isn't a rehearsal. You're living on the same planet as everyone else so wake up and smell the coffee. And I mean it."

Margie looked up Norbert on the Internet again. Northland Oil. He'd inherited from his father a chunk of an island off the Norwegian coast that turned out to have vast oil fields under it and from that he'd earned a small fortune. Like a true Norwegian, he kept his cards close to his chest, and the two bios she found were vague about amounts, but he'd given two million to the Tulsa Art Museum, so there was serious money around. She thought she should tell someone. Father Wilmer. Or Carl. In the past three months, she had, barely lifting a finger, realized a half million dollars. Success Comes to Margie Schoppenhorst.

She had accepted the $150,000 for herself and Carl to go to Rome on a patriotic pilgrimage to honor an American fighting man who'd given his life for his country, along with the members of her book club. She was not stingy. No, not at all. She had called up Father Wilmer one afternoon, and told him, "We're going to Rome the end of March. You want to come with?"

"Oh, that's too kind of you," he said, and she could hear him about to say *Sure, you bet*, getting ready to spit it out. "You can find someone who's a lot more fun than me. I'd only make people uneasy. Especially the Lutherans."

"No," she said. "We have a spot for you. I want you to come. Please come along. I am happy to pay your way."

"Well," he said, "a person only gets this chance once. I do have some cash squirreled away in a pastoral retreat budget. This sounds like just the ticket." But she had offered to pay—she didn't hoard her good luck. She had not offered to pay for the others, but then Mr. Keillor took care of that, so it wasn't a problem. But she hadn't been greedy. She had shared.

And now she felt no moral qualms at all about collecting a windfall. She had done the neighborly thing and reached out to Mr. Norlander in his last days and she had brought closure to an old story in his life and lent him some peace as he rode off into the sunset. And she had reaped a bucket of gold. Good for her.

BEAUTIFUL MAN

‹❦›

Vacation days! Free to go where you please. She was in high spirits all day and the next. Carl and Daryl wanted to go on a double-decker bus—*Fine! Go!*—and off they went. Eloise collapsed into bed and so did Clint and Irene. Okay for them. Let the sleepers go sleep, she could sleep when she got home. Weariness is only a feeling, you don't have to obey it. Sleep can be postponed. There's coffee. That helps.

She visited the Keats-Shelley house, a tiny shrine with a lock of Keats's hair, a pair of his socks, a box of his shoes, two letters from Byron, a teacup, a golf club, a 5-iron.

She and Maria had planned to meet for coffee at a café near the banks of the Tiber. She walked and walked toward where she thought the river was, but didn't check her map, for fear of looking like a tourist. Finally, she saw the coffee bar and stepped through the open door into a beehive of people coming and going. A narrow room. A pleasant aroma of coffee and oranges. She took a deep breath and felt a buzz in her head. No lounging around. Customers stood at the long bar of granite and stainless steel and ordered their coffee from the barmen bopping back and forth between the espresso machine and the cooler, a hundred bottles of booze on shelves against a mirror, and when your coffee came, you downed it and out the door you went. There was room for a few loungers at three small tables along the wall. Next to a cold chest full of ice cream. Photographs on the wall of Rome in horse-and-buggy days. From the radio came a throbbing baritone singing about his broken heart. A box of breath mints by the register. She took a pack and put down a ten-euro note and ordered her coffee and, *bing bing bing*, a tiny cup was set down in front of her and her change, and she dropped two breath mints into the coffee and stirred it. The man next to her was studying her but he said nothing. She drank the coffee in one gulp and it wasn't bad. It could've been worse. She ordered another, and then her phone rang. It was Maria saying she couldn't make it because her mother had taken a turn for the worse.

She looked around and thought the man next to her was on the verge of talking to her. He was looking at her in the mirror, through the rows of liquor bottles, and when their eyes met there, he looked down at his drink. It smelled of licorice. He was a beautiful man in his thirties with black hair slicked back, tortoise-shell glasses, a black jacket, jeans.

Her coffee came and this time she didn't put breath mints in it. She sipped it. Bitter, but in a good way. The man next to her ordered another drink. Maybe he was getting up his courage to ask her to go somewhere with him, come to his home and see his etchings. Maybe this happened all the time in Rome. And what if he did? What if he said, "You're an American, aren't you? I thought so. I love America. I've been there a dozen times. I live not far from here. Would you like to come and see my artwork?

I am a painter. I'd love to paint you. Have you ever been painted? I think you'd be magnificent. The light is still good. What do you say?" Would she go? Yes, she might. And an hour later, she'd be sitting naked on a couch and he'd be gazing at her body, a big canvas in front of him, a palette in his left hand. And then he'd offer her a drink to relax her. And then . . .

The man said, "You're American?"

"Yes, I am."

"*Bellissima.* We were delighted when you elected Obama."

"So were we."

"And then the inauguration. My gosh. Aretha Franklin singing in front of the Capitol. And what a speech he gave!"

The man was Italian. Paolo. They shook hands. He was slight, with beautiful hands with long fingers. He taught American literature at a university in Milan. He loved Fitzgerald, Updike, Flannery O'Connor. Did she read those writers?

"I do," she said. "I teach high school English. We read *The Great Gatsby*. And an Updike story, 'Pigeon Feathers,' they like. Not O'Connor. Too dark for my kids."

He wanted to talk about Fitzgerald, she being from Minnesota and all. The movie *Benjamin Button*—had she seen it? (No.) And she wanted him to be somebody who would take her to a building with a tiny cage elevator and up they'd go to the fifth floor and into an old high-ceilinged studio with skylights and canvases stacked against the walls and she'd undress for him and sit on a couch, her knees primly together, her arms folded over her chest, and he'd look at her fondly and say, "Ah, *bellissima*." And she would lie down on her back on the sofa, one foot on the floor, her arms up over her head.

"Do Americans spend all their time on the Internet?" he said. "I've heard that."

"I don't, but my younger daughter told me she goes online after supper and she might be on the computer until three in the morning."

Hmmmmm. His handsome face darkened, he shook his head.

"She can be in four or five chat rooms at once. She keeps up her Facebook page and MySpace and HisSpace, which is a Christian web site, and then there's FriendLink and One-plus-One. And she's updating them every day and answering e-mails and trying to be amusing and smart and, my gosh, the work. The sheer amount of typing. Keeping in touch with all these people she's never met and never will meet . . ."

"So strange, so impersonal," he whispered. "I prefer this. The human touch." He put his hand on her arm.

She said she probably should be going, but she didn't go. And he leaned toward her and said, softly and simply, "My hotel is near here if you'd like to come up and have tea." He almost put his hand on her hand, on the counter. He was going to put his hand there and then it stopped short, in midair.

And she heard herself say, "I'd love to."

His hotel was called Il Paradiso and it was smaller than the Giorgina, a tiny lobby, no couches, no bellman, just a hallway with a little office for the clerk, and he led her into an elevator so small she felt suddenly joined to him. Her bare arm touched the sleeve of his jacket where they stood facing front.

"Do you write poetry?" he said.

"A long time ago. But I ran out of things to write about."

"You could write about this."

"About meeting you?" She smiled. "Well, I hope I will."

"You've lived all your life in Minnesota?" The elevator stopped and the doors opened. Yes, she said. He walked down the hall to the second door on the left and unlocked it. She stepped in. There was a double bed and a chair and a desk, a door leading to the bathroom. "I want to get out of Milan and start something new. First, I must earn some money though. I don't think my parents are going to die anytime soon and I don't think they will leave me much." He gestured toward the bed and she sat down. He picked up an electric teakettle from the floor and took it in the bathroom and ran water into it.

"I've stayed around out of habit, I guess," she said. "Can't think of another reason." The single window at the head of the bed looked into a small empty courtyard.

"I don't think people live by habit," he said. "Everyone has a sense of adventure, don't you think? You must. You're a poet. Poets have to be brave." He plugged the teakettle into the wall socket and set it on the chair. He sat down on the bed beside her. He put his hands in his lap and looked at her legs.

"I'd like to read your poetry," he said. She said she didn't have any with her. He nodded. "I hadn't written poems in years and then the other night I woke up with a poem in my head and oddly it was in English. I spent a year at Indiana University. I sometimes dream in English. Still. All these years later. So I dreamed the poem and then I woke up and wrote it down."

He put his hand on her knee and said, "*Your face and your green eyes. My knee pressed against your thigh where you sat crosswise. And the next three hours flew by and my life was made new by you, my lover, that fragrant night. Nothing to do but love you, and when it was over, we lay together, me and you. Like horses in the summer sun, we happy two."*

"That's very lovely," she said. Surely he could feel her pulse pounding with his hand on her knee like that. He was gently squeezing it. She was going to tell him to stop, but if she did, then what had she come to Italy for?

"What did you write poems about?" he said.

"Things I thought about when I was a girl."

"How could you run out of things to write about?" He was feeling around her kneecap. He was thinking about moving up her right thigh, she guessed. She was thinking about stopping him.

"I had children, I had other things on my mind."

"Are you married?"

"Yes," she said. Yes was the correct answer, wasn't it? She and Carl were married. But she almost had said, "I don't know."

"Did you ever write poems for your husband?" She shook her head. She couldn't remember if she had or not.

He turned to her and put his right hand against her left cheek and kissed her very lightly on the lips. And then a second time.

"That was nice," he said. "Thank you."

She nodded. Did she nod? Yes, she did. She hadn't meant to, though.

And then he put his right hand on her breast. She quailed. She whimpered.

"What's wrong?"

"I'm scared like a little rabbit."

"What are you afraid of? Are you afraid of your own feelings? I won't hurt you. I'll only admire you and when you tell me to stop, I will stop."

He opened her shirt and pulled down the cup of her bra and kissed her breast and licked her nipple.

She stood up. It took all her effort but she made it and didn't fall down or have to brace herself against the wall. "Thank you," she said. "I really should go. They're expecting me. I'm in charge of a large group. I don't want anybody to get lost."

He unplugged the teapot. "Can I see you again?"

She whispered, "Where?"

"At the coffee bar. Tomorrow."

"I will if I can get away."

"Otherwise, this is my phone number." He handed her his business card. "You are a very attractive woman. I hope you know that. I would say—magnificent. I was so lucky to meet you. I want to see you again." He smiled. "Do you and your husband ever make love?"

She blushed and opened the door. "See you tomorrow," she said. He closed the door and she rang for the elevator. She could hear the engine humming far below. Yes, she and her husband made love. Months ago. It was the day after Christmas, the kids had all left, and she and Carl toppled into bed around 4:00 P.M. and he rolled over next to her and caressed her, and slipped his hand up her blouse. She reached over and unzipped his pants and put her hand down and there it was, all ready to go. And when he pulled her skirt up, he was in a hurry to get inside her. He got on top and thrust hard and it was over in a few minutes but it was okay. Very much okay.

The elevator door opened and she got in. Had she just committed adultery? She wasn't sure. Should she ask Father Wilmer what constitutes adultery?

GUSSIE MOVES IN

⁕

Dear Lille Bror,

The German front is falling apart and our Second Corps is heading north on Highway 7, and we're also busting out of the Anzio beachhead, and this made the Brigadier sad because he had to give up his ritzy quarters and take to the roads. He was playing Duke Ellington records last night and feeling very moody. He is afraid of getting whacked by an American mortar. His best friend, a Captain Merrill, was hit by a mortar shell while squatting over a latrine and there wasn't enough of him left to bury so they just covered over the latrine and stuck a cross in it. The Germans are retreating but very craftily, and our line advances, it waits, it moves, it waits, it waits, and so we are edging toward Rome. Nobody expects the Germans will put up a fight there. They'll make their stand farther north. General Clark let the Germans escape across the Tiber so he can put on his parade past the Colosseum and get his headlines. When we get to Rome, the Brigadier is hoping for a Palazzo. He has got his heart set on it. One with paintings and a gilded ceiling. Tonight we are bivouacked near a soccer field outside the city, a stone's throw from Highway 7. It is quiet. Thousands of aircraft and tanks and trucks in the vicinity and a half million men on our side and a hundred thousand on the other side and it's quiet as Sunday in Minnesota. We found a stone hut and the Brigadier is inside sleeping on a pile of electrical cables and I am sitting in the Jeep writing by lanternlight. Maria was assigned to go into Rome to mark the good locations for the newsreel cameras and I am sick from worrying that she will get shot or raped and be left bleeding in the street. I stand at the window praying to the God who doesn't exist to watch over her. The Brigadier got very drunk today. He dreads the sight of dead bodies and today we drove through a little valley where there'd been some hard fighting an hour before and the carnage was still there to be seen. A tank driver who got roasted hanging out of his forward hatch and the flies crawling on him. The Brigadier closed his eyes and I drove around the tank and on we went. The historians will take an aerial view of the war but here on the ground it just looks like cruelty and stupidity rolled into a ball, a rolling opportunity to do despicable things and be admired for it. And in the midst of it, this woman whom I love who wends her way on the outskirts of horror. She sees the worst, fratricide, Italians preying on each other, partisans hunting fascists, patriots chasing the collaborators, and it's pure cruelty under a thin veneer of principle. I don't believe in any of it anymore, but I do believe in her. She is my true heroine.

Your brother,
Gussie

WHAT IS HIS PROBLEM?

❧

The pilgrims were resting in the lobby of the Giorgina when she came back, all except Carl who was upstairs napping and Evelyn who had eaten a doughnut from a street corner vendor that turned out to be a meat pie and it hadn't agreed with her. And Mr. Keillor—"He went to visit friends," said Irene, raising her hand with uplifted pinky. *La-di-da.* "Too good for the likes of us," said Wally. "The more I see of him, the more I wonder, *Where did this guy come from?*" said Clint. "You know what I mean?" They did, indeed.

For years the man had spoken in a plummy semi-British voice that bore no resemblance to how anybody in Lake Wobegon talked—had he learned it from old Charles Laughton movies? Of late, he seemed to be aiming for boyishness (a little late, at 66) and greeting people with a big warm howdy and a wink. The producers of his show had teamed him up with a chimp named Bombo who was supposed to humanize him somehow (according to a story in the paper). Margie wondered if he might've been fired from *A Prairie Home Companion* and if his traveling with them to Rome might be out of desperation, to cushion the shock. What if he were devastated and on the verge of taking a fistful of pills and what if he called her at 3:00 A.M. one of these nights, sobbing, and asking why he shouldn't just kill himself right now and save everyone the misery of his presence? What would she tell him?

"How are you doing, Margie?" said Lyle.

"I am having the time of my life." And she was. Three days in Rome and she didn't see how she could possibly go back to being the little country mouse she used to be. A Lake Wobegon woman was expected to go along with things. If people snub you, smile and move on. Smile at insults. Water off a duck's back. If men say stupid sexist things in front of you, be a good sport, laugh, and move on. Boys threw snowballs at you. They called you names, said you were ugly, stupid. Smile and turn away. Don't make an issue of it. Drop it. Grandma Schoppenhorst gave her a plaster plaque for her birthday, the Blessed Virgin in her blue smock and underneath BLESSED ARE THE MEEK FOR THEY SHALL INHERIT THE EARTH and like Grandma, Margie was well-schooled in meekness. Last fall she went in to see Dr. DeHaven about the lump in her breast and his secretary Gloria called Margie up to the counter and as she approached, Gloria sang out, "So this is about the bladder leakage?" And all around the room, people with their heads buried in *People* made a mental note, *Margie Krebsbach pees her pants. Guess that's why she gave up wearing white ones. Too bad. Must be embarrassing for her. My uncle had that problem, but he was eighty-three.* And she wanted to turn and announce to the room, "No, I don't. She's got my mother-in-law's folder, not mine. Myrtle suffers from occasional incontinence. She is pushing eighty. Or pulling it, we really don't know. I am fine. If you must know, I do have a little problem with hemorrhoids, and if you'd like a close look, let me drop trou and bend over, okay?" But she smiled and said, "No, that's my mother-in-law, Myrtle."

"Oh!" Gloria shrieked. "You're here for a boob check then?"

What could you do with these people?

But now she was a new woman. She had had an illicit meeting with a man she met in a coffee bar. It happened in slow motion, giving God time to alter events unless—what?—did God intend for it to happen? And now she was considering divorce and pondering what to do with half a million dollars. Maybe she wouldn't go home at all. She could take twenty grand out of the bank and find a room to rent, enroll in Italian class, advertise for work on Craigslist, and get to know Paolo better and better. Maybe move to Milan. Her kids didn't need her. Mr. Halvorson could find a sub to finish out the year. There would be talk—*She stayed in Rome. She and Carl are separated. Irene thinks she met someone there. Isn't that unbelievable?* She'd need to find friends. But she had found a close friend. In just a couple of days, Maria had become her closest confidante.

A miracle of a sort. Buried all her life in Lake Wobegon, now she had (sort of) shacked up with a man she'd just met— sat on his bed and let him touch her in the Hotel Paradiso. Would Audrey have done this? You bet your boots she would've.

She tried to visualize life without Carl. The man who lay next to her reading yet one more book about the Civil War, blue pajama bottoms, the furry chest, the sheer Carlness of him, his bouquet of sawdust and motor oil and Mountain Lake deodorant. If she wanted him to come over, she used to be able to simply touch his arm, and he'd snake his foot over and find her foot and then she could snuggle up close to him, put her chin on his shoulder, and if he was in an amorous mood he'd turn the light out and they'd neck in the dark and then undress and follow their routine—Missionary, Spooned On Side, Cowgirl, All Fours—and for years it was always on Tuesday nights until Carla's basketball games knocked them off the pace. But no more. He had gone across the hall. His choice. So if he wasn't going to return to duty, why not give him his discharge papers?

Last winter, she caught an old movie on the movie-classics channel, *Lassie Brings The Pie*, about the couple who split up and the dad moved to San Francisco, far from the mom and kids in Idaho. They missed him on Thanksgiving Day and Lassie, ever sensitive to human feelings, took a pumpkin pie that the mom had brought home from the bakery and trotted down the street with it. It was in a box, tied up with string, and Lassie held the string in her teeth, and carried the pie through a blizzard and over rickety swinging bridges and fought off a cougar and over the Sierras and down to the Bay and across the Oakland Bay Bridge, trotting between lines of rush-hour traffic, too late for Thanksgiving but just in time for Valentine's Day, and found the dad, who was about to go out on a date with a sexy model. He saw Lassie and burst into tears. "You never told me you had a dog!" the model said in a pouty voice. "I'm allergic to dogs." Lassie set the pie at his feet and untied the string and the model sneezed and stepped in the pie, and fell down and fractured her leg, and in the next scene the dad and Lassie were on a bus heading for Idaho and he was singing "Let the Rest of the World Go By."

Maybe Carl's problem was stress. He'd promised to build that huge lake home for Mr. Ladderman, a handshake deal—Carl assumed that a big Minneapolis investment mogul who drove a Lexus was good for the money—and then in November, Ladderman's wife found the letters he'd written to Honey Bunny and the wife fired both barrels at him as he jumped naked out a second-story window of their home in Aspen. He suffered buckshot wounds in his left calf. "How can you fire both barrels at a man from fifteen feet away and just hit him in the calf?" said Margie. "How could you not get him in the chest?" Had the man been killed, Carl would've been paid off by the estate, but now Ladderman was sued for divorce and was living in El Paso under an assumed name because the bloodhounds were on his trail as his investments tanked and his notes came due and he was six months in arrears on payments to Carl for this monstrous half-finished structure that Carl had stopped work on and mortgaged his own home (for the first time in his life) to keep the business afloat, and now was getting urgent calls from Hjalmar at the bank to come in and talk, all of which might take a man's mind off the pleasures of the flesh.

Maybe he had wilted in the hot sun of parenthood. It happens. You're in love with a woman and the next thing you know she turns out to be the mother of three children. And dang it, they're yours!

Sleep apnea?

Claustrophobia?

Allergy?

A side effect of cleaning chemicals? Perhaps the fumes rising from her sparkling clean floors had denutted her husband and turned him into a hermaphrodite.

She called Dr. DeHaven and asked him straight out if Carl's prostate medicine might affect his sex drive and Dr. DeHaven said, "No. Why?"

"Just curious," she said.

How about fear of vaginal entrapment?

Maybe he was just trying too hard. You start down the slope, kissing and touching, and it picks up speed, and then what if you think "What if I can't?"—it becomes self-fulfilling. The woman is breathing hard, panting, rearing up, and crying, "Do it! Do it, Baby! Pound that nail in! Sock it to me, big boy!" And the poor man lies there with a wilted daffodil in his pants.

And then there are wood ticks. One of them crawls up your leg and finds a place where the moon doesn't shine and feeds off you and at the same time releases a toxin that attacks your libido. It's the wood tick's way of protecting itself—if you don't undress in bright light, you're less likely to find it—and that's why Thoreau didn't date girls and that's why our rural population is shrinking.

Could Carl be gay? Had he lost interest in her because he had discovered Another Side of Himself?

She found an ad in the back of *Christian Cavalier* magazine for a "love potion" that gave a man "more energy and sustaining power" but it was offered by a company that also made a metal disc to put in your mouth that enabled you to sing in perfect pitch, "no more whinnying or quavering."

In high school they spoke of Coke and aspirin having aphrodisiac powers, but not for men, only for girls. A man was supposed to have those powers in his back pocket. She Googled "aphrodisiac" and found an article about garlic and Cajun dishes such as blackened catfish ("Spicy food can backfire. Passion is a fragile mood and may be disrupted by stomach gas.") and alcohol, of course ("It is easy to overshoot the mark when plying a lover with drinks. Alcohol reduces a woman's level of judgment to where her affection for you doesn't mean so much."). One article said that an exchange of clothing between lovers can stimulate hitherto unexpected levels of passion, that a small-town banker in Illinois who, in the privacy of their bedroom, tied one of his wife's long silk scarves around his neck, suddenly stripped the clothing from her body and also from his own and cast himself down at her feet and engaged in various exciting actions with her toes that inexplicably made her cry out with pleasure and thus began ninety minutes of loud and passionate entanglement that wound up in a climax that, according to his stopwatch, lasted for thirty-seven seconds.

Or maybe Carl had never loved her, in the sense of actually truly loving her, in the sense of searching high and low for the Beloved and finding her and crying out, "I want to be with you for the rest of my life, O you magnificent one." In Lake Wobegon, you worked from a small pool of appropriate partners and a man stepped in where the woman had signaled a vacancy and if she thought he was okay, not an incipient drunk or child molester, she didn't dismiss him, which was the Lake Wobegon equivalent of falling in love, and thus, quietly, obediently, like schoolchildren falling into line two by two by two on a field trip, people formed pairs and marched to the altar.

Except for some, like her older sister, Linda, who escaped to become a flight attendant for Continental, lanky Linda, hair dyed bright red, devoutly single, jetting off to Delhi, Rio, Copenhagen, Rome, phantom Linda who returned home rarely, who existed in postcards and the 4 A.M. phone call. She called from Beirut in February, to ask how things were, and for once Margie told her the truth. "Take him on a trip," Linda said. "Shake up the routine. You people get so deep in your trench, you can't see over the side." Linda was bisexual. Women were more pleasant to be with, not so scary, and there wasn't the erection problem or the semen to deal with or such dreadful diseases. No strings attached. You just lay together, the two of you, and then you said thank you very much and moved on. Or vibrators were nice, too. Or you met a nice man who knew how to show you a good time and then go away. Linda had no desire to have children. God, no. She loved hotels. She loved to take a nice hot bath with a stack of magazines on the edge of the tub, and lie in bed with a good novel, and then turn out the lights, pet the cat, and go to sleep. Dreamland. Who could ask for more?

BAD BAD BAD BAD

S he had Paolo's phone number in her pocket the next morning as she and Eloise, Daryl, Marilyn, and Lyle trudged through the ruins of the Forum, a junk pile of imperial history, and snapped pictures of each other standing before a single column rising above the scattered stones. Once it had been part of a temple and now, orphaned, a mere memoir of ancient glory. Nearby, stairs rising to the six columns of the façade of a temple, the temple itself gone. Vacant pedestals where statues had stood. Cornerstones half buried in the turf. Marilyn stopped and said it reminded her of church. The old people sitting around at coffee hour talking about their kidney stones. "You don't dare use the word 'prostate' or you'll draw a crowd. Don't even say 'interstate' because their hearing isn't that good either, and they're likely to pull out their prostate and give you a look."

"What does that have to do with the Romans?" said Lyle.

"Well, we read Romans in church," said Marilyn.

They stopped to look at the great arch of the Roman Senate, which put Lyle in a funk. "All gone," he said, softly. "A whole civilization. Gone. And soon we will be too."

"What do you mean by that?" said Daryl.

"I read that stars get hotter just before they collapse and that's what is happening to the sun. In a billion years, it'll burn about ten percent hotter than it does now, which means that Earth will be uninhabitable. Isn't that a horrible thought?"

"No," said Daryl. "It's not. A billion years is a long time."

Lyle threw his arms out, to embrace the Forum, the glory, the history, the classics, Virgil, Horace, Caesar, the works—"We're all going the way of these guys. In the end, we're going to turn into cinders."

"In your case, it isn't going to take a billion years," said Daryl. "I'd say fifteen, give or take a couple."

"You don't understand! All the glory of the human mind— art, music, architecture, science—it's all futile. Why do we bother? It all ends up as a small dead scorched astral body drifting in space. That's the ultimate story. It's all ashes."

Margie said, "So what should we do, Lyle? Become nihilists?"

He didn't know. But the enormity of it stunned him. All your life you strive to accomplish something. Aim for the stars. And for what? For nothing.

"So what were you going to do instead of teach biology? Sit and play Solitaire?"

They moved on to the Colosseum, its walls intact, the arena floor gone except for the stone ribbing below and the brick-lined remnant of an ancient sewer, and through narrow alleys to the Villa Borghese, a dusty park, Daryl setting the pace, Lyle trailing behind, contemplating Man's Fate, Eloise wishing Fred would call her. "I can forgive him," she told Margie, waiting for Lyle to come out of the men's toilet. "I can understand someone you love having a crazy fling with someone, can't you? It probably happens all the time!"

"Oh yes. Of course."

When Lyle emerged, Daryl was in the mood to make a speech. Right there in front of the Temple of Venus, weeds growing in the pavement. "We're stronger than we know," he said. "We will endure. I believe that." *Oh please,* thought Margie.

"When my dad lost his right hand in the corn picker, he just picked it up and came back to the house and asked Mother for a bucket of ice to put his hand in and a dish towel to bind up the stump. He said he'd drive in to St. Cloud to find a surgeon to sew it back on.

"She asked if he wanted her to drive him in. He said, 'No, I can manage. But I'll need to take your car. It's got automatic transmission.'

"She said, 'Can I make you a sandwich?'

"He said, 'I'm not so hungry and besides, I don't see how I'm going to manage a sandwich, Mavis.'

"She said, 'You could steer with your knees.' And she made him a cheese sandwich and off he went. That was Dad. He came back six hours later, his hand sewn on, and within a couple weeks he was wiggling his fingers. He never regained full usage, never could put a minnow on a hook or shuffle cards and it took him a while to button up his trousers, but it was good enough."

Margie ducked into the women's toilet and into a back stall and called Maria and told her about Paolo and Maria said, "Call him. What can it hurt? You're here for fun. So have fun. You want to see him? Flirt with him? Kiss? Maybe go to bed, maybe not? What's the harm? Do it." And so she did. She called his phone and before she could change her mind, he answered. He was delighted to hear from her. He had been thinking about her. "I want you to come meet me," he said. "You could come to my hotel now. Or if you'd rather, we could meet at the coffee bar. Either one is fine by me."

"The hotel is good," she said in a small voice. "I'll be there in fifteen minutes. Can I bring something?" Thinking: pastry, fruit, perhaps a couple of ham croissants. "All I need is you," he said. "Beautiful you."

She told the others that she was going back to the hotel—not specifying which hotel—but Eloise clung to her. "Please don't go. I need you right now. You're the only one I can talk to. You understand." Eloise was sure she had done something terrible to drive Fred away (*O, please stop*, thought Margie) and now God was going to make something very very bad happen. Something involving terrorists. "I know you think I'm crazy, but I keep seeing women with backpacks and one of them came and stood next to me and I about crapped in my pants," she said. "Am I crazy?"

"Yes," Margie said. "A lot of people carry backpacks. Americans and everybody else. They're as common as dark glasses."

"I just have this feeling that I'm about to be blown up."

"Then don't stand too close to me."

"I mean it feels like a dangerous city. And the cops don't seem all that alert, if you ask me. Somebody could put a suitcase full of dynamite into the back of our van and blow it sky-high."

"Somebody could dump a hundred bowling balls out of an airplane and one of them could hit you on the head and we'd be mopping up your brains. Same thing."

"I'm serious. Everywhere I look, I see liquids and gels. A plastic explosive the size of a bar of soap, if it's placed in the right place—one minute you're looking at the ruins and the next minute you're a big grease stain."

"Just get a grip. Nobody's going to blow us up. We're not that important." It made Margie feel like a heroine in a war movie, a nurse during the Blitz, telling her charges to buck up, cheerio, stiff upper lip, do your part for queen and commonwealth, nice cup of tea, duckie, pull up your socks, comb your hair, it'll all be right as rain.

He was waiting for her in his pajama bottoms and a T-shirt. A bottle of wine sat opened on the table and two white tapers were burning. She had never done this before. *Done what before?* What she was thinking about doing. She didn't think she ought to do it but she thought maybe she would anyway. How else do you find out about these things? Mother said, *Oh Marjorie*, and started weeping. *When are you going to wake up?* Mother, I never tried adultery before. Maybe it's not the answer, but who knows?

Anyway, it was the direction things were headed unless she turned around and left right now. Which she didn't do. She thought she might but then it turned out that she sat down on the bed instead and when he poured her a glass of red wine, she said, "Thank you very much, Paolo."

"It's a Spanish wine. I spent a couple weeks in Spain once and met a girl in Madrid. She was American. From Idaho. We decided to travel together."

"How old was she?"

"Her name was Lucy. She was twenty-four, studying to be a doctor. A nice girl but so self-centered. Very immature. Younger women are highly overrated. Anyway—"

"Do you keep in touch with her?"

He smiled. "I don't believe in keeping in touch," he said. "I believe in the moment. The beautiful moment. Life is a series of beautiful unforgettable moments and the beauty is in the moment itself. Keeping in touch—why? Retrospect only makes the moment ordinary."

"I love you," he said. "You're so delicate. The way you tremble when I kiss you."

His lips tasted of smoke and wine, and then his arms were around her and he laid her down on her side, facing him, in his embrace, and he kissed her face and her neck, and then he unbuttoned her shirt and kissed her collarbone and bared her shoulders and kissed those. And then they lay, looking into each other's eyes. His were green and very steady and she saw kindness in them and she kissed them, first the left eyelid, then the right.

"What are you thinking?" he said. She said she was thinking that it was very nice to lie there with him and how lucky to meet him.

"I think so, too. Would you like to get under the covers?"

No, said Mother. *Where are your brains?* But Carl said nothing. He lay reading a book about the Battle of Shiloh and the carnage of the Civil War.

She didn't say yes and she didn't say no. But when he sat up, she sat up, and when he pulled back the covers, she pulled back her side of the covers. He took off his pajama bottoms, and he moved over to her and unzipped her jeans and helped her out of them. She wore white panties with little cherries on them. He kissed her behind the ear and whispered, "You're delicious, my American."

Fifty-three and a man in his thirties wanted to make love to her. That was some kind of accomplishment. Nothing you'd get an award for at a Thanatopsis banquet, but it made her feel pretty good. He raised his T-shirt over his head and she looked at him. He was rather in good shape, a patch of black hair on his chest, hairy legs, and a small rose tattoo on his shoulder. She touched it. She kissed it. And then she reached down and took his penis in her hand. She was sort of shocked that she did this. It wasn't the Marjorie Schoppenhorst that people in Lake Wobegon thought they knew. It was another Margie, one whose story was yet to be written.

He was quite hard in her hand and now a sense of urgency came over him. He undressed her quickly and he eased her down on the bed on her back and opened her legs and got busy down there doing things that she had read about but were not part of her lovemaking history. No, sir. He was down there for a couple of minutes and it was exciting and then almost unbearably exciting and then he stopped and he was pressing himself inside her and he was lying gently atop her and rocking to and fro and gently biting her shoulder. "Is this nice?" he said. Yes, it was. It was very nice. It wasn't what she should be doing right now but that wasn't the question. It was very nice. He rocked forward and back and she raised her legs and then he knelt and grasped her calves and raised them high, rolling her rump up in the air. Himself very deep inside her, looking deeply into her eyes, going on and on, riding, riding, riding, and then the warm wave in her sexual plexus and she arched her back—"Yes," he said. Oh yes indeed. To hell with caution. "I want you to come inside me," she whispered. Her hands on his shoulders as he leaned down, eyes closed, the whole length of him pushing, pushing, and she cried out, "Oh yes. Yes yes yes. Oh my God." And he gave out a great groan and she felt the hot wet of him inside her and her legs convulsed and she grabbed him by the neck and hauled him down and she sobbed— for pleasure—she lay and wept big tears of pleasure and looked at him, his nose on her nose, and said, "That was pretty great."

She dressed in the bathroom afterward, not looking at herself in the mirror. He was lying under a sheet on the bed, smoking, a full ashtray balanced on his chest. "Sit down," he said. "Talk to me. What's on your mind?" She sat on the side of the bed and he put his arm around her butt and stroked her thigh.

"I'm thinking about staying here," she said. "Renting a room and studying Italian and figuring out my life."

"For how long?"

"For as long as it takes."

"If you do, I hope I'll be able to see you."

"I'd love to see you."

"But I must tell you. Rents are exorbitant. You're actually better off investing—I've earned a lot of money buying and selling apartments. Rome is hot now. Property is affordable. Huge demand. Middle Easterners wanting to get out of oppressive Muslim countries, enjoy themselves."

"I don't know if I can afford it."

"You'd be surprised." He pulled her down. "Kiss me," he said. She kissed him on the mouth, hard. "You're the best lover I ever had," he said.

And he threw the sheet off to invite her back in, but she jumped up. "Gotta run." And out the door. She had to wait a full minute for the elevator and then it still didn't come, so she ran down four flights of stairs and out the front door, in a daze of pleasant bewilderment—the pleasure of the adventure and also a low throbbing voice *Bad Bad Bad Bad*—and right there on the sidewalk were Eloise and Lyle and Daryl and Marilyn.

"Where were you?"

"Went in the hotel to get directions."

"Where you going?"

She looked up and caught sight of a sign pointing to the Trevi Fountain, fifty meters. "The Trevi fountain," she said. So they trudged over there, though the four of them had already seen all there was to see of it.

Fresh from Paolo's bed, his juice trickling down her leg—she felt alien in the mob of tourists obsessed with cameras, posing in front of the fountain, the torrential billows of water, the marble seahorses and giants blowing horns, mounds of coins in the pool, a hundred camera flashes per second. "My God, let's get out of here. The tourists!" she said. "But we are tourists too," cried Eloise who wanted Lyle to take her picture. She stood, her back to the fountain, about to toss a coin over her shoulder, as Lyle examined her camera. "Just point and shoot!" she said.

A man in a black silky jacket, his hair slicked back, stepped up behind Lyle and said, out of the corner of his mouth, "Fifty feet from here, pal, ten beautiful girls waiting for you, the most beautiful girls in the world and none of them has a stitch of clothing on her body whatsoever, not even a pair of socks—they are au naturel, stark naked, topless, bottomless, and one hundred percent nude or your money back—check it out, check it out."

Lyle was engrossed in the camera and paying no attention.

"None of them over eighteen years of age, we have certificates to prove it," the man muttered.

And just then Eloise recognized people she thought she knew from a seminar in Minneapolis years ago—she didn't dare say hello to them because she couldn't remember their names—so they beat a retreat and Daryl led them up the Palatine Hill and the Capitoline Hill, reading from the guidebook all the way. Here was the Villa Medici where mad King Ludwig of Bavaria pranced around in the nude, waving sparklers. Here was the Villa Minesoto of the aristocratic family from Minneapoli (Little Naples) who sent a son to America in 1831 to explore the upper Mississippi. Here is the Church of St. Stephen Rotondo (Stephen the Plump), who was martyred by squeezing. *We are doing the same thing that millions of people have done before us,* she thought. *Looking at the same things, thinking the same, following the trail. Like migratory birds on the flyway.*

"I can't walk another step," said Eloise, so they sat down to rest at a little outdoor café. Margie liked Eloise much better jet-lagged, grieving. All her leadership qualities leached out of her and now she was purely human again. She was getting over the terrorist stuff but she was thinking about calling Fred for a heart-to-heart. Fred had a videocam on his computer, thanks to the new girlfriend. Eloise could call him and have a video conference. She'd need to put on lipstick first and do her hair. "Don't torture yourself," said Margie, "let go of it. Forget Fred."

"What are we trying to forget?" said poor Lyle. He had retired after forty-two years of heroic attempts to teach biology to teenagers, a losing battle, the learning retention rates terribly low, and now, just when he should be enjoying his freedom, he was losing his mind. "I know we're here for a reason and I forget what it is," he said.

So she told him. "We're here to put a picture of Gussie Norlander on his grave. He died a hero in the war a long time ago and his old mother wanted people to know who he was."

"Right. Of course. Who's Fred?"

"Fred is my former boyfriend who stuck a knife in my back, but I still love him," said Eloise.

He put a hand on Margie's leg. "I love you," he said. "I have always loved you and I always will. I even have impure thoughts about you. You're remarkable, Margie."

"You're so sweet." But she thought, *Look out. No more late-night walks with Lyle. We've got a loose cannon on the deck. Please don't let him stand up and expose himself. Please.*

They stopped in the Church of St. John and saw the Scala Sancta, the sacred stairs that Jesus walked to the upper room where the Last Supper took place and also the Sancta Sanctorum Cucina, the kitchen where it was prepared. And the Palazzo sant' Angelo where Pope Leona lived in the tenth century, the legendary female pope (or *papessa*) who came up in the Church as Giovanni di Nebuloso (John the Vague) who, while a holy man and all, did not give concise answers to questions. And he loved to sing *un forte tremore soprano* and spin around and around in a *pinafore*, but they didn't question him on this because he was a holy man, or, as it turned out, a holy woman. One day, saying high mass, he let out a cry and squatted by the altar and gave birth to a baby girl, who was named Immaculata and became the prioress of the Abbey of St. Estiva, and meanwhile what to do with Pope Leona—

rather than go through a big inquisition and cause scandal and give ammunition to the enemies of the faith, they pronounced the birth a genuine miracle, which any birth surely is, and put the pope into a cloister where she lived a perfectly holy life, and died, and when the Church Fathers met in conclave to elect a new one, they sat in the nude, a tradition carried on to this very day.

Heading home to the Giorgina, they stopped and looked at a sidewalk artist's charcoal portraits. He watched them coolly from his canvas chair, green cap shading his eyes, orange corduroy shirt. The portraits were good, Margie thought, and she said so. "A hundred euros, though," said Daryl. "Pretty steep. And why do it when we have a camera?" She leaned down toward the artist and smiled and said, *"Scusi."*

"Good evening," he said.

"Would you do my picture for sixty euros?" He offered one for seventy-five. "Then make me look like Audrey Hepburn," she whispered, putting the bills in his palm. And he did, sort of. An Audrey with rounder cheeks and pursed lips. Daryl took half a dozen pictures of her posing for the artist who worked swiftly and rolled up the picture and put it in a cardboard tube. "My, you are a brave one," said Marilyn. "Bargaining and everything. I wouldn't know how to do that."

"It's easy," she said. "Everybody wants more than they're entitled to and sometimes you get what you want and sometimes what you're entitled to." She thought of the beautiful man whose perspiration was still on her body, whose seed had dried on the side of her leg. He was not an entitlement. She thought she would take the portrait to a printshop and make a copy for him and sign it, "To Paolo, with love from your American, Marjorie."

ANNIVERSARY

Carl was half awake when she got upstairs. "Have a good day?" he said.

"Excellent," she said. She wondered if he could smell Paolo on her and what if he could? Would he become enraged and smother her with a pillow, like Othello? It was hard to imagine Carl in a towering rage. "I've got a headache," he said. She offered him an Advil and he shook his head. "It's the Ladderman business," he said. The bank had faxed him a rather brisk letter, asking him to call at his earliest convenience. "I can't call them, I don't have anything to say. The guy hung me out to dry. If I'm going to lose my shirt, I don't want to know about it yet."

She closed the bathroom door behind her and got out of her adultery clothes and examined the shiny trail of dried semen on her leg. This was something that was supposed to happen to you at twenty-one, not fifty-three. She was living life out of order. You should go to Italy for your junior year and meet your Paolo at the Hotel Il Paradiso, have a big wonderful affair—have several of them, six or seven; heck, fifteen—and then go home, meet your Carl and marry him. That was the right way. But what could she do? She wanted to live a rich full life and the door had been closed until now. She'd had the meat loaf and gravy and now someone offered her the shrimp appetizer and the spring roll and the wonton soup. She took a sleeping pill that night and put in ten hours of good sleep and dreamed that Eloise was pushing her cart through Ralph's Pretty Good Grocery and said, "I like your hair that way." And she awoke and bounded up from bed and showered and dressed while Carl lay bleary eyed, restless. He'd been kept awake by bad dreams. Men with dogs chasing him into a dark swamp toward a cliff. "Hey. Isn't today our wedding anniversary?" she said. Of course it was. How had *that* slipped her mind? She'd never forgotten it before.

He asked her what she'd like to do on their anniversary and she said, "We're here, together. That's enough." Okay, he said. She wished he'd suggest making love. And then she wasn't sure she wished that at all. Too confusing, two men in 24 hours.

There was a bouquet of daisies waiting for her at the front desk, with a note from Maria:

Are you coming over? Mother is asking. Whenever I say the words "Lake Wobegon" she smiles. Her mind is fading but she sure remembers Papa. She is wearing that Whippets jersey you sent me in January. The jar of rhubarb jelly broke and that messed up the postcards but I cleaned them up and she sits and looks at them, wearing her jersey with the dog on the front. By the way, why do they call it the Chatterbox? Is that a typical name for a café? And the Sidetrack Tap? What is a "sidetrack"? Ring me up and let's have coffee.

She called Maria from the lobby. "A sidetrack is a railroad siding where they park boxcars that aren't in use. And a chatterbox is someone who talks a lot."

"And the Sons of Knute? Who is Knute?"

"He was some old Viking ruler or somebody. And they're a bunch of old men who get together to eat codfish and drink aquavit and sing sad songs in Norwegian about how much they miss the fjords and mountains, which, in their case, they've never seen."

Maria said that her mother was not having a good day but that she, Maria, wanted to see Margie, so they made a date for lunch at a little café near a church that Maria wanted to show her.

She stepped into the long breakfast room off the lobby hoping to eat alone but there in a blazing rectangle of sunlight was Father Wilmer waving to her, with Wally and Evelyn. So she filled up a plate with two hard rolls and cheese, boiled egg, yogurt and corn flakes, and a mug of strong coffee. Through the sheer curtains she saw passersby on the street, meeting each other, ducking, stepping through each other like dancers in a complicated reel. A busboy stood at attention, brass buttons on his green jacket. An elaborate brass chandelier hung over Father Wilmer's table, the green and white tablecloths freshly starched. "The yogurt is excellent," he said. "It's from Greece. You pour honey on it."

"Father was just saying that there is a dress code at St. Peter's," said Evelyn. "No shorts, but they allow slacks."

Wally said that Evelyn wanted to get a papal blessing for her aunt in Owatonna who was ninety-two and nearing the end, but nobody knew where you could get them, did Margie? No, she did not, but it can't be so hard to fool an old lady, can it? "Give her a little St. Christopher's medal, tell her he kissed it, she'll die happy."

Evelyn shook her head, "I can't believe you'd say that. What's gotten into you?"

Father had pictures of Santa Maria del Popolo where he'd just come from early Mass and was still stunned from the experience. "Such beauty, such reverence," he whispered. The pictures were out of focus. "Our young people want something contemporary and instead of the Sanctus beautifully sung by a choir, they want people bouncing around with guitars singing, 'Our God is a wonderful wonderful God'—sing seven words eleven times and clap and grin—they just don't understand the beauty of Latin. It's fading so fast that in ten years nobody will remember what a Sanctus sounds like. Don't get me wrong. I'm as progressive as the next person. But—the classics are the classics."

When Carl came down, she asked him where the Whippets had gotten their name. "I don't know where the name comes from. They did once play against dogs, though. It was a traveling exhibition team, called the King and His Rooks, with a one-armed pitcher named John 'the King' Kramarszuk, who lost his right arm in a robbery. He stuck up an armored car and told the guard to hand over the money and instead the guard threw it back in the truck and the King reached in for it and the electric door closed and sliced it off at the elbow. He learned to pitch left-handed during his eight and a half years in Stillwater Prison. He's the pitcher and there are two outfielders and two dogs, Pete and Repete, who cover the infield, and the catcher, Blind Boy Thompson. The King throws a pretty good screwball and he shut out the Whippets for five innings before Ronnie hit a double but one of the dogs bit him as he headed for second and Ronnie was mad and tried to stretch it into a triple and the dog took the throw in his jaws and tagged him out and then the dog did a backflip."

They set out from the hotel at 10:00 A.M. in a downpour, two by two under big black umbrellas, and she tried to hurry them along. She was going to meet Maria. She walked alone, Carl behind her, under Daryl's umbrella. They were teammates on the Leonards basketball team that lost the District trophy to St. Agnes in 1974. Daryl went to the free-throw line with the score tied and one second on the clock and he missed two free throws; one hit the backboard *bonk* and the other bounced off the rim, *bwang*. He attended Augsburg College with hair down to his shoulders and a serape, read *Steppenwolf* and searched for his true self outside the restrictions of society, and the day after graduation he and Marilyn walked around Lake Wobegon with lilacs in their hair talking until 4:00 A.M. and sat down on the steps of the Central Building. He said, "I met an old alumnus, class of 1964, and that seems so long ago, but it won't be long until 1984 is as far in the past as 1964 is to us," and from this profound observation they decided to marry, and now he had the same flattop haircut as in high school. He had told this story the night before, standing in the hall outside their room. It was the first time Margie heard it. He was telling Carl about Yorkshire hogs, their durability and their excellent conversion ratio of feed to meat, and their superior loins. "That's where your profit is, in the loins." Now, walking along, Daryl bent and picked up a wet paper napkin and casually tossed it into a trash barrel fifteen feet away, *ker-plop,* and she remembered the St. Agnes game and how she sat in the bleachers with a crowd of Lake Wobegon girls and on the *bwang* they all looked at each other and spontaneously burst into tears. They collapsed in toward each other and sobbed and walked out, arms linked, weeping, like women grieving for lost miners, and onto the cold bus. He was supposed to toss that napkin in the barrel back in 1974 against St. Agnes. *Life happens out of order sometimes.*

Evelyn had developed the irritating habit of saying aloud Italian words she saw that were close to English, such as *libreria, gastronomia, informazione, vino,* which she assumed the Italians had taken from us and adapted to suit their own peculiar notions of spelling. She stopped to admire a window display of beers and read them aloud. *Birra Moretti La Birra Italiana, Nostro Azzuro, Doppio Malto.* "Double malt," said Lyle, dictionary in hand. "You see?" she said. "*Qualita Tradizione*—a tradition of quality. But why put the words backward?" She shook her head.

Carl stopped in front of a hardware store, its displays spilling out onto the sidewalk: ironing boards, ladders, brooms, gardening tools, balls of twine. The building itself seemed about to collapse from the Glory That Was Rome. Everywhere he looked, he saw shoddy workmanship. The old Roman brickwork had survived but the new stuff . . . "My gosh, look at how they slapped that together," he said, poking at a marble tile on a café wall. He looked like he was about to pull it off and fifteen more along with it. He looked down and saw concrete that hadn't been properly cured. In their hotel, the wood paneling in the lobby was crooked. "Look at that," he said, running a finger along the gap. The molding in their room was off-kilter. The caulking around the pipes in the bathroom, the electric switch, the carpeting—"It's like they hired fifteen-year-olds to do the job"—it bothered him. "You're not the local housing inspector," she pointed out. He shook his head. "I just don't understand how people can build like this."

He wanted to head back to the Forum. You could find a tour group and tag along and listen to the guide for free. He and Daryl had done that yesterday. It was neat. And cost nothing.

"The Catholic Church is earning a million bucks a day. The Pope is collecting money online, did you hear?" said Daryl. "It's called PayPal." The others groaned.

She stopped. "I'm sorry. I forgot something at the hotel. Don't wait. I'll catch up later."

"What?" said Carl.

"It's a female thing. I'll find you later." And she slipped away. "Hey!" he was saying, and then she was around the corner, slipping through the throngs, and made her way to the little coffee shop where Maria sat waiting, pouring sugar into an espresso. She was all dressed up in a white jacket and slacks, a gray sweater, a big straw hat. She looked as if she'd spent a couple hours putting herself together. She stood up and they embraced and Margie smelled a faint aroma of sandalwood. Maria grinned. "It's my papa's aftershave. Mother's very fond of it. She's a rather stubborn thing except when she smells this and then she's—what's the expression?—a piece of cake."

A BEAUTIFUL IDEA

The waiter brought Margie an Americano. Maria leaned back and lit up a cigarette. The smoke drifted up into her face and she waved it away.

"You're my friend and friends have to be honest," she said. "I've got two pieces of advice for you. Call me crazy, tell me we're no longer friends, but I have to say this. I think you should leave your husband and I think you should buy an apartment in Rome."

Margie laughed. "No halfway measures, huh?"

"You're fifty-three. You're in your prime. It doesn't last forever. You gave him thirty . . . what?"

"Thirty-five."

"You gave him thirty-five years. That's half your life. Americans believe in therapy. It works for some things, it doesn't work for this. Love is a mystery and it comes and goes, nobody has ever understood it. People long for permanence. It's a beautiful idea but it doesn't exist. Because experience changes us. It's not in our natures to be stable. People crave stability until we get a good hard look at it and then we long for freedom and the next adventure. So we have to adapt, or else go crazy."

"Why should I buy an apartment?"

Maria stubbed out the cigarette and leaned forward and laid her hands down on the table, her fingers spread. "Number one, you will love living here. Rome is an international city. You will find things here you could not dream of. Or things you could only dream of. The light of the ages. Magic. Freedom of the spirit. All of your needs satisfied. I can show you if you want to see for yourself, but number two, I have bought and sold four apartments for myself in the past eight years and it was the most fantastic investment I ever made."

She leaned forward and whispered, "One hundred fifty percent profit over eight years. One hundred fifty. The stock market is broken. Banks pay next to nothing. Gold is for the Swiss. Diamonds, art, rare musical instruments—nothing compares to real estate.

"I have friends in the business. I can get discounts," she said, leaning back. "But only if you want. I don't want to sell you anything you don't want. It's neither here nor there to me. I only offer as a friend."

And then she leaned forward and whispered again. "The hotel where Papa and my mama made love and created me—it has been made into condominiums. Very nice. Not far from here. The room they occupied that night—on the fourth floor, looking toward St. Peter's—it's for sale. Do you want to see it?"

Yes, actually she did want to see it.

"The day after tomorrow. Tomorrow I'll talk to my friends and see what deal I can get. I'll give you the address." She wrote it out in a big hand—*No. 25 Via Maggio*—and gave it to Margie and leaned forward and took her into a big warm embrace. "I am so lucky to find you," said Maria. "I always wanted a friend like you. An openhearted American friend." She signaled the waiter and asked for a Campari and soda. "We'd be even dearer friends if you lived here.

"A well-adjusted person needs two cultures, not one," she said, clinking the ice in her drink. "This is the place where you can become you. This is your safe place. Your holy place. There is a great spiritual depth here and not just the church. Pagan spirits too. The spirit of the immortal past can illuminate your soul. It sounds hocus-pocus but it's the wisdom of Italy. The past is fertilizer and we blossom from it."

She wasn't sure about pagan spirits illuminating her soul, but the idea of divorce—maybe she should think about it.

Well, actually she was thinking about it.

A woman in Sartell got a divorce last year because her husband was always chuckling. She told him to stop and he couldn't. Or didn't. So she told him she was leaving him and he chuckled. It was in the paper. So what about emotional abandonment?

She went to an Internet café and Googled "divorce, grounds," and found that in marriage, nothing is trivial. People had split up over the failure of one spouse to use coasters. A woman in Wisconsin had divorced her husband for beginning every sentence with the word "So." "So," he'd say, "we going to town now or what?" "So," he'd say, "what's for supper then?"

Snoring was grounds for divorce, and farting, and peeing in the shower, but about emotional abandonment, nothing. She found a web site called Divorce Q&A for Women.

Q: My husband got into a snit because I asked him to turn down the sound of the basketball game which he and his friend Mike were watching in the living room. We live in a mobile home and I work an early morning shift as a crossing guard at an elementary school on the other side of town and must leave the house at 4 A.M. to take two different buses to get there and then walk ten blocks, all to work four hours at $8/hr, so I need my sleep, and there he was drinking beer at 10 p.m. and hollering about a stupid basketball game, and I asked him to please be quiet, and he went to Mike's house and has spent nights there for three weeks. Is that abandonment? (He returns home in the mornings after I've left.)

A: If he comes back, it is not abandonment.

"I've always been fascinated by the law myself," said Lyle, looking over Margie's shoulder at the screen. She jumped and tried to close the Q & A window.

"How's everything going?" said Marilyn, pulling up a chair.

"Fine," said Margie, closing the window.

Marilyn said, "Don't worry. You're not the first person to think about divorce. I've thought about it fifteen times. So has Lyle, I'll bet." He nodded.

"Not so much since I hit my head, but before that, I did."

IN THE PIAZZA

To the Piazza Navona in the rain to look at the fantastic fountains—a naked man stabbing an octopus who has grasped him by his thigh; big-butt bare-breasted ladies riding winged turtles; cherubs clinging to a wild-eyed horse galloping in the surf. And above the square a billboard for vacuum cleaners, a happy housewife hoovering away, her glad children cheering her on. Clint stood in the rain and shot picture after picture, the sheer drama of the fountains, the swash and splash of water, the pool pricked by thousands of raindrops, puddles on the pavement, the gray and cream and salmon buildings beyond, their balconies decked with broad-leafed tropical plants.

"Remember the fishing opener that year?" said Wally, studying the pool.

"The year we gave up fishing openers? We sat in a boat in a cold rain, the coffee was cold, the sandwiches were wet, and we watched our bobbers bob for a couple hours, and we said to hell with it, and I haven't been fishing since," said Clint.

"What's the difference between rococo and baroque?" said Eloise, reading a guidebook. "Rococo is like baroque," said Margie, "except more so."

A woman in white stood at a high window facing the piazza, and when Clint aimed his camera up, she pulled the drapes. Margie had read about the piazza in *O Paradiso*, it was where Joanne the farm widow met the mime Alfredo who told her with his hands and eyes that he loved her soul and then he struck a heroic lover's pose atop a wooden crate and held it for seventy-five minutes as passersby dropped change in the straw hat on the sidewalk and Joanne watched him for those seventy-five minutes of perfect stillness.

Lovers see the world with fresh exuberant eyes. They make a strip mall into the Alhambra and a Midwestern Main Street into the Boulevard of Beautiful Dreams. Lovers scatter blessings wherever they go, their keenness, their hunger and passionate gentleness, the music of touch—and when I looked at Alfredo, he was no longer a forty-three-year-old street mime who lived in the backseat of his Fiat, he was the spirit of generosity let loose in the world, whom I had found on a wooden box in the Piazza Navona.

"On the west side of the piazza stands the former friary of the Augustinians, a favored trysting spot for Pope Julius of Orange and his mistress, Queen Christina of Sweden," Eloise read from the guidebook. "A young German friar named Martin Luther lived in the room below the papal chamber, and the loud cries of the splenetic, hunchbacked, beetle-browed Julius and his short, stout, pockmarked paramour may have been what triggered the Reformation."

Margie led them into the church of St. Agnese with its high dome and fruit-salad arches and columns, and in the vast dimness a statue of the saint standing in flames, hands outstretched, looking only mildly perturbed, as if to say, "This, after I just had my toenails done." Tourists shuffled across the marble floor, stood at the brass railings, gazed at the balconies, and tried not to gawk at the few devout women kneeling and whispering to God. Though you had to wonder about the young woman whose shoulders shook, her muffled sobs clearly visible. What was up with her? Love troubles, most likely. She didn't look pregnant, at least not from the rear. Maybe her lover had done her wrong and she had shot him, and, before descending to the dungeon cell, she was making amends with the Lord. The pilgrims stood together, looking at her, kneeling, weeping, rocking to and fro.

"I wonder how many people actually attend this church. I hear church attendance is very poor in Italy," said Clint.

Father Wilmer said that attendance isn't the mark of success. That the church has no mark of success. And if you want success, probably this isn't the place to find it.

"Okay," said Clint. "Thanks for the information."

Everywhere you looked, statues of saints looked mournfully or beatifically or thoughtfully at you, or gazed up toward heaven, or gazed at you and directed you to look up toward heaven. The Blessed Virgin stood by a rack of candles, sympathizing with each person who came to light a candle and say a prayer.

"Father Emil once fired me as the Virgin Mary from the

Christmas pageant because I didn't say my lines loud enough," Margie said. "He yelled at me, 'Don't just stand there like you're a statue. You're the Mother of God, for crying out loud. Speak up.' I burst into tears and ran out of the room and he yelled, 'What's the matter with her?' and then he got somebody else. Mary Magendanz, who was stiff as a board and mumbled. It was humiliating. Especially for my mother."

She had said this to Carl, who was not listening. He was whispering to Clint. "Pretty amazing for a Lutheran to see this, huh?" Clint nodded.

"We Lutherans always were pretty plain. No incense, except for Old Spice, and no statues. Though of course some members are less physically active than others."

"The statues are so you know you're not alone if you come in here alone."

"Lutherans don't go to church alone."

"Strength in numbers, huh?"

"Not really. But we get strength from each other."

"Well, there you are. We believe you come to God alone."

"Well, yes, of course. And we believe you come before God naked. But that doesn't mean you have to take your clothes off."

"Thank God."

"The church was built by Pope Giovanni della Cancelleria (John the Omitted) about whom little is known," read Eloise. "St. Agnese was an early church organist and, in a fit of spiritual ecstasy, she played without ceasing, even after ordered to stop, whereupon they attempted to suffocate her with seat cushions, then stoned her with shoes, and finally set her on fire, and she played and sang until consumed."

St. Agnese reminded Clint of his mother as she canned tomatoes in August, pulling the hot jars out of the pressure cooker.
And also his mother's cousin Ruthie who used to go to Clearwa-
ter, Florida, every winter with her husband, Arthur, because, she
said, the Lord had led them to witness the resort-goers, which
they did, walking along the beach in long white paper gowns
with Bible verses painted on in big black block letters, warning
of eternal hellfire if people did not repent immediately, which
most sunbathers, already a little scorched, declined. Ruthie and
Arthur always wore broad-brimmed hats and plenty of sun-
screen. A verse in Deuteronomy had warned them about skin
cancer, they said. They spent several hours a day trudging the
beaches, and if anyone looked at them and smiled, they stopped
in their tracks and stood so as to permit the sunbather to get the
full benefit of Scripture truth. . . .

Clint told this story to Carl, standing near the statue, and as he
got into the story, Clint's voice got a little louder, and people in far
corners of the sanctuary turned around, startled—the acoustics
were such as to make him seem to be talking right into their ear.

One day Ruthie was moved by the Spirit to kneel at the foot
of a chaise longue occupied by a fat man in a bright red bathing
suit who had scoffed at her—said something like, "Get out of the
way, fattycakes. You're blocking my light"—and she cried, "I am
bringing you the light" and knelt down, not seeing the hibachi
in the sand on which he was roasting his knockwurst. She prayed
for him loudly and then felt the heat of the paper Gospel dress
going up in flames. . . .

"Do you realize how loud your voice is?" said Irene. "People
can hear you all over. You may as well climb up in the pulpit."

Arthur tore the burning dress off her and there she stood in her foundation garments, but she felt no shame at all. None. She felt the sudden powerful indwelling of the Holy Spirit and she cried out, "Thank you, Lord Jesus, for taking away my shame!" She felt changed forever. She had been freed once and for all from the condemnation of the law and given the true sense of liberty that is the birthright of the true believer—free from the mere decorum of piety, free from moral fastidiousness—and she started dancing around in her underwear, a sort of born-again Charleston with some Grizzly Bear moves thrown in. Arthur told her to stop for God's sake, that people were watching, and she cried, "Don't you see, Arthur? God has delivered me into a state of pure blessedness!" and she snatched up an alcoholic drink from a table and drank it and cried, "Praise the Lord!" And then she unsnapped her brassiere. . . .

"Please come outdoors," said Irene. "People are staring. A priest just looked out of that alcove over there. They are going to call the cops." "They *have* called the cops," said Mr. Keillor, who had been walking by the church and heard Clint's voice and came inside.

"Where have *you* been keeping yourself?" she said. "Did you pick up your traps and move to the Ritz-Carlton?"

"Are you talking to me?" he said. "I've been seeing friends."

"Maybe you ought to move here, if you have friends here." She beckoned him closer with an index finger. "As a friend, I think you should consider starting a new life," she said. "You might be funnier in Italian."

The author could not understand where Irene's anger was coming from. So unrelenting, after all these years. What had he *done*? He decided not to ask. Too many possible answers. She had been a close friend of his first wife's cousin, and perhaps she had heard things about his restless, reckless twenties and thirties, but why take it out on him *now*? Have mercy. He backed away and bumped into a pew and sat down in it and pulled his brown Moleskine notebook from his jacket pocket. *She drilled into him with her dark pencil-point eyes, bitter scorn writ large on her thin lips, hands on her hips, her jaw jutting out like a fist—and suddenly he remembered the scene on the beach when they were seventeen. Irene in a (rather unrevealing) two-piece suit, he in bloomerish swim trunks and a bilious green shirt to cover his bony chest, she talking about a book that changed her life and handing it to him,* Air and Space *by Kahlil Gibran, and he opened it to the sentence, "The longing that we feel within will lead us to the light and to the sacred togetherness of the creation and the universal soul which is not the Other but which is through you and before you and over you and also with you in all of your comings and goings." She had thrust the book at him and told him to read it and he accepted it, though it was pure gibberish, and then what? That was forty years ago. Oh my God, he thought. He had forgotten to return her book! It had joined the togetherness of a pile of junk and been hauled away by the trashman. She was angry at him for rejecting the book that had changed her life!*

Clint was not done with his story—Arthur had not been liberated. He still had his Gospel smock on. He tried to restrain Ruthie from going around bare-bosomed and hugging people. She was a robust woman and he had a hell of a time wrangling her back to the tourist cabins and when he finally got her there, she was buck naked and shouting out praise to the Lord. The next morning, after a restless night of prayer and praise, he got her into the car and headed for Minnesota. She said, "Quench not the Spirit, Arthur." She kept saying it. "Hold fast to the truth. Quench not the Spirit." And Arthur replied, "Abstain from all appearance of evil, such as running around naked." And she said, "Take no thought for what ye shall wear. The life is more than meat, and the body is more than raiment. Consider the lilies how they grow: they toil not, they spin not; and yet I say unto you, that Solomon in all his glory was not arrayed like one of these. If then God so clothe the grass, which is today in the field, and tomorrow is cast into the oven; how much more will he clothe you, O ye of little faith?"

"The carabinieri have pulled up in front," reported Wally. "I'm not talking that loud," said Clint. "It's the acoustics," Irene hissed. The pilgrims got hold of Clint who kept saying, "I was not talking that loud!" and herded him out the doors and down the steps. Four officers of the law stood around the car labeled CARABINIERI, its blue lights flashing, and waited for further instructions. The pilgrims maneuvered Clint around behind a fountain, the one with naked nymphs and giant sea turtles.

Arthur got confused about his directions—this was before we had GPS and Magellan and these Australian women guiding us around the backroads—and he saw a café all lit up called Lilies of the Valley Café and she said, "Stop right here." And she went in and came out with two big bags of food. It was a Chinese café run by Christians and the owners had felt that the Lord was about to send special visitors, and when Ruthie walked in, they emptied their larder and gave her buckets of Kung Pao chicken and Chinese barbecued ribs and a rather spicy shrimp dish, a whole gallon of it.

Arthur and Ruthie were new to Chinese food, but this was divinely sent for their refreshment, and they chewed on the ribs as Arthur drove, and they tore into the shrimp dish, which scorched their palates, but still, they knew it was God's Will that they partake. They drove on, in tears, sobbing from acid reflux, trying to fathom what God was showing them, thinking they might be the first martyrs to perish from seasoning, and then Arthur slammed on the brakes and there in the road stood a fifteen-foot alligator.

Arthur pulled over and Ruthie said, "Thank you, Jesus. Thy Will be done, Lord." The gator stood twenty feet away, blinking its big yellow eyes, flexing its claws. She cried out, "Lord, Thy Will be done and if I am to join You today in heavenly glory, I give praise for it." When she opened the car door, the gator smelled the food in the car and lumbered over and Arthur rolled down the window and tossed out the big bag of ribs and the bucket of spicy shrimp and the gator scarfed it all down and stood motionless for a long moment and groaned a mighty groan as if something powerful were underway in his lower digestive tract. He lay down and ate some grass and he gave Ruthie a baleful look where she stood praying for her deliverance into Glory at the Lord's right hand, and the gator gagged a few times, and then his bowels opened, and he slid away leaving behind a trail of greenish scat. It was Arthur who noticed the slip of paper poking out of a pool of green poop, and it was Ruthie who picked it up. It said "At all times, let us give thanks, and again I say unto you, let us give thanks." And on the other side, "Lilies of the Valley, noon to 9 P.M., M–Sat. Free delivery."

Irene poked Mr. Keillor who stood a few feet from Clint, writing quickly in his notebook. "That's not for you," she said. "Leave it alone. For crying out loud."

"So what happened to these people?" said Lyle. "I don't think I ever met them."

"They never returned to Lake Wobegon. The experience convinced Ruthie that God could not be known through the language of men, only by miraculous revelation, and they left the Sanctified Brethren and settled in Florida and became sun worshippers. Someone ran into them a few years ago and they looked like petrified people except they could walk and talk. Their skin was dark brown and horny and crinkly like an alligator's. And that's all I know. I suppose they're dead. This was years ago."

By now, they had scooted across the piazza under their umbrellas to an outdoor café and were drinking red wine and they clapped for Clint as the story came to an end. A heckuva story, with nudity, religion, marriage, mysticism, gator poop, and Chinese takeout in one tale. It was still raining hard, but it didn't matter. Their long table was covered by two tan canvas umbrellas twelve feet in diameter as the rain poured down. The big menu card posted on the sidewalk showed pictures of the entrees, in case you didn't know what lasagne was. Carl ordered two bottles of Amarone. "It's our wedding anniversary," he said, and everyone clapped. "Speech! Speech!" said Wally. "Don't tell us everything!" said Daryl. The waiter brought a chocolate cake with HAPPY ANNIVERSARY MARGIE & CARL in green icing. Eloise's doing, judging by her proprietary air. She snatched the knife from the waiter and cut twelve slabs and flopped them onto pie plates and ordered a gallon of vanilla ice cream. "Presto!" she cried. "Or pronto!"

Daryl rose to make a toast. "I grew up on a farm where nobody would ever talk about what a good year they had, if they had a good year, which sometimes they did, despite themselves. It was considered bad luck to celebrate. It was too much like boasting. So there was plenty of grumbling and grousing, fretting and fuming, bellyaching, wailing, and gnashing of teeth, and lots of sarcasm and ridicule and caustic comment, but they'd never admit success. My dad was a dark Norwegian, don't you know. Failure was inevitable. No such thing as progress. A good year just meant the postponement of disaster. The posse is going to catch up with you eventually. That's the philosophy we all grew up with."

"Get to the point," said Marilyn. "Don't give us your life story."

"So we tried to escape from that, and brought up our kids to believe in creativity and self-expression and being happy. My dad, if there was something I said I wanted, he'd say, 'People in hell want ice water.' That was his philosophy: You want it, you're not going to get it. I wasn't brought up to be happy, I was brought up to do the right thing. But if you did the right thing, you weren't praised for it, you weren't allowed to feel good about it, because there was no such thing as success. Success was just the postponement of disaster. My kids are happier than I was. Lois sent me a picture of her with her friends in her backyard in Santa Barbara, flowering bushes under the trees and a table with white linen and a platter of salmon with dill and lemon and whole-wheat couscous and her crusty bread rolls with chunks of brie—"

Marilyn: "Wind it up, pal."

"And we always worry about Lois and why doesn't she have a husband and kids by now, and here she is with four others, all of them tanned and grinning and raising their glasses, and they're happy, damn it, and they know it and they dare to *be* happy instead of grumbling and grousing the way I do and the way so many of us do."

Marilyn: "Just make the damn toast."

He raised his glass. "I'm only saying, congratulations to Carl and Margie for a great marriage and I wish you happiness." He sat down, to murmurs of agreement.

"Let's hear from the bride and groom," said Marilyn.

Carl and Margie looked at each other. She said, "We've been accused of having a great marriage. What do you have to say?" He said, "You go first."

She was feeling good about the red wine. A hearty Italian red wine and it did something for her that coffee could not. Her chest was filled with warmth, her head with light. She felt almost emboldened to stand up and sing

> When the world seems to shine like you've had too
>   much wine
>   That's amore. . . .

Instead, she stood up and told the story of Darlene and the Saskatchewan man she met on WebMatch who drove down to meet her for dinner and how could you deny a guy willing to drive 1,100 miles for the privilege of meeting you? His name was Orville Bledsoe and he had enormous eyebrows and wore a green plaid sport coat with suspenders and had a belly on him big as an anvil. But she went out for dinner with him at the Moonlite Bay Supper Club and it was clear that he loved her. He was too shy to say so, but he did. He was humming to himself and winking and blushing and he wrote "Sweetheart" on his napkin and passed it to her. But she couldn't love those eyebrows or that enormous gut. He talked about how wonderful Saskatchewan was and his house on the creek and his six dogs and his snowmobile and she could tell he was imagining her living there with him and it simply wasn't going to be. She said good night, grateful that he didn't lunge at her, and when he called at midnight she let it go to voice mail. "I hope you had as good a time as I did," he whispered. "You are magnificent." She met him for breakfast the next morning and brought two loaves of banana bread as a going-away gift. He stood by his pickup truck and said good-bye and he knew that this was good-bye and that all of his hints about taking a fishing trip to the Yukon were for naught and his heart was broken, he knew she was the love of his life and there would be no other, so his eyes were full of tears, and just above were those eyebrows. Actually one continuous eyebrow, like his head had cracked and someone had put a strip of black tape across it. He put a hand on her shoulder and leaned in to kiss her, that big hard belly up against her, and she turned her head and his lips grazed her cheek and she felt his teardrops land on her cheek. Burning hot tears. It left a red mark.

Marilyn took out a hanky and wiped her eyes. Eloise was crying too.

"What are you trying to say?" said Daryl, pouring himself another glass of wine. They had finished off the two bottles of Amarone and Carl was looking around for the waiter.

"I think it's sort of a miracle when two people get together, even if you have all the usual problems—you have to remember what a miracle it was that started you out. Two people joining up and worried they're making a huge mistake but they have all the right ideas about making a feast of love—"

"Hogwash," said Irene. She stood up. "I've had two glasses of wine," she said, "so take that into account, but—you remember my brother Richard. What a bookworm he was, and girls scared him to death. He was brilliant, went to Carleton, then Berkeley, loved San Francisco, lived in the Sunset neighborhood, and everyone assumed he was gay, especially gay men, but he wasn't. Every day, some beautiful man would make eyes at my brother, touch his arm, ask him out for coffee, compliment him on his hair, but all the time he was longing to speak to a young woman who always sat at her laptop in the corner of a coffee shop called The Beanery and never looked up. He was afraid to walk over and introduce himself because he was thirty years older, maybe more. He gazed at her from across the room, and drank espresso until his stomach burned. Finally, in a torment of jealousy because a young bearded man sat down next to her and spoke to her, he followed her home, got her name off the mailbox, and arranged for a Poetry Telegram—a messenger dressed up like Dionysus in a golden tunic and sandals, with golden hair, knocked at her door, as Richard watched from across the street and when she opened it, the messenger cried, 'Come live with me and be my love midst valleys, woods, and fields, and we will all the pleasures prove that this brief summer yields!' and opened a box and released five hundred golden butterflies that flew up in a cloud, and he had the card with Richard's name on it, but she didn't care, she put her arms around the god and cried, told him how much it meant to her, and invited him up. Richard stood across the street for two and a half hours.

He saw them in her apartment window and then it went dark. That was four years ago and he is still in love with her."

Daryl held up his hand. "And the moral of the story is what?"

"Don't count on it. It can go either way. At any time. What you call love and romance may just be the cosmos playing games with you."

Evelyn shook her head. "What?" said Irene. Evelyn snorted and looked away. "Say your piece," said Irene.

Evelyn stood up and looked up and down the table and said, "This may surprise you, but my first husband—"

Her first husband? Did she say "my first husband"?

"She was married to a guy in Willmar for a year," said Wally.

"Three months," said Evelyn. "Anyway, he loved repairing radios, and he was good at it, too. I didn't know until I married him that his house was full of radios. We courted on the porch; he never invited me inside. We were married by a justice of the peace in Morris and we drove home at top speed and into the house we went and I was expecting him to—well, you know what I was expecting. But what he wanted to show me was how he'd rigged up a battery-powered radio you could use to turn another radio on. It was the forerunner of the remote. He was thrilled by this. 'Look,' he said—I was standing there in my slip and garters—'you can turn it on without getting out of bed.' And he explained how it worked. It took him awhile and by that time I was naked as a jaybird and lying in bed, but it didn't matter to him. He wanted me to know what a great thing he'd done. And then he had to demonstrate it. Except it didn't work. Which, of course, got him going, trying to fix it. He got out his screwdriver and took it apart and fussed with it for a while, and didn't notice that I'd gotten out of bed and dressed. I said, 'I'm going to my mother's for awhile.' 'Okay,' he said, 'I'll have this fixed in a jiffy.' 'Take your time,' I said, and I went to Mother's. Heard from him a month later. He'd gone to Chicago to buy parts. I don't know where he went from there. I got the marriage annulled three months later and married Walter."

"I know nothing about electronics," said Wally. "That was a selling point right there."

Margie's cell phone rang. She got it out of her pocket. Mr. Keillor was calling her. Where was he? He had not come across the piazza with them.

"Oh God, no, don't answer it, let him stew in his own juices," said Irene, but Margie did. "Where are you?" she said. "You disappeared. We're at a café in the Piazza Navona. Come and join us."

Mr. Keillor had been taken into custody by the police. He had tried to explain that it was not he who was shouting a ribald story in the church, but they shushed him and told him that he could either spend the night in jail with the pickpockets and male prostitutes, or he could pay his fine there and then. Two hundred euros. That's why he was calling. He had no money or identification. His billfold had been stolen inside the church.

Margie explained his predicament to the pilgrims and put a fifty-euro bill in an empty breadbasket and passed it. Irene put in a five and Wally a ten. "Oh come on, people. Give it up. It's only money." Daryl put in fifty and Father Wilmer forty and then Clint dropped in a hundred and headed off in the rain, ransom in hand, to rescue the poor man from prison.

The waiter brought two big bowls of olives and a basket of bread and poured olive oil onto a plate to dip the bread in.

"I would like to make a speech," said Father Wilmer. He rose unsteadily to his feet and grasped the table. "It was three years ago when my sister Willa was supposed to come up from Chicago to visit. The weepy one with the hammertoes. I love her dearly, but you have to keep your distance with her or she'll take over your life. I was a little worried because she was talking about wanting to leave Chicago and what it means to be family and how we have to stick together as we get older. So I was afraid she was thinking about moving in with me. A week before she was due, I was driving back from giving Last Rites for the fourteenth time to Mr. Hudepohl and I ran into a big buck on the county road coming past Hansen's. He leaped up into my headlights and *whammo*, the airbag blew up big and pink and I slammed into it and the car slid into the ditch. I sat there in shock and Frank Sinatra was singing—

> *I've got you under my skin*
> *I've got you deep in the heart of me*

"The impact turned the radio on. And then the airbag deflated and I was looking into the big brown eyes of a dead deer, his head had bashed through the windshield, his antlers had missed me by inches. My cell phone rang and it was Willa, saying, 'Where are you? You said you'd call me an hour ago. I've been worried sick.

Why can't you call if you say you're going to call? All I'm asking for is a little consideration.' And then she heard Frank singing and she said, 'Are you in a bar?' And that was how I got Lyme disease. I was laid up with aches and a high fever and the doctor said it must be the flu that's going around except this didn't go around, it stayed put. It took six months out of my life." He stopped and looked down at the olives and cleared his throat.

> Out of the night that covers me,
> Black as the Pit from pole to pole,
> I am the master of my fate;
> I am the captain of my soul.

"Or something like that. . . . I forgot what I was going to say," he said.

"Maybe it'll come to you later," said Carl.

"No, you know what you were going to say," said Eloise. "Tell them what you told me last night." He looked at her, blushing.

She said, "Father fell in love with that nurse who took care of him. Suzanne. And he's still in love with her and she's waiting for him to decide what he's going to do about it."

They sat, stunned by the news. Their priest, deliberating whether to pull off the collar and be flesh and blood like the rest of them.

"I'm not good enough for her, I know that," he murmured. "We don't want to rush into anything." He was in tears. Suzanne made him bacon spinach salad with vinaigrette dressing and latte with a touch of caramel. She was a gentle woman who wrote poems in a journal with an Elliot Porter photograph of a tree on each left-hand page. She sat at his bedside and sang to him as she played a guitar, and before his afternoon nap she read Thackeray to him, and every night she poured him a glass of chardonnay with overtones of fescue, goldenrod, meadowlark, and Gorgonzola. And then one night she crawled into bed beside him and said, "Is this okay?" It was more than okay. It was truly splendid.

Father confessed all. He'd been to a therapist who gave him a test—he flashed slides on the wall and you said what you felt about each one, dread, fear, mild dismay, and so forth. "I suffer from demophobia, or fear of crowds," said Father. "Also, monophobia, the fear of being alone. And theophobia, the fear of God. I am the last person in the world who should be in the priesthood. The absolute last! I am scared in the pulpit, and scared at night in the rectory, and also I think God is going to punish me for being a bad priest." Suzanne was his great consolation. She was unmarried, 47, smart, sweet, and they liked to go for rides in her car and take pictures of old deserted farm sites. To avoid suspicion, they rendezvoused on a deserted stretch of country road near Holdingford and he parked his car in a dry creekbed and covered it with branches. He wanted to marry her but she was agnostic and felt very guilty about keeping company with a Catholic, what with the church's long history of persecution and intolerance.

Margie put her hand on his and whispered, "Good luck, Father." What could you say?

"I think it's so wonderful that all of us have gotten along so well," said Evelyn. "I am having a wonderful time. Trips can be so stressful."

"The wine helps," said Irene.

"This is why people travel," said Margie. "To learn new things.

To learn how to love each other." She looked straight at Carl as she said it and he smiled uneasily.

Irene said that she couldn't of course speak for others but that she would not mind leaving this café right now and finding another one so as to spend this precious time with each other and not with Mr. Keillor, who she spotted across the piazza, getting out of the police car. She would be happy to take full responsibility.

"You do as you like," said Margie, "but I told him we were here and so I'm going to stay put."

So they stayed. Mr. Keillor came walking through the rain, Clint holding the umbrella over part of him.

Marilyn stood up and dinged her glass and said, "When we left home, Corinne had just gotten her Prom dress, a pale yellow silky off-the-shoulder thing, and of course she looks fabulous in it. When strangers see her and they look at us, you can see them thinking, *What is that beautiful Korean girl doing with those big white people?* But you know, inside, she really is even more Norwegian Lutheran than we are. She said to me, 'Mom, I'm not going to go to the Prom with anybody. I don't want to make these boys feel bad.' She got asked by six or seven boys, and when she told them no, that raised the hopes of the ones on the B-list, who've been helping her with her 4-H project, which is maple syruping. She's got taps in about thirty trees. When we left the house, there were fifteen boys collecting wood for the fire and there she stood, stirring the sap in a big steel pan like a witch with the black hair streaming down her back and all these boys under her spell and her doling out tastes of the syrup from a wooden spoon. That was what we saw, as we drove away. Our daughter surrounded by suitors. What they don't know about her is that she is so deeply Lutheran that she is repelled by flattery. This stunning beauty—I can say that, since she's adopted—and if someone tells her she is, she's offended, and if a boy moons around, all damp-eyed and dreamy and writing poems about her raven hair and china skin and so forth and so on, she only feels pity for him. The boys think they're pursuing her and actually she is mothering them."

"What's your point there?" said Daryl.

She looked at him coolly. "The point is: when it comes to love, we just plain don't know. Nobody knows. It makes no sense. I'm with Margie. It's a miracle when it happens. And if it doesn't, you can live without it."

Mr. Keillor sat down, damp and extinguished, and said, "Thanks for bailing me out. I was afraid they might raise their price." And then the pizza came, four enormous discs of pizza, and they dug in. The rain let up a little as they ate. Irene passed a plate to Mr. Keillor who said he was not hungry. "Don't be a martyr," she said.

She said, "I shouldn't say this with Mr. Author here, but if he repeats this, I will kill him with my bare hands and that's a promise. The first time they served pizza for hot lunch at school, it was sort of like fried silage with chunks of boiled owl, and anyway none of us were used to it, and by the time school was over and we went to confirmation class, we were full of gas. I remember kids sitting perfectly still in their seats, not leaning to one side or the other, but now and then some gas would escape and sound like a bassoon solo and we'd all smell it and look around and scowl so everyone would know it wasn't ours. We were trying hard not to laugh, and when you try to hold a laugh in, it will explode on you, sometimes in the form of a fart. Which happened to me. I had my cheeks clamped shut and I was afraid this fart could explode and I would load my pants. And then Pastor Tommerdahl asked me to stand and read today's scripture and I said, 'Could I please go to the toilet first?' and a couple boys busted out laughing, and I stood up and read the verse about Pentecost in Acts, the second chapter, it says, 'And when the day of Pentecost had come, they were all together in one place. And suddenly there came a sound from heaven as of a rushing mighty wind, and it filled the whole house where they were sitting.'

"And I exploded. It boomed like a cannon and two big strands of mucous shot out of my nostrils and hung there like spiderwebs and I covered my face, the smell was horrible. And you, Clint, you yelled 'Evacuate!' and we did. That was when I thought seriously about leaving home and never coming back. I wanted to join the Air Force and move to Colorado. Or the Navy. In Norfolk, Virginia. Indecision was what kept me at home. Couldn't make up my mind where to go."

"Then you fell in love with Clint," said Eloise.

"Actually she was in love with two other guys," said Clint. "Couldn't decide between them. So—there I was."

The waiter brought the check and Carl reached for it, but not with blinding speed, and Father Wilmer got it first. "My treat," he said. They protested, mildly, and he whipped out a credit card. "It's such a relief to have you in on my secret," he said.

"And not have Mr. Keillor here, taking notes," said Irene, giving Mr. Keillor a cautionary look.

"What a beautiful evening. Thank you so much," said Margie. And she took Carl's arm and stood up and sang and he sang along

with her, quietly, and Eloise joined in, and Father Wilmer, a love
song from their childhood.

> *Du du liegst mir im Herzen,*
> *Du du liegst mir im Sinn.*
> *Du du machst mir viel Schmerzen,*
> *Weisst nicht wie gut ich dir bin.*
> *Ja ja ja ja.*
> *Weisst nicht wie gut ich dir bin.*

"What does it mean?" said Daryl, though he knew, of course.
*You live in my heart. You bring me joy and sorrow. You'll never
know how dear you are.*

LOOKING FOR GUSSIE

They had arrived in Rome on a Thursday and now it was Tuesday and—Carl reminded Margie—they hadn't found Gussie's grave. She said, "We'll get to it." She wanted to tell the truth—that he had slipped on ice while AWOL and died of a brain injury and was buried a mile away—but Eloise had made so much of the Medal of Honor citation, Margie thought it was impolite to contradict her. Eloise had passed a photocopy of the citation around the breakfast table, and they each pretended to read it. Though they had heard it read almost every Memorial Day since they were kids. Eloise said, "Here we are, just ordinary people no different than anyone else, and yet here is this story of someone who was just like us and his deed of valor that just boggles the mind. To put a chain on a bomb and swing it like a censer . . . "

And Gussie's heroism was the reason Wally and Evelyn had come to Rome, as they reminded everyone. "Not here for my own pleasure," Wally said. "Here to honor a young man's sacrifice."

It was hard for Margie to stand up and look the legend in the face and say, "No, folks, the truth is he slipped and fell after he made love to his girlfriend and bumped his head and there were no Germans anywhere around, they'd all headed north because they didn't want to be heroes either." So Mr. Columbo would drive them out to Anzio and Nettuno in the afternoon to look at the landing site of the Allied invasion and search the American military cemetery. Carl was very uncertain about the adhesive Norbert had supplied for the plastic engraving of Gussie's picture. Carl tried to glue a beer cap to the pavement with it and it wouldn't hold. "We can stick it on with double-sided Scotch tape, take a picture of it, and we're good to go," said Irene. "Send the picture to the brother and he'll be happy."

"His brother died Sunday night," said Margie, "and he died thinking we would do what I told him we'd do."

"Well, that settles it," said Wally.

She'd ask Maria to find them a good hardware store. Maria hadn't been heard from since she and Margie had coffee that Friday morning, and then she called after breakfast on Tuesday. Her mother had died. Gussie's great love had died in her sleep wearing a Whippets jersey. Maria seemed distracted. "No, no, no," she said when Margie offered to come over and help. The burial would be Wednesday afternoon. "No waiting around. Mama wants to join Papa in the cemetery."

"We want to come," said Margie. Maria said that would be fine.

The pilgrims were in the Pantheon under the ancient roof, looking at its ancient gray walls pocked with holes from cannon fire, when Maria called. Margie sat on the steps of a church and talked, and then two Gypsy women approached, hands outstretched, begging, sobbing, keening, pushing strollers with fat dark-skinned weeping babies, and the pilgrims fled around the corner and down an alley past an Egyptian obelisk and a statue of an elephant and into a small church. Margie slipped off to a side altar and lit four candles and said a prayer for the soul of Miss Gennaro and was about to ask to be forgiven for the sin of adultery and then thought, "Not yet. Later." Ten wooden confessionals stood along one wall, green curtains, brass grilles—inside one, rolled-up carpeting, and in another, cleaning supplies. Once upon a time, a priest sat in here, leaning toward the grille where a sinner spilled the secrets of her heart. Lust, greed, anger, pride. Now, only dust mops and soap and plastic buckets.

Outside and across the street, a little shopwindow displayed crucifixes and manger scenes and little plaster angels. "Can we go in?" Evelyn asked Margie, as if she were the teacher. So in they went, except Margie who looked at the window next door, stacked with books. Big leather-bound, gilt-lettered tomes, all different languages, in tall stacks, Cervantes, Dickens, Balzac, Dante, Tolstoy, Zola, the world's great literature carelessly gathered in a big heap. No marketing (*Read literature and become a better person*), just heaps of books. Next door, a fancy shop, advertising Hermès jewelry, Chanel bags, Annick Deligny perfume. A poster of Meryl Streep for Dior. "I didn't care for her in that movie where she was the Iowa housewife," said Marilyn. "She's better as a mean person. I think all of us would be more interesting if we were meaner." *Huh?*

"I mean it. We're brought up to be so sweet and accepting and—we're so goddamn *Lutheran*."

"I'm not," said Margie.

"You are, actually. Italy is a real Catholic country—in Minnesota, you Catholics are just Lutherans with statues."

She stopped and Daryl bumped into her. She ignored him, and waved her hands in a big sweep of Rome. "Catholics are in a struggle with God. A losing struggle but they fight back. Those guys who went to Saturday night Mass and afterward they went off with a girl and a bottle of vodka—they were fighting back. We Lutherans just keep our heads down and hope God isn't paying real close attention."

"I'm not with her," said Daryl. "I don't know who she is."

"Remember Lonnie? She used to date Catholic boys. She'd go out to her dad's hunting shack and sit there and wait for them. She'd invite three or four to make sure somebody showed up. And she kept a loaded pistol behind the sofa cushions just in case things got out of hand. Lonnie's mother was Lutheran but she married a Catholic, so Lonnie was sort of out there on the borders, searching, and meanwhile, she liked to drive boys crazy. She wasn't that good-looking but I suppose in candlelight she was presentable if you were eighteen and drinking vodka. She told me, 'Come on out on a Saturday night and see what a good time is like.' Being Lutheran, I didn't go, but she told me all about it. She had sex with anybody who was in the mood. She was wild. Wore little short shorts and a T-shirt and no bra, and back then, the sight of a woman's nipples was more than a novelty. Some boys got overexcited and that was the reason for the pistol. Lonnie told me that a shot to the chest was the only way to go—don't mess around aiming for the knees." She tapped her sternum.

"I know nothing about this," said Daryl. "I was not there."

"One night, there were three guys there and—well, wait just a minute." She turned around. "Carl, you were there. You tell."

"I was where? At Lonnie's cabin?"

"With Donnie and Mark."

"I was the designated driver," Carl said. "I never went in the cabin. I stayed with the vehicle."

The pilgrims had stopped, waiting for more details. "Just 'fess up," said Irene. "Nobody's going to tell."

Carl said that, so far as he could remember, Donnie was with Lonnie and Mark was in the outhouse throwing up. Donnie and Lonnie were entwined on the couch—so Donnie said later.

Marilyn interrupted him. "They were going at it like a couple of bunnies and she was worried about the pistol and she put her hand down there to put on the safety and the gun went off and blew a hole in the sofa and Donnie was halfway across the room in a single bound and she looked at his member, which had suddenly deflated, and she laughed and he grabbed his coat and out the door he went and a year later he was in seminary."

"This was Donnie Schoendienst," said Carl. "Not my brother Donnie."

Margie checked her watch. Eleven-fifteen. She was thinking how nice it would be to see Paolo. Last night, after the festive anniversary supper and the speeches and all, she'd gone hand in hand to the Giorgina with Carl and he kissed her and said, "Thanks for thirty-five years." She took a shower, put lotion on, dressed in a red negligee, and came out of the bathroom to find him asleep.

He woke up when she climbed into bed.

"You know something? I'm really tired," she said. "I'm going to turn out my light." So she did. He didn't move. She said, "You don't mind if I just go to sleep, do you?"

"No, that's fine," he said. They lay quietly, looking at the ceiling.

She said, "Do you ever wish we hadn't had kids? Do you?"

"Of course not. What a terrible thing to say."

"Sure, you do. Everyone wishes that. Sometimes. Of course you do."

"Well, if you know I do, then why do you ask?"

"Just admit that sometimes you have wished that we hadn't had children."

"Don't be silly. What would we do without kids?"

She could think of things. But the look on his face—plain incomprehension—a good Catholic father. Childlessness would go against God's Will for our lives. God knows best what we need for our happiness and that is why He makes us fertile. *What would we do without kids?* We would have a romance, that's what we would do.

And a moment later, he was dead to the world, on his back, mouth open, snoring. And the worst of it was that she felt relief at not having to make love. She gave him a shove and he rolled over, the rumbling and rasping stopped, she rolled over, her back to his, and fell asleep.

And now she was imagining Paolo, imagining him with another woman—younger, sleeker, cooler, like one of those young mammals on the Spanish Steps, hundreds of young women reclining in the sunlight like a colony of seals on the rocks, young bulls flopping beside them, nuzzling, moaning, and in the piazza below them a great stone boat of a fountain. What did Paolo see in her anyway? She was old. Fifty-three. No longer so interesting to a man. All the more reason to use what charm she had before she turned into an old hag.

Margie walked ahead, into a street of stucco houses, burnt sienna, golden umber, blood orange, pumpkin, houses the colors of squash and rutabagas and potatoes, past a squash house with green wooden doors and a Laundromat (WASH & DRY, LAVA RAPIDO) in a building with a fresco of Apollo chasing Daphne.

Lunch was at a pizza cafeteria and, as always, some of the pilgrims took forever to choose their food. Evelyn pondered the menu as if she were about to purchase a house. So Margie skipped lunch and got a cappuccino out of a machine. She sat down by Marilyn who had chosen a slice of sausage pizza and thought it was not as good as Domino's, frankly. Lyle was lurking nearby. He had been staring at her all morning. Whenever she turned around, there was his big round face, his dark eyes blinking. She had told Ardis she'd take care of him. So she walked over and put a hand on his shoulder and told him to get a slice of pizza. Her treat. He said he needed to talk to her. "Later," she said.

"Get a load of this," said Daryl, and thrust a copy of the Rome *Daily American* at her, his big finger pointing to a personals ad (M 4 F):

Easygoing overachiever here, VGL, HWP, no games or drama, looking for life partner. I will listen when you need it, hold you if you want it, and respect you always. Words women use to describe me: intelligent, kind, charismatic, dynamic, dependable, unique, and erotic. I have a lot to offer. Literate, educated, but also love doing anything outdoors. We'll never know what could be unless we go for it, so don't be shy.

He smirked at her as if this were some huge joke, a man advertising for romance. Or was it the word "charismatic"?

Or was Daryl letting her know that he knew about her You-Know-What?

"What's so funny about that?" she said.

"I just thought you'd get a kick out of it. Imagine if people did this in the *Herald Star*."

"Not a bad idea. A man telling you what he's got to offer—"

"Unique? Erotic?"

She leaned toward him and whispered, "Sometimes modesty is used to cover up real inadequacy."

"Huh?"

She thought that a dependable, erotic, intelligent man sounded like a good deal.

Mr. Columbo came after lunch to fetch them.

Carl was in possession of the plastic engraving and the adhesive materials, though he still seemed jet-lagged. What if he glued his own fingers to the gravestone and they had to call in a chemist to break the bond?

Mr. Columbo jumped out of the van and they jammed inside, except Eloise, who stood on the sidewalk, surveilling the passersby. "Have a good time," Margie said, but Eloise didn't budge. "I have a premonition," she said.

"Get in the van."

She got in the van.

"You're not coming?" Carl said. "I have to lie down," Margie said. "Jet lag hit me." And when the van pulled away, she went off to lie down with Paolo. She went to the coffee bar and called his number and he picked up on the first ring and said, "Hello darling

Margie" with a hard *g* and said he'd been hoping she'd call. Well, she had. "Would you like to come over?" Well, yes, she would. She headed for his hotel, armed with clear directions—down a narrow street with many little restaurants and a bar called Luigi's on the corner, and turn left past a modern art gallery—but Luigi's never appeared. She turned and retraced her steps, but evidently not—the street didn't look the same going in this direction—and she stopped, and was about to ask for directions. *Dove si trova Il Paradiso?*

The weight of the question struck her: which way to paradise? And a little voice within said, "Not this way, that's for sure." She was lost in more ways than one.

She was a bad person. Perhaps God had put a price on her head even now, and should she dare to take Communion when she returned home, the Body of Christ would stick in her throat and she would choke to death. Of course one could avoid Communion, make all sorts of excuses, but bad things do happen to guilty people, no matter what they say. It's true. Call it "bad karma" or call it Nebraska, but a sinner has every reason to be paranoid. Something awful could be just about to happen. Cheryl could marry a man with obsessive-compulsive arsonist tendencies and Carl Jr. take up parachuting and Carla give birth to a dwarf.

She could imagine a sorrowing Sister Arvonne approaching her, hands outstretched. (*Don't take life into your own hands, my child. Don't throw away all of God's gifts and two millennia of the wisdom of the Holy Mother Church in favor of your own restless heart. If you don't believe, that is okay—faith comes and goes— but don't destroy the temple that God has built in your heart. Your parents, your grandparents, your teachers, all of the faithful,*

have worked and prayed and sacrificed to make you the good
woman you are. Don't throw it all away for an hour of pleasure.)

She was lost, looking for paradise. Paolo had carefully pointed
her toward it and she must've taken the wrong passageway
because she came into a piazza full of parked cars, a sort of
fifteenth-century parking lot, where an eager young man stood
with a big steel hoop around his neck on which hundreds of car
keys hung. He had made the piazza his parking lot. A red Fiat
drove up, a lady hopped out, he parked the car in the mass of
other cars, and added her keys to the hoop. Across the square, the
high marble front of the church of Sant'Agostino, and she crossed
over to look at it. Four slender pilasters with carved capitals (she
read in her guidebook), the crests of a bishop and a cardinal on
the façade, a fresco of St. Augustine himself ("Known for his
work with the care and conversion of prostitutes, the church was
built in what was then Rome's red light district."). A church designed for women just like herself. She opened a small side door
and walked into the dimness. When her eyes adjusted, she found
herself standing next to the archangel Raphael, a gown slipping
rakishly off one shoulder, holding a black marble half shell with
holy water. She dipped her fingers in it and crossed herself.

In the dimness she could make out gilded baroque columns and
colored marble, carved birds and plants, busts in niches, frescoes,
an explosion of color—odd, to have such a gaudy display and so
poorly illuminated—and then her eye met the eyes of a man in a
black suit standing thirty feet away in the aisle, his right hand in
his pocket, holding (it looked like) a pistol. A second man stood in
a pew near him and a third and fourth in the side aisles, all of them
in dark suits, dark hair swept back, and then she noticed, in the

middle of them, the man kneeling in prayer. Four hoodlum body-guards protecting a sinner. They made no motion toward her and she stood stock still for a moment and then, seeing the statue of the Blessed Virgin a few feet beyond Raphael, stepped over to it and knelt on the cushion. If they wanted to shoot a woman at prayer, then so be it.

She asked to be forgiven for the sin of adultery, enjoyable though it had been. She asked that her love for Carl be restored to her heart, difficult though he is. She asked that she not be shot and killed, especially not in a state of sin. She prayed for her mother and father, that they have a peaceable old age. She prayed for the happiness of her children, though she had no clue what that might involve. She prayed for the well-being of her fellow pilgrims, that light shine into their hearts. She prayed for the new president and his family.

And then she prayed for the existence of God. She said, "I would feel so foolish talking to You like this if in fact You are simply a myth or a superstition. And think of how the people who built this church would feel. I mean, look at the work involved. The expense. The artistry. Does this not create some sort of an obligation to be real, Lord?

"I'm not demanding that You walk out of a cloud and talk to me, though I wouldn't object to it either. I just wish I believed in You more. I was brought up Catholic, You know. Which is pretty strict. Maybe not to You but to us it seemed pretty tough. All black and white. Do what you're told and don't slough off. You can't be a half believer. That was my preparation for life. And now here I am, riddled with doubt about You and the Life to Come and also what to do about this one."

And then a door clicked shut. She looked around. The men in dark suits were gone.

So she got to her feet and continued living her life. The Holy Mother sat under a halo of gold stars, the infant God in her arms holding a bird in His hand, a silver leaf over His genitalia. Just beyond, in a little chapel, a large painting of an elderly man and woman kneeling in the dirt before the Madonna ("Note the famous dramatic lighting of Caravaggio, which emphasizes the Madonna's everyday clothing and dirty feet [scandalous to many in the seventeenth century] as the pilgrims kneel before her."), just as she had just done, and light shone on her. Her phone beeped. There was a voice-mail message. It was Paolo. "Darling, did something come up? Did you decide not to come? It's okay. I'd love to see you whenever you can. I love you."

"He drove us around the battle sites but they're all gone," Carl told her that evening. "Just a lot of ugly high-rises and shopping arcades and pizza shops, gelato stands, gas stations. No monuments to be seen. Anyway, the Americans and British landed there at Anzio on the twenty-second of January, 1944, and fought inland through light German resistance up the beach and into the Padiglione Woods where the fighting got heavier. They had moved a couple miles inland by January twenty-fourth, but then the German commander, Kesselring, brought in two Panzer divisions and stopped them cold right there. There was an Anzio Beach Landings Museum but it was closed. So we stood around where the boats had come ashore and tried to imagine what it was like, thousands of men wading through the surf holding their rifles up over their heads, the landing ships coming up on the beach."

"Did you find the grave?" she said.

"He's not there. We looked all through the American Cemetery outside Nettuno, about eight thousand Americans buried there and the names of three thousand missing written on the memorial walls. No Gussie."

"I'm sorry," she said.

"Well, it's not your fault."

But it was, of course.

She hadn't shown them Gussie's letters. Better to keep the mood lighthearted, she thought, than face up to Gussie's bitterness about the entire Italian campaign, the senselessness of it, the arrogance of the American command, Lieutenant General Mark Clark in particular. Probably Gussie was right and Clark was an ass, envious of Eisenhower's stature, aware that the D-Day invasion of Normandy was slated for early June, and anxious to get to Rome before D-Day put the Italian campaign on the back pages. The strategic importance of Italy was nil. The crucial thing was to demolish the German army, not to capture Rome. Clark let the Germans off easy and set his sights on a triumphal parade through the Eternal City. That's how Gussie saw it. He'd come ashore at Anzio and hooked up with the brigadier and seen and heard a lot. His next-to-last letter to Norbert began:

Dear Lille Bror,

The Germans have skedaddled and the Second Corps is all jubilant about that, all except the Brigadier who's sad because now he must give up his deluxe accommodations and hit the road with the hoi polloi and take his chances elsewhere. He was playing Duke Ellington on his record player last night and feeling very thoughtful and after his fourth Armagnac and soda, he said, "I am not cut out for war. The killer urge is not in me. I am a thinker, maybe too much so. I see too many contradictions. The morality of the thing and so forth." And he passed out on a pillow and slept the sleep of the confused and I removed his boots and leggings and finished off the Armagnac. The Germans are smarter than we are and they know that Italy means nothing in this war and so the more they can make us pay for it, the better. The war will be won or lost in France and Germany. Were it not for the Russians, we'd be sunk. They bled Hitler white on the Eastern Front, which is the real story of this war and the one you won't read in the history books. Churchill will write the history of this war, just wait and see, and it will be all about Churchill and the Spirit of the British People and the little boats rescuing the Army from Dunkirk, which is all well and good, but if Hitler hadn't made the boneheaded decision to attack Russia, the Wehrmacht would be parked in Piccadilly and we Americans would be negotiating a treaty with the Huns and the Japs and feeling lucky to have a big ocean on either side of us. Everybody knows this but nobody says it. If we are winning the war, it is because the Fuehrer is even stupider than our generals, if that is possible. So here we are moving toward Rome a month late, all fat and happy, having failed to wipe out Kesselring's army, and General Clark shall have his parade tomorrow. Tonight he is rehearsing his lines so he can speak them with his head tilted up and a nice strong jawline which will look good on the front pages of all the newspapers, much better than pictures of American GIs torn and crumpled in the mud, which is the price of Churchill's bullheaded insistence on an Italian campaign and General Clark's being outgeneraled at every turn. Ten thousand Americans dead, blown up, bayoneted, and all to win a rocky peninsula of no strategic importance. Like launching an invasion of New York by attacking Miami. This is what wartime censorship accomplishes: it enables stupidity to continue unhampered. But I am out of the war now. I signed my own treaty and I am waiting for dark when I will make my own invasion and find my darling Miss Gennaro who sent word that she found us a lovely little hotel near the Gate of St. Paul. She bought us a bottle of wine and some ham and cheese and she is wearing a white nightgown passed down from her grandmother. Do you get the drift? She wants me. I've been playing it cool and avoiding her and this is the payoff. Oh what's the use of pretending? I'm in love with her. I adore her. I am never coming back to Minnesota. I'm going to marry her and settle down and become Augustus the Roman and make a family. And in two hours I am going to be in her arms. Kesselring's army can't stop me.

More tomorrow but don't expect me to tell you everything.

Gussie

BOYFRIEND

C arl was very courtly to her that evening. *Did he know about Paolo? Had she been spotted? Rome wasn't so big you could assume secrecy.* "What did you do today?" he said, in a kind way, not accusingly. "Just living my life, walking around, seeing the sights," she said. *True enough.* "Glad you're having a good time," he said. He had unbent from his pissy attitude toward the Italians and he'd even adopted some of their style. He opened doors for her, bowing slightly, and offered her his hand up stairs, a courtier in a green nylon jacket and chinos. Once, offering her a chair in a restaurant, he even kissed her hand. Tuesday night, there he was in a sidewalk café near the river, sitting by her side, chatting her up, charming her with witty asides. Affecting a certain Continental style, a *knowingness.* Everyone had been content to stick with Chianti and then Carl out of the blue ordered a bottle of Tignanello. And pronounced it without hesitation. The waiter was impressed. He uncorked it and poured a splash into a glass and Carl swirled the wine around in a professional manner and tasted it.

"How is it?" said Wally. "Looks like wine to me."

"I like it. It's more complex," he said.

Carl had never commented on the complexity of wine before in his life. Nor had he ever indicated a preference for complexity, not in wine or anything else. And then he drank the wine and said, "One thing you get the sense of, being here in Rome, I must say—you get the feeling that there is a great great deal about life in this world that we will never understand and maybe we should stop trying to and just enjoy what we have."

"Let me write that down, Shakespeare," said Wally.

"I'm serious. Americans think we can understand everything and then solve it. Italians are different. Maybe it's enough just to live your life."

"Thank you for the poem," he said to her on the way back to the hotel. She had sent him the poem that ended, *I hope you know, my darling one / I love you, after all is said and done.*

"That's nice that you're writing poems again."

"It's not finished," she said.

They made love that night. He lay in bed reading and she took a shower and stood by the bed toweling herself dry, one leg up on the bed. It felt like an Audrey Hepburn movie, except more explicit. He peered over the top of his book at her. It was *Beachhead in Italy*, about the 1944 campaign, bought used at a curbside book table for one euro, a small triumph for Carl. She dried her legs and spread cream on them and pulled on her green warm-up pants and her IF YOU'RE COLD, PUT ON A SWEATER T-shirt. They lay side by side reading and then he turned out his light, and they lay on their backs for a while. "You having a good time?" he said. She said she was. "Everybody seems to be doing okay." And then he turned toward her and put his arm across her belly, and hitched his leg up over her leg, and she turned toward him and slipped her hand under his T-shirt, and the rest came flowing along naturally. A miracle. Pure divine intervention. She had said prayers to St. Helen, the patron saint of older women and the lovelorn in general, and the good saint, who had received her martyrdom at the hands of Eskimos in Greenland who set her adrift on an iceberg, came to Margie's aid, and suddenly Carl was her boyfriend again. It was nice. Very nice. And when it was over, he pulled his pajamas on and she put her head on his shoulder. And almost said, "That was wonderful." Could have said it. But did not. She said, "Remember the time we went to Chicago for our anniversary and stayed at that famous hotel that turned out to be a welfare hotel with thousands of cockroaches that stampeded when we switched the light on, so we drove around and went to the Drake and you said, 'Hang the expense,' and we sat in that bar with about a thousand photographs of famous people nobody ever heard of, and it was just us and the bartender and the pianist with black horn-rims and a guy back in the shadows who when our pupils adjusted to the light we saw was Robert De Niro. Remember?" He shook his head.

"He wore a tan raincoat. I smiled at him and he smiled back."

"You must've been with someone else."

"Darling, I've never *been* with someone else. The next night we saw *Chorus Line* and you hated it."

"Maybe you dreamed it."

"No. Sorry. Not *Chorus Line*—*Forest Time*—that musical about the magical grove where people never grow old. It was really really bad. But there was a song called 'Mr. Happy' and you said, 'I'm so happy that I was able to talk you into marrying me.' Remember?".

He shook his head.

She sang: *"We've got love in our hearts, and sweet melodies, and we're dancing our way through the trees."*

"Never heard it," he said.

"Do I know you?" she said. "Did you father those children or was that someone else?"

He had already turned over and was lightly snoring. She stood at the window, naked, arms folded, looking out into the little courtyard. The dry fountain, wooden benches piled against it, workmen's toolboxes. How incomplete life is and unceasing. Three months she had waited to make love—longed for it, imagined it—and now there it was, done, and. . . life is still incomplete.

Nothing changes. We're still standing at the window, wishing for something else. You get your kids raised and out the door and realize you don't know any more than when you started. The Pope says High Mass and then he sits down and eats a cheese sandwich. You go to Rome for the experience of a lifetime and then it's time to go home and put in the tomatoes.

The next morning, she poked her head out of the bathroom, toothbrush in her mouth, and said, "That was nice, last night." He murmured, lying in bed, his nose in *Beachhead in Italy*. She said, "It's been such a long time. Why?"

"I thought you weren't interested."

"And that's why you went and slept in the guest room for three months?"

"Sorry."

"I'm not upset, I'm just asking. Is that why you left our bedroom?"

He looked up. He wasn't good at this sort of conversation. She knew that. But hey, it's life. You're fifty-seven. Get used to it. "I just wished that sometimes you'd say that you wanted to make love with me."

"And you were waiting for me to say that?"

He nodded.

So he had simply gone on strike. He had withdrawn his services until she asked for them to be resumed. And that led to the romantic getaway to Rome and that led to a half million in cool cash. Everything connects.

And down to breakfast they went. He took her hand, which had a coffee cup in it, and pressed it to his lips and whispered something like "love of my life" and then bowed and went back to the men's table where they were studying a map of the Allies' advance toward Rome through the Padiglione Woods and the Alban Hills. Wally was reading a history of the Allied campaign of 1944. The hilly wooded terrain favored the German defenders who retreated slowly, making the Americans and British pay dearly for each hill. It took five months of bitter fighting before General Clark got his picture taken parading into Rome and marching up the stairs to Michelangelo's City Hall.

She said good morning to Wally and Evelyn and Father Wilmer.

"How are you?" she said.

"Someday," said Father, looking down at his scrambled eggs, "women will have their eggs removed, and fertilized in a labora-

239

tory, and after the embryo has developed for a few days, they'll go in and rearrange the chromosomes to give people what they want in a child—math ability, resistance to colds, physical agility, verbal skills, blue eyes, small feet, you name it, you can have it. Every child will be a designer child. No flaws. I saw a program about this on TV last night. The BBC. And let me just say: that is a paradise I will be glad not to be living in."

Miss Gennaro's burial was at 10:00 A.M. and the pilgrims were all on deck at nine, dressed for the occasion, though Margie had told them, "You don't have to go. You really shouldn't feel obligated. None of us ever met the lady. I'm going because her daughter is the one who called me in January and told me about Gussie. Her mother was a friend of Gussie's, the old lady who died."

"How did she know Gussie?" said Eloise. "She was Italian."

"They were very good friends. I'll explain later."

Eloise pulled back the curtain and looked out at the street. "That white truck has been parked there all night," she said. "Isn't that suspicious?"

Margie ignored her.

"Don't you think about a terrorist attack?" she said, eyeballing the humanity passing by. "What if a bomb went off? We'd be blown to pieces."

"Depends on how close you are."

"What a ridiculous way to die—blown up on a trip that I never wanted to take in the first place."

"You never wanted to what?" Margie laughed. "You were all over this from the moment I told you. You were flapping around like a hawk on a rabbit. Nobody twisted your arm. So what's your problem now?"

Eloise said she was sorry. It was just lack of sleep. Anxiety about her kids. Anger at the Fred situation. "And I'm worried about you," she said.

Well, that was a new one. "Worried about what?"

Eloise looked at her. That serious maternal look. "Are you seeing someone while you're here?"

"I'm seeing all sorts of people. I'm looking at you right now."

She smiled. "You know what I mean."

"Of course not," she said. But there was a telltale hesitation before she said it. And not enough astonishment written on her face.

"Be careful, darling," said Eloise. "Don't blow up your house for a little excitement, you can get enough excitement from books." And she got in the van.

So Eloise knew. Someone had told her, and maybe that someone had told someone else. And if that second someone were Irene or Evelyn, then likely there would be a scene. A righteous woman confronting the sinner. Carl would get wind of it. He'd be terribly hurt. He'd pull back into his shell and it would be up to Margie to resolve the outcome—go home to Minnesota? Stay in Rome?

That afternoon, she called up the American Overseas School on Via Cassia. Who, a kind lady with a New York accent informed her, were not hiring teachers now, but maybe she should try the Thavis School of Language ("The gifts God gave us are nurtured at Thavis") so she did and a young man told her that indeed Thavis was looking for a native English speaker to teach full-time starting immediately, salary of $43,000 a year. "Think about it," he said. Oh, she was thinking about it. Yes, indeed.

THE FUNERAL

It was raining when they got to the Protestant Cemetery. Mr. Columbo handed out a few black umbrellas and the pilgrims stood around in the walled graveyard under the cypress trees. Music played softly over loudspeakers in the trees, the Pachelbel "Canon" and then "Ave Maria." Gravel walks radiated from the entrance, following along boxwood hedges, laurel and oleander. Crosses and upright tablets marked the graves, swathed in green. Signs pointed the way to the tombs of Keats and Shelley. Off to the left was dense vegetation, vines and shrubs overgrown, but most of the plots were neatly set in low stone walls like plant frames. There were a few aboveground crypts but mostly the dead lay in the earth and let nature take its course. One large cypress leaned seriously to one side, loose dirt around its roots, the casualty of a storm, and it looked likely to fall and maybe spring a corpse or two into the air like tiddlywinks.

Flat slabs of granite lay over the tombs. Some upright columns with busts atop them. A Celtic cross. A manly angel stood on a pedestal, a loose drape hung from his belt and covered his manhood, and nearby a female angel lay facedown on a gravestone, weeping inconsolably for an Evelyn Story (1882–1919) who lay moldering in the dirt below.

"If you had to die, this'd be the place to be buried," said Clint. "I'll bet my kids would visit my grave more often if it were in Rome than if it were back there where it's going to be."

Keats's marker said:

This grave contains all that was mortal, of a YOUNG ENG-LISH POET, Who on his Death Bed, in the Bitterness of his Heart, at the Malicious Power of his Enemies, Desired these Words to be engraven on his Tomb Stone: Here lies One Whose Name was writ in Water.

Poor Keats, consumed by self-pity as he lay coughing his heart out, imagining his Fanny in the arms of another, pretty sure that the "Ode to Melancholy" was not a big hit.

The usual inscriptions (*Blessed are the pure in heart for they shall see God. Blessed are the merciful for they shall obtain mercy. Qui riposa in pace*). Englishmen from Somerset and Swansea. A Norwegian who died May 19, 1944. James of Charleston, South Carolina, died in 1844 at age seventy. An Ursula Dimpflmeier, 1920–1973. Fifty-three, same age as Margie. An orange tabby cat leaped from stone to stone and Margie's eye followed it as it landed on a large marble tablet:

Requiescat in Pace
Sacred to the memory of
AUGUST NORLANDER
Of Minnesota

Pause here a moment, all ye who read
The writing on this fine erection
Which honors a most generous deed
By a fighting man of great affection
Who enriched Rome by his own seed
And now awaits the Resurrection.

"Did you know he was here?" said Daryl. "Did we make that trip out to Anzio for nothing?"

"I thought he was here but his brother thought he was out there," said Margie. "So we had to eliminate one before establishing the other."

Eloise said she was confused. Why would they bury him here and not in a military cemetery? Wally was confused too and hoped somebody would clear this up. "Was it because Gussie was not a Catholic?" Margie shook her head.

Carl got out the plastic engraving of Gussie. "Look. When you tilt it, he smiles," he said. He showed them and sure enough, Gussie put his head back and grinned. At the bottom it said, OFFICIAL. DO NOT REMOVE UNDER PENALTY OF IMPRISONMENT. The adhesive was supposed to bond plastic to any stone surface, but Carl wasn't sure that the plastic engraving of Gussie would stick to the stone, seeing as it was so wet. Evelyn thought the stone was so beautiful, it would be a shame to deface it with a piece of plastic.

"We promised," said Margie. "That was the whole deal."

They looked at the stone from all angles.

"That's an odd inscription," said Clint. "The part about erection and the donation of seed?"

"Maybe it's about seed corn," said Margie. "I'll ask around."

"Stick the picture on it," she told Carl. He got out the adhesive tubes and squirted a line of pink gel on the stone above the RE-QUIESCAT and let it sit for a moment, then squirted a thin spray of clear liquid onto the pink. It sizzled. He pulled the plastic engraving of Gussie out of his pocket and pressed it onto the adhesive and pushed.

A man in a blue suit came running out of the cemetery office, yelling at them. The pilgrims shrank back. "Do not deface the monument," he yelled. "Or I'll call the police."

"We aren't defacing it, we are refacing it," said Margie.

He pointed at the plastic. "That was not there before."

Margie stepped up and poked him in the chest. "That is an American war hero who died in the fight to save Rome from the Nazis. You remove that and you insult me, you insult General Eisenhower, you insult Duke Ellington and Frank Sinatra, you insult Barack Obama."

The man stepped back. He looked around at Marilyn and Daryl, Clint, Irene, Carl, Wally, Evelyn, Eloise, and then his glance landed on Father Wilmer. The man bowed slightly. He said, "Father, don't let them do bad here." Father Wilmer nodded to him. The man marched back to the office. He locked the door. Twice.

"Is it tight?" said Daryl, reaching for the plastic. Margie

grabbed his arm. "Don't touch it." And she took Carl's camera and snapped two, four, six, seven shots of it. It looked okay. From a certain angle. A short person would walk in here someday, a boy of ten or eleven, and look at the picture and rise up on his tiptoes and Gussie would smile at him. And the boy would keep this a secret until one day he'd show it to a girl. *Look. A dead man smiling at us.* A joke on a tombstone. Amid all the drippiness, an American grins and winks.

As they stood in the rain, a procession came through the gate, led by a man playing a violin, playing very badly, a woman holding an umbrella over him, and six men carrying a coffin on their shoulders, followed by a priest and four mourners. They bore their burden toward the old Roman wall at the back of the cemetery where two gravediggers stood beside an open tomb. The marble cover had been removed and stood against the wall. It said GENNARO.

Margie led the pilgrims up the path behind the mourners. All four were women dressed in black, three wearing long black scarves and Maria wearing her black wool cap.

The pallbearers laid the coffin down beside the crypt, on the wet grass, and stepped back. Margie stood, hands clasped, as the priest intoned a prayer. When he finished, he stepped back and Maria stepped up and said,

> To see a World in a Grain of Sand
> And Heaven in a Flower,
> Infinity in the palm of your hand
> And Eternity in an hour.
> Every Morn and every Night

Some are Born to sweet delight
Man was made for Joy and Woe;
Thro' the World we safely go.

The pallbearers stepped up and gripped the handles and hoisted the coffin up high and over the open crypt and then gingerly lowered it, bending down, and it came to rest, Margie thought, rather unevenly, as if it had been placed in on top of someone else's bones. The mourners then took handfuls of dirt from a blue plastic bucket and tossed them in and a few yellow blossoms, and the gravediggers and the pallbearers took hold of the marble slab and lifted it up to shoulder height and carried it to the crypt and set it down with a great dull thud.

Maria turned and smiled at them. "I wanted them to be in the same tomb together, like Romeo and Juliet, but the cemetery wouldn't allow it. Anyway, they're close enough, they can whisper to each other at night."

"I'm so sorry for your loss," said Eloise.

"It's all right. She was anxious to go. She had been thinking about him a good deal lately." She turned to look at the crypt and then suddenly turned back to Margie. "Would you have lunch with me?" she said. "And we can look at that apartment."

"Should I bring my husband?"

Maria frowned. "No. Why would you? Men don't know what we want. We have to figure it out and tell them."

FATHER JULIO'S STORY

The restaurant was called Café Lucca. It was off on a narrow brick-paved street with a cluster of motor scooters parked and bicycles leaning against the building. A cupboard of wine at the entrance and a cold chest with wheels of cheese, a little dining room, about thirty by fifteen, with family pictures on the walls, weddings, christenings, fat babies, under a high arched ceiling. Small square tables, and they sat down at one, Maria and Father Julio and Aunt Magdalena and Margie. VIETATO FUMARE, said the sign. Smoking Forbidden. But people smoked anyway. The waiter was a man with white hair swept back, tattoos on his arms, a bowl of spaghetti in one hand, a small child in the other.

"I'm glad Gussie didn't die out in the Aleutian Islands somewhere. Or Siberia. If you want people to visit your grave, Italy is the way to go," she said.

Maria beamed at her. She sure had Gussie's nose and his big grin.

"I want to know all about Lake Wobegon," Aunt Magdalena said. She said that Maria had drawn thousands of pictures of

Lake Wobegon when she was a little girl, crayon drawings of dogs playing baseball and Boy Scouts fighting Indians on horseback, giant fish leaping from the lake. A grain elevator operated by a woman with white gloves and you got on the elevator with a bag of grain and she took you to your floor. The Sons of Knute lutefisk dinner, the fish playing guitars. The Norwegian Lutherans were all handsome like Gussie and carried skis. The German Catholics were small and fat and wore pince-nez glasses and carried whips. The Catholic church was as big as St. Peter's and full of paintings and sculpture and an ancient American pope was carried in a sedan chair through the streets, lined with pine and spruce. Men with tommy guns rode in long black convertibles, and blonde babes in slit skirts lounged under lampposts.

Margie asked how Gussie had gotten written up as a war hero and Aunt Magdalena said that the brigadier had done it. He had been visiting a bordello the night Gussie died and he blamed himself for what happened and set about to make it right by inventing a lovely story of heroism under fire. "I liked how he had him swinging a censer that contained a hand grenade. And the part about his vestments turning crimson. That was a nice touch."

In fact, Gussie had slipped on a patch of ice and fallen and hit his head and died of brain trauma.

"I was with him," said Father Julio. "It happened like this. I was a friend of Miss Gennaro's family and they knew what she was planning and asked me to go and bless the unborn child. There is no rite of the Church to consecrate the union of unmarried, so I had to make one up, and I followed the American to Miss Gennaro's hotel room and when he went inside, I waited in the hallway. When it was quiet inside, I let myself in and sat by the door to her chambers. I sat there, and heard the joyful sounds of their intertwining, two very passionate individuals, and her sighing and singing, and then at the moment of ultimate joy, I thanked the Lord for His marvelous gift and asked Him to protect the young life and bring it safely into the light of the world to receive the new birth of baptism, and then I fell asleep. The American woke me up. The sun had come up. He said, 'Forgive me for I have sinned,' and I said, "Don't worry. It's covered. Let me buy you breakfast." Miss Gennaro was asleep. He covered her with a blanket and tucked it in around her chin and kissed her and left her a note saying he loved her and would see her in a few hours, and he and I walked out to this very café. The Café Lucca. We had an excellent breakfast together and he sat and wrote a letter to his brother and then we left. It was on the sidewalk in front of the café where he died. They had given a party for the liberation the night before and served ice cream and to keep it cold they had many pounds of dry ice which they now had dumped out on the street to melt and as the American and I walked to the café, we didn't see the ice. He was just telling me how much he loved Miss Gennaro and Rome and how he would learn Italian and start a tour company to take Americans around Rome and show them the sights and he was very excited about this and he raised his hands to gesture to me—'It's going to be beautiful!' he cried—and he slipped and fell backwards and hit his head and was unconscious. He lay on his side and I ran to the café for help and then went back and blessed him. He looked very blessed already. His eyes were closed and he was peaceful. He died in the hospital of San Giovanni and I said a prayer for him there. I knew an undertaker from my childhood parish and he did the job. I came to the cemetery with Miss Gennaro and the brigadier and saw the American lowered into the ground. It was a sunny morning. She was nauseated. She was sure she was pregnant. She carried an American flag and the bed linens from when they had made love. She was going to bury them with him but couldn't bear to and kept them folded under her arm. The brigadier was a kind man but not so smart. He gave a little speech about his friend and his aide-de-camp. He said that Corporal Norlander was a gentleman and a scholar and that America had lost a good man. He said that he would remember him forever, to the end of his days. And then he stopped. He had more to say but he had forgotten it. And then he bent down to drop flowers into the grave and his shirt came out of his trousers and I saw the deep crevice of his buttocks. Miss Gennaro said nothing. She was feeling quite distressed, full of grief and also rather ill, so I helped her toward the car. She vomited alongside the wall and again at the curb. Her apartment was in a hotel six kilometers from there. The brigadier gave us money for a taxi but there were no taxis. He didn't think to offer us a ride. He shook my hand and wished me good luck and away he drove in his Jeep, seeing how he drove down the street, I was glad we weren't with him. I could hear the clutch grinding when he shifted gears and the Jeep bounced off the curb and almost turned over. We started to walk and then Miss Gennaro stopped. She said, 'I'm afraid of losing the baby.' So I carried her in my arms through the Gate of St. Paul and into the city toward the Colosseum. She was quite light and not hard to carry, but I felt the worst carnal temptations holding her body against me. I had my hands under her thighs and she had her hands clasped around my neck. Her thighs were delicate and my hands slipped almost to an indecent position because her dress was silky and it rode up and soon I was clasping bare flesh. I was trembling with excitement. I prayed for victory to St. Benedict who subjugated his own desires by casting himself naked into a thicket of briars and rolling around until he was bleeding all over and thereby conquered the flesh and made possible the great harvest of virtues, but I gained no victory at all. My manhood was quite insistent. People laughed to see us, a priest carrying a beautiful young woman. Rome was very festive that day. The sidewalk cafés were full of people. Strolling accordionists played American songs and she said, "Why couldn't God have let him see this day?" I carried her to Via Maggio and went into the hotel. People laughed and whistled at me, a priest carrying a girl into a hotel, and little did they know how sorely tempted I was. I laid her on a divan in a parlor off the lobby. She lay there, weeping. 'I am terrified I will lose the baby,' she said. 'If I do, I will kill myself.' I went to speak to the superintendent. 'The elevator is broken, I have a lady who is with child.' He shrugged. Nothing could he do with the elevator. He offered to carry the woman. No, no, no, I said. I didn't want him to touch her with his big rough hands. So I had to carry her up six floors, resting on each landing. She was crying on my shoulder. The room was tiny and had an old brass bed and a ragged blanket. A picture of the Blessed Virgin on the wall. She turned the picture toward the wall. She said, 'I wanted the baby because I knew it was the way to keep him, and now I've lost him and only have the baby. I can't bear to be alone. Don't leave me alone. I'm afraid.' I didn't dare stay with her, because of my carnal desire. I said, 'God will be with you.' She said she hadn't believed in God since she was eleven and her father died. So I stayed with her. I slept on the floor and she slept on the bed. Twice I got up and looked at her with lust in my heart and I kicked my shin against the bed until the pain drove the lust from me. I still have the marks." Father Julio raised his right pant leg and they examined the scarlet dents in his pale skin. He turned to Maria. "So you are not my child, my child."

"Let me take you to that hotel where August and Maria's mama made love," he told Margie, and off they went. It was a white brick building, six stories, and the apartment was on the fourth floor, overlooking a courtyard. A hall divided the apartment, a large bedroom and living room on one side, a kitchen and bedroom on the other, the bath at the end. A little balcony in the kitchen and another in one bedroom. Oak parquet floors. Gas heat. New electrical wiring—Maria pointed out all the features. "And in here is where the young couple made love," said Father Julio, opening the door to the smaller bedroom. A double bed with a white bedspread, a picture of Christ the Good Shepherd hung on the wall over it. "Here is where your countryman spent the last happy hours of his life."

"Six hundred thousand is the asking price, but I can get it for you for five," said Maria. "Keep it for two years. If it hasn't increased in value, then I'll buy it back for six hundred thousand."

"How can you do that?"

"For you, for a friend, I can do that."

Margie called Associated Federal in St. Cloud and got hold of the cashier. "I need an international bank draft for a half million."

"Wire it," said Maria. "It's so much easier." She wrote down her account number on a slip of paper and Margie read it to the cashier.

"And now—you are a Roman. One of us," said Maria, and they embraced. A golden sky, the dome of St. Peter's in the bedroom window.

AT THE VATICAN

<hr>

The pilgrims went to Vatican City the next morning and as they approached St. Peter's across the vast brick plaza ringed by colonnades, several thousand tourists were massed on the steps, waiting to enter and view the wonders within, all of them snapping pictures of each other snapping pictures of St. Peter's. At the periphery of the vast mob, tour groups stumbled along like convicts, each of them following a dapper gentleman holding up a metal shepherd's crook with a totem tied to it—a yellow flower, a stuffed lion, a plastic cardinal—as a beacon in the ocean of humanity. A group of Japanese went by like a herd of penguins, headphones clamped to their heads, listening via radio to their group leader, a tall Japanese lady in a kimono, jabbering away into a silver microphone, telling them what they were seeing. Margie could only imagine what they saw here—an enormous pagan temple where guilty Westerners (like her) came to tremble in the presence of the Three-Headed Divinity, one Head of which had been hung up on a pole and left to die and then, magically, had risen in the air on golden wings, accompanied by other avian creatures.

Carl clutched at her arm as they neared what seemed to be the end of the line to get into the basilica—which was still far in the distance—but it wasn't exactly a line: other groups leapfrogged past and still other groups pushed ahead of them. A group of elderly dark-skinned people in strange colorful cloaks stood by, dazed, tired, swaying. Were they beggars? Pigeons scurried around them as if waiting for them to collapse. The bells of St. Peter's began to clang and some car alarms started whooping, triggered by the bells. An ambulance raced by, screaming, and four buses passed, their engines grinding.

"I can't do this," Carl whispered to her and turned away. Claustrophobia had hit him in a couple of churches and he felt waves of unbearable anxiety looking at St. Peter's. He walked away and she walked with him. "You can go in if you like. I'll wait out here. . . . " He waved toward the street.

"Don't be silly. We're here together."

She was glad not to go in. She felt guilty about Paolo but even guiltier about buying an apartment without asking Carl, though it was her money, given to her by Norbert. But still—her motive was to have a place to go to escape from him. She was tingling with guilt. She had been brought up to feel that something horrible would happen to her if she set foot in a holy place when she was in a state of sin. Which she was.

Carl waved her away. Told her to go into St. Peter's—silly to come halfway around the world and not see it—but she took his arm and led him out of the plaza. "We'll come back," she said. "You'll see. We'll come back when it's less crowded. I think maybe we should buy an apartment here."

"Why in the world would we ever do that?"

"A romantic getaway."

"We can't afford a getaway. We may not be able to afford to stay at home."

The words "romantic getaway" sounded a little silly, hanging in the air. But wasn't it worth it? What price do you put on love? A half million dollars for a sweet little two-bedroom apartment with white walls and wooden shutters, looking out on a narrow street in the heart of Rome, in an 1845 building with excellent water pressure—an apartment listed for $600,000 that Maria had obtained through her friends for an enormous discount. She wanted to take him there right now. "I have a surprise for you," she'd say, and they'd take a taxi to Via Maggio and up the stairs and there they'd be—"Our love nest, Carl!" she'd say—and maybe they'd do it right then and there. Drop their clothes on the floor and hop into bed and take the long climb up the stairway to heaven and *boom* and then lie curved against each other.

A man in a bearskin hat was selling tickets to a guided tour aboard a van that drove through the Vatican Gardens and Carl thought he could tolerate that fairly well so off they went on a narrow brick-paved alley along an ancient stone wall and around the corner of a palatial mansion where the van stopped. The driver got up out of his seat and motioned to his belly and groaned—international sign language for nausea—and off he went and did not come back. Fifteen minutes, by Carl's watch. The six other passengers seemed content to bide their time but Carl was feeling claustrophobic and had to evacuate so she went with him. They stood beside the bus for a few minutes and then he suggested they walk around and have a look. They stepped over a low brick wall and into a grove of bamboo and found a path that led them through a dense thicket that opened onto a bare patch of dirt where an old man was turning over the soil with a shovel. He wore a white shirt and white pants and he wore a white beanie.

"Good morning," said Carl. The old man, startled, turned and said, "Good morning."

"Looks like you're going to put in some vegetables."

The old man looked down and said, "It is our hope to put in a few rows of corn. The sweet kind that one boils and then eats with salt and butter. We call it *mais di grande dolcezza*."

"Sweet corn?"

The old man nodded. "We have received gifts of two packs of seeds from the good people of Dubuque, Iowa."

Carl shook his head. "Not to tell you what to do, but Iowa corn is for hogs, it's not for people. You'd bust your incisors on that stuff. You want the Anoka Super Sweet from Minnesota. That's the one worth the eating."

"Minnesota—," said the old man. "It gets cold there, doesn't it?"

"You need cold weather for corn. Everything needs to have a dormant period to rest up. Your soil in the south is all exhausted. Sweet corn, potatoes, apples, onions—it's all better in the north."

"Where would I get this Anoka Super Sweet?"

"I'll send you some soon as we get home."

So the old man wrote an address down on a scrap of brown paper. And just then four men in blue suits strolled up and took hold of Carl and Margie—gently, smiling, nice as could be—and led them back up the path to the van.

Father Wilmer came out of St. Peter's early. He had seen a man on a high ladder replacing a lightbulb and had to leave. "Like Earl Magendanz that time," said Carl. "Yes, like Earl." And Father told them the story.

"Earl loved ladders even though he was seventy-five years old—"

"I know, I know," said Carl. "I was there."

"So anyway, he went up to change the little spotlight over the Blessed Virgin Mary, which was forty feet in the air and required him to stand on the very top of the ladder on his tiptoes, and we begged him not to, on account of his recent fainting spells, but up the ladder he goes with me behind him—so if he fell, both of us would break our necks, I guess—and he got to the top and was swaying slightly as he reached way up to unscrew the old bulb. And that was when the bird flew in and around the sanctuary and flapped around Earl who waved at him with a damp rag and the ladder swayed and the men steadying it down below hung on for dear life—"

"I was one of those men," said Carl.

"Anyway, I said, 'You okay?' and Earl says, 'Yeah, I'm fine.' And then he noticed the stranger in the big black overcoat walk in and kneel down in front of the Blessed Virgin Mary and burst into tears and cry out that he had fallen as low as a man could fall, meanwhile the bird is flying figure eights around Earl who is looking down at the man and up at the socket and I have hold of his legs and I am perspiring so hard the sweat is running down in my eyes and I have to let go of him and wipe my eyes and the ladder is swaying—"

"Actually it was pretty steady," said Carl.

"And now Earl is starting to sing, '*Pack up all my care and woe, here I go, singing low, bye bye blackbird,*' and two guys climb up past me and grab Earl—"

"That was me and Roger," said Carl.

"And Earl is saying, 'I'm okay, get your hands off me' and in the struggle he falls thirty feet from the ladder—"

"Ten feet," said Carl, "and I had hold of his wrist and that broke the fall. Also broke the wrist."

"And he lands on the big black overcoat guy, knocking him out cold—and when they went to loosen his clothing, they found dozens of billfolds in the lining of his coat. The sheriff came and the thief turned out to be a former child actor who played Timmy on *Friendly Neighbors* on WLT and he'd gone through the Chatterbox at noon and picked pockets, including yours."

"That is true," said Carl.

"Anyway, in St. Peter's, I was looking around at the beautiful art and marble and I walked into the ladder. I heard someone yell and looked up and he was almost directly above me, and I thought he was going to jump on my back, and I hightailed it out of there."

Daryl took pictures of St. Peter's and when the pilgrims reunited in a café that afternoon, Carl looked at them on the camera—the long nave, the great marble canopy over the altar, the celestial light filtering down from the dome, the crowds of carved angels, apostles, bishops, saints. "Nice," he said, and looked over at Margie. "What are you reading?"

"Just a letter about Rome," she said.

Dear Lille Bror,

The Germans are gone up the Tiber Valley so there is nothing to do in Rome but catch a nap and read Stars and Stripes and admire the girls who are, of course, all beautiful in their clean white dresses. But I have Miss Gennaro, so I don't look at them too hard. She is beautiful too and quiet, brown eyes, honest, even-tempered, nothing silly or flirtatious about her and now that we are lovers I am a man on a mountaintop and everything is clear to me and I know more than generals or reporters or the Pope himself and am about to make great pronunciamentos. I suppose this will not last long.

I have lost my Jeep and suppose I should tell the Brigadier about it before he reports me but I think there is time. He has attached himself to OSS now and may not even notice I'm gone. The owner of the café is bringing me eggs and bread and a piece of meat for breakfast and I reach into my pocket for money and he waves it away. "Grazia, grazia, grazia." My feeling exactly. The eggs are delicious. I will eat breakfast and then go back to my lady and collect her and go underground. Don't worry about me, I am in love and nothing bad can happen to a man in love, he is impermeable. I will stay out of trouble and trouble will stay out of me.

Oh my God I am so happy. And the coffee is good too and the sun is shining. I will dump this khaki which has earned me this good breakfast and I will become a Person Unknown and make my way through life accepting whatever compensations are offered and also whatever hard knocks. Think of me, little brother, as a great lover striding through a great city, and if any of the old gang asks about me, tell them I am thankful for their thoughts and think of home with due reverence, especially the beautiful snow and the glittering trees after an ice storm, which I have described to my serene and lovely Miss Gennaro. The love for life, my brother! Let it never be extinguished. And if they try to send you to the Front to wade through the mud and suffer for their blunders, the heroic thing is to refuse. This war will be forgotten but love will endure and poetry and stories and the sound I hear right now which is a boy playing with hesitation a love song on a piano. How beautiful! To hear his cautious notes, like a man walking out onto a newly frozen lake, testing his footing, and now I hear trucks approaching, and I must say good-bye. I'll give the letter to the breakfast man to mail, and wish you well, and as they say here, "*Pazienza!*" Patience. And tolerance and skepticism and frankness! I am O.K. Whatever happens, I will not be gone for long. I have extra cigarettes and soap and chocolates and whiskey.

We may hide out in the Apennines and live in the forest for a while in a little stone cabin, and surface when the coast is clear. Love is subversive, always. I hear a band approaching, the appalling strains of Sousa, the thump of the drums. I am eating my eggs with one hand, writing with the other. Hurry, hurry.

Good-bye. Good luck. Ciao. Buon fortuna. Whatever happens, know that I was never so happy as I am this very instant.

Love from your brother,
Gussie

THE HOMEWARD LEG

~~~~~~~~~~~~~~~

At 0900 Mr. Columbo arrived with the van to take them to the airport to fly back to America. Maria could not be there to bid farewell but sent a beautiful bouquet of pink roses.

They had assembled in the lobby at 0630, their luggage in single file. They were a little crestfallen at the thought of returning home though nobody said so, all of them comfortably dressed for travel except Lyle, who wore a black suit, black shirt, and white tie. Irene said, "You look like a boy I knew in high school, he had Roman hands." Daryl remarked that the high point of the trip for him had been the ruins of the Forum, just to walk where Caesar and Augustus had walked, and now he was going to read up on Roman history. There had been lengthy discussion about How Much Time to Allow and Margie had argued that two hours was more than enough but the more cautious won out, so they were leaving at 0900 for a 1400 flight.

"It can't hurt to get there early," said Daryl, and others nodded in agreement.

"Maybe we should have left last night," said Margie. "Or

Tuesday. Well, one last breakfast then." And they all trooped in to the familiar buffet, the crusty rolls, the parade of cheeses and cold cuts, the juice tank, the corn flakes, the interesting yogurt pot.

They arrived at DaVinci at 1015. Margie gave Mr. Columbo an envelope with five hundred euros and thanked him and there was a group picture and he thanked them and off he went. They checked their bags and got in the security checkpoint line, which reminded Evelyn of the Magendanzes' trip to Mexico, seven of them, and all of them nervous about traveling out of the country—especially about the danger of losing their passports— so they gave them to Marie for safekeeping, also their billfolds, and she put them into a plastic bag, which the hotel maid thought was garbage and off it went, and the Magendanzes chased off to the dump to search, and tripped an alarm, and took off running, and didn't dare return to the hotel. They made their way north, hitchhiking, not much Spanish between them, but they got by, doing odd jobs, mowing lawns, cleaning houses, reached the Rio Grande and crossed at night into El Paso, made it home in one piece, and there they found a package from the Mexican hotel with their passports and billfolds.

And now the pilgrims came to the checkpoint, removed their shoes, their jackets, swept through the detectors, headed for the gate. *Can't hurt to get there early?* Guess again. The concourse was an aviary of nervous excitation, passengers fluffing themselves up, strutting back and forth, yakking on those dangly cell phones. She could see Carl getting agitated, jiggling his leg, taking deep calming breaths that didn't calm him at all. A man and a woman sat down near them. She was weeping. "Oh, for crying out loud," he said. "Grow up." She told him to go without her. "How long is this going to go on, Doreen?" Evidently she was afraid of flying, which infuriated him. She was a slight woman with reddish hair, a brown raincoat, a green scarf, and tears in her eyes. He told her that if she didn't get on the plane, that was it, he was done with her, and he meant it.

That was too much for Eloise.

She swiveled around and glared at him and called him a name—a simple two-syllable word for a part of the lower digestive tract that all of us have, whether we use that word or not. He pretended not to hear her, so she said it louder. And then she jumped up and circled around the row of seats and the man jumped up and ran into the men's room and stayed in there. Eloise stuck her head in the men's room door and yelled, "I'm out here and I know who you are and you're not going anywhere!"

It was the old Eloise, back to good health.

She came strutting back to her seat and grinned at Doreen, plopped down, and leaned in toward Carl and Margie. "Did I ever tell you about the time Fred came home from the poker game in Sartell at 3:00 A.M. with a cut over his left eye?"

She had told them, but so what? There was time to kill.

"We'd just broken up and when we were apart, of course, we got along just fine, so we decided to give it one more chance and then he went off to play poker with his old buddies. He comes back to my house around 3:00 A.M. with a big story about how he was winning and couldn't leave. Well, Mr. Lundberg was waiting outside the house. You remember when the Lundbergs used to sleepwalk. After they went to that revival service in the tent up near Nashwauk. You didn't know that was why? Well, it was. They stopped in because they were curious and the evangelist was a sweaty man waving a big black Bible and he had two big black dogs who came after the Lundbergs when they refused to kneel down and accept Jesus. They said, 'We're Lutheran,' and the dogs chased them and they'd had dreams about it ever since and that was why they went sleepwalking in their pajamas. So here was Elmer Lundberg out sleepwalking when Fred came sneaking home at 3:00 A.M. with a big gash over his eye, bleeding into a towel, and Elmer tried to grab him and Fred just about pissed his pants. He had invented a story about helping a man fix a flat tire and the jack handle hitting his forehead but seeing Elmer put the fear of God in him. He told me the whole truth. He'd been hit by a mirror that fell off the ceiling of a motel room where he'd gone with a girl named Amber who had a thing about older men. He hadn't gone to play poker, he'd gone to poke Amber and there they were reclining in the Jacuzzi and looking at themselves in the mirror overhead. He opened a bottle of cheap champagne and the cork flew and bounced off the mirror and suddenly their reflections got bigger and bigger. The mirror cracked her on the shoulder and she bled and screamed and somebody hit the fire alarm and pretty soon there were six firemen in yellow phosphorescent jackets piling into the room and when they saw Amber they called for reinforcements."

"Well, looky looky," said Irene under her breath, and then Mr. Keillor was there, smiling down at them from his great height, in black sweatpants and black sweatshirt (AMOR VINCIT OMNIA), his hair rather long and swirly, his eyebrows enormous.

Get those puppies trimmed, she thought. He put his hand on her shoulder. "Good morning," he said in his honeyed radio voice. "How's everyone doing today?"

"We're flying back to face the resentment of our friends and neighbors," said Irene, never one to mince words. "But that means nothing to you. You're flying first class. You're on the gravy train."

"They upgraded me because I'm platinum," he said.

"I don't doubt it for a minute," she said. "And poor Lyle here has Alzheimer's. Think about that for one minute. He had such a good time flying over, he's been looking forward to the return." She motioned for him to hand over his boarding pass.

"It's not Alzheimer's, actually I just hit my head on a low beam," said Lyle.

"Please," said Mr. Keillor. "I need the legroom. I have work to do."

"I don't doubt for a minute that you do. Let me see that notebook in your back pocket." He took a step back and clapped his hand over the pocket. "You've been writing down what we say, haven't you, you little sneak."

"I'm keeping a journal," he murmured.

"Heck you are. You're writing it all down so you can put it in a book and make us look like idiots on parade. Am I right? Well, tell me, what gives you the right to do that? You're a member of a group, whether you know it or not, and one of the rules when you're in a group is that you don't go around blabbing your mouth about what you saw and heard. That is just basic decency. About time you learned it."

He sighed. The woman was merciless. He closed his eyes. She

reached over and pulled his boarding pass out of his shirt pocket and handed it to Lyle, who started to protest and then thought better of it. Mr. Keillor felt the boarding pass slip away and did not bother to open his eyes. He held out his hand and she put Lyle's boarding pass in it and he picked up his briefcase and trudged toward the Jetway. He headed for 38F—a middle seat— and there in 38E was a woman who beamed to see him. "I can't believe this," she said. "Look at this, Wendell. It's the man from the radio. I've listened to you since I was a child. Your stories take me home. Would you mind if I give you a big hug?" she said. He winced. She reached over and patted his shoulder. "Now you tell me if I'm talking too much," she said. "You just say, 'Stifle it, Mary Louise.' Oh my God. I am so excited. Wendell, get the camera. Do you mind if we take a picture? Tell me—how long do you think you'll keep on doing the show?"

"Forever, I hope."

And as he said it, he knew that the End was near. A person always imagines there will be more, and then the steel doors clank shut. He closed his eyes. "I should let you be," she said. "You probably hate this, being pestered by strangers. I can imagine how hard it is, meeting people you don't know *whatsoever* and they know all about you from your books and stories. I mean, I know about the Sanctified Brethren and how you always were the last one chosen for the softball team, I know about your fear of water and how that girl laughed at you when you tried to kiss her and I know what kind of hand lotion you used when you masturbated. Jergen's. Remember? You mentioned it somewhere. I've read everything you ever wrote, I know all that stuff. Your fear of damnation. Your ignorance of the names of plants. The time you spilled on the lap of your new seersucker suit. Your agonizing memory loss. Your self-consciousness about your thin wrists. The animosity of your ex-wife. It's all there! You've shared yourself so generously with us fans and now we know you better than we know our own siblings! It's true! I have no idea what my brother's sexual fantasies are, and I know a lot about yours. Sometimes I feel like I'm your therapist! I really do! Honest! Your dream about falling off the cliff in the Faeroe Islands into a vast dark abyss—I think I could work with you on that. And your dream about standing onstage at a microphone and the audience like stone statues and nobody comes out from the wings to help you. Oh that was so telling! So evocative! I mean—if you want to sleep, okay, but if you want to talk, I really think we could work on some of these issues."

It is two and a half hours from Rome to Amsterdam and then an hour until their nine-hour flight to Minneapolis and Lyle was concerned that due to headwinds or engine malfuntion or whatever, they could easily lose an hour en route and land in Amsterdam too late for the flight to Minneapolis and have to explain their predicament to the Dutch who would put them up in a hostel fifteen miles away in a sleazy neighborhood full of drug addicts. "It's the little things that kill a trip," he told Margie. So she asked the gate agent if perhaps they could get on the earlier Rome-Amsterdam flight leaving in thirty minutes. The agent was a stocky woman in her midfifties and she looked at Margie as if she were a second-grader and not one of the bright second-graders. "That flight is full," she said.

"Maybe there are people on that flight who wouldn't mind switching with us. Couldn't you make an announcement on the PA and ask for volunteers?"

"Sit!" the woman cried. "Enjoy the view! Talk among your friends. Tell each other stories. Sing if you like. We can find you a guitar. You can sit here in the gate area for a few hours and have a beautiful time. Enjoy!"

Margie had put a Placidol in Carl's apple juice and he was still a little twitchy, so she gave him another. He had brought a book to read and then on page thirteen there was a plane crash. He read it in the waiting area and it struck him as more than mere coincidence. Flight 1302—plane crash on page thirteen, second paragraph. Could God make this message any clearer? Panic began to flower in his chest, his pulse throbbed, his heart danced in his chest. Sweat ran down his forehead and into his eyes. He remembered the senior class play, *Our Town*, with Cheryl as Emily Webb, and how overwhelming to see his girl marry George Gibbs and then die and go up the hill to the cemetery, and now he could see himself, holding a black umbrella, sitting next to her. He tried to settle down but heard a grinding sound and turned and saw a small albino child riding a coin-operated whale and Carl put two and two together and clearly he was the Jonah and if he boarded the flight, it would crash.

The agents announced general boarding. He told Margie, "I can't go. I'll have to find a boat." She told him to keep calm. "Take a drink of this liquid protein, see if it doesn't make you feel better," she said, and put it to his lips. She tilted the bottle up and he gulped it down. She had dissolved another Placidol in the drink and five minutes later he was quite manageable. She put him in a wheelchair and rolled him through the door and though he let out a little *meep* as he bumped over the threshold, she got him into seat 37A and herself into 37B and pulled out a pillow for him and a blue blanket that he held against the side of his head. It seemed to comfort him.

"You're just fine, honey, you did fine."

"Are we on the plane?"

"This is the plane."

"This is."

"Yes, all of this is the plane."

"We're going home," he said. She nodded. "Would you like to come back to Rome?"

He shook his head. "Then I'll come back with Ramon." She'd never known a Ramon, but it sounded intriguing. "Oh," he said. He looked out the window at the ground crew moving the jet bridge back. "Do they need help?" he said. And then he closed his eyes and was gone.

She had brought Mr. Keillor's novel *WLT* to read on the plane, and opened it, and when she woke up, the plane still humming along, someone next to her was touching her. It was Lyle, his big black horn-rims slipped down on his nose. "I know we went to Rome," he said, "but did we do what we went there to do?"

"Yes. We put the picture on Gussie's grave."

She pulled her camera out of her purse and scrolled down the display of pictures and punched one and handed the camera to Lyle. "See? We did it. It's right there."

"I'm sorry," he said. "I'm only trying to get it straight in my own mind. I must be going crazy."

"We'll take care of you, so don't worry."

In Amsterdam, the flight to Minneapolis was delayed on account of engine problems, so the pilgrims reconnoitered in a little café. Margie was having serious buyer's remorse about that apartment. She was astonished, thinking back on it, at her own impetuousness. Good God. It was a lovely apartment, but where was her common sense? She'd walked in, taken a quick look around, fallen in love with her own romantic fantasy, and shelled out a half million dollars in less time than she'd take to shop for a silk purse. Daddy used to say, "Only hard work will teach you the value of a dollar," and he was right—money you get for free has no weight or value—and now she was one of those foolish heiresses she used to read about who'd burn through Grandpa's hard-earned wealth in a typhoon of greed and wind up in a welfare hotel in lower Manhattan with needle tracks on their lovely forearms. *Did she really need to own an apartment in Rome, Italy? Who was going to clean it? When was she going to live in it? She'd spent her entire windfall on it and had nothing left over for airfare or maintenance or taxes. . . .* O God, the sheer idiocy of it.

"What's wrong?" said Eloise.

"Nothing. I'm fine."

The vastness of the stupidity of it. Her husband needed her. He was struggling for life under a crushing debt, a man trying to carry a house on his back. And she had floated away in a silver balloon and danced on the dew-beaded buttercups and swanned around in her gossamer gown, adored by hummingbirds and katydids, and feasted on rainbow cake and sunrise tea, and opened her heart to the Milky Way, and whispered intimate thoughts to the wind, and now she was sitting with people who thought they knew her and O God they did not but they were about to know her much too well—she was twelve hours away from Lake Wobegon, and when she rode through the snowy fields and over the hill past the Farmer's Union Grain Terminal and up Main Street past the Sons of Knute and the Chatterbox, the piper would be there, hand out, waiting to be paid.

Services will be held Wednesday at 1 p.m. for Marjorie (Schoppenhorst) Krebsbach, 53, of Lake Wobegon, who died suddenly last Sunday of asphyxiation while taking Holy Communion at Our Lady of Perpetual Responsibility, where her last rites will take place.

She was an English teacher at Lake Wobegon High School, from which she had matriculated in 1974. She had just returned from a trip to Rome with her husband Carl, who survives her, and a party of ten others, including author Gary Keillor, host of *A Prairie Home Companion*.

She is also survived by her children, Carla (Mrs. Bradley) Hoffert of Santa Barbara, California, Carl Jr. of Seattle, Washington, and Cheryl of Minneapolis, her parents, Gottfried (Gus) and Lois Schoppenhorst of Tampa, Florida, and sister Linda of New York City.

Reached at a beach house north of San Francisco where he is vacationing, Mr. Keillor expressed regret at Mrs. Krebsbach's untimely demise but confessed that he was not surprised. Not at all. In the mellifluous baritone voice so familiar to millions, he said, "She tried to fly too high too fast. I may as well tell you the truth—you'll find it out anyway. She glommed into a half million dollars from a dying man in Tulsa and flew to Rome, at my expense, and there she had an affair with a stranger she met in a coffee bar. She slept with him the day before her thirty-fifth wedding anniversary, and then she blew the half million on an apartment. . . .

She stepped out of the café into the busy concourse. A flight to Moscow was announced and another to Seattle. She walked upstream into the mass of humanity and ducked into an alcove where three men sat on the carpeted floor, their laptops plugged in, tapping away, and she called Maria in Rome to ask her to please, please cancel the purchase. If there was a penalty, fine, Margie would pay it, but she had no use for the apartment, the idea was insane. The number rang and rang and then a woman answered in Italian.

"Is Maria Gennaro there?"

The woman said what sounded like a question.

"Maria Gennaro."

"No," the woman said.

"Is she coming back?"

There was something in Italian that sounded like a list, maybe a recipe.

"*Inglese?*"

The woman hung up.

Margie dialed the number again. It rang and rang and then a click and a man's voice, a recorded message in Italian.

She called Paolo's number. Six rings and then a click and a

recorded message. The same man's voice. She wrote down the words as she heard them, and called the number three more times to make sure she got them, and she sat down at a coin-operated computer and fed the words into an Italian-English translation program and some of the words it recognized: *Americano, andare casa*. American, go home.

In the café, the pilgrims were trying to come to grips with the true story of Gussie. Margie had told Eloise and she told the others. She was a little stunned still by the revelations, having given a big speech to the high school kids about the boy of nineteen who left these very halls and shipped over to Italy to fight for his country and died a heroic death, and why should they now hear otherwise? Father Wilmer said he thought the truth should be told, but he would be willing to leave it to a vote. Margie didn't care one way or another. The vote was 11–1 for silence. "You get that?" Irene said to Mr. Keillor. She lowered her big head and gave him a long cold basilisk stare. He was writing as fast as he could in a little brown notebook. He didn't look up. He said that he had not come all this way to hear a story that he now could not repeat. "I told you we shouldn't bring him," she said. Daryl said that by coming along on the trip, he was implying that he would abide by decisions of the group. "No such deal," said Mr. Keillor.

"You want to destroy this town, don't you?" said Evelyn. "You've always wanted to. And now you have a story you can use to make young people cynical and want to leave town and before you know it, we'll have grass growing in the streets."

"I was brought up to tell the truth," he said.

"Why start now?" said Irene. She tried to grab the little note-book out of his hands but he got it away, except for one page that she ripped out. She looked at it. "What does this mean, *a long cold basilisk stare?*"

He looked up, his ballpoint poised over the notebook. "I hope you didn't write down all of that about Suzanne," said Father Wilmer. Keillor looked away. Irene snatched at the notebook again and he whisked it away. "You hand that over or else," she yelled. He shook his head. He stood up and retreated around to behind the chair and she snatched at him and grabbed his left arm and pinched him so hard he yelped. "You are not going to make a book out of this, you big cheater." But he certainly was. He'd heard everything and he was now going to tell anybody who cared to know and, if he was lucky, earn back the money he'd spent on the trip.

On the plane coming home to Minnesota, Margie thought of Gussie, the smiling man from Lake Wobegon, a coward in war and a hero in love. He went to the hotel and spent the night with Miss Gennaro and left with a light heart and was taken away from the earth.

In the Minneapolis airport, she finally came to grips with the fact that she'd been cheated of a half million dollars by a desper-ate woman who had played her cards right and gotten some of her dead father's fortune. She didn't want to think so, but then Paolo called.

"I'm sorry," he said. "This must be very painful for you. And I apologize for the pain. But it wasn't your money, of course. It was hers."

"How did she know about it?"

"She talked to her uncle and asked him for what was coming to her and he cursed her. He cursed Italy and all things Italian and told her he would burn in hell before he would give her one penny. He was furious. He told her that he was giving it all to you instead. An American."

A half million dollars. She had been snookered out of a half million dollars.

"So you were in on the plot, Paolo."

"Actually, my name is Gianni. She asked me to meet you and talk up the real estate. The seduction—that was my idea."

"Did you enjoy it?"

"I did. And so did you."

"And the mother?"

"She died ten years ago. We bought the empty coffin for the occasion and we sold it back to the undertaker."

"And Father Julio?"

"That's Mario. Maria's friend."

"And you are also Maria's friend."

"I am. Our mothers were friends and I've known her since I was in college. We were lovers for a while and then not and now we are again. And again, I am very sorry about all of this. When I agreed to help her, I had no idea you would be such a wonderful woman."

Well, there didn't seem to be anything more to say so she said good-bye.

A fortune in her fingers and it fell out. Simple as that.

Everyone had heard about the eight-year-old girl in Avon who figured out how to go online and trade derivatives, having gotten $600 from her dad's Visa card, and in five days she turned it into

$37,000 and when he asked her how she did it, she showed him the stock market listings in which she saw shapes of animals and wherever the animal's left hind foot was, that's where she put her money. He decided to let her go on investing and in about a month, she was worth a half million dollars. And then she simply lost interest in it. They coaxed her but she was all engrossed in dolls. So her dad tried to employ the left-hind-foot strategy and he lost all the money in three days. *Unbelievable*. That's what everyone thought at the time.

And now Margie had gone and done the same thing.

The day they arrived home, a heavy wet snow fell, good snowball snow, and three projectiles hit them, *wham, wham, bam,* as the two airport vans pulled up in the parking lot of Our Lady of Perpetual Responsibility and the pilgrims got out and stretched and looked at the pile of luggage and were reluctant to disband. It was dark, almost 7:00 P.M. A thin crescent moon like a raccoon's toenail. Clusters of tiny white lights blossoming in trees and a blaze of light beyond from the skating rink on the lake and faint music, an old waltz. From downtown came the grinding sound of Bud's snowplow blade. One by one they stepped up to thank Margie for putting the trip together and she shrugged and said it was nothing and she was glad if they had a good time. "Did *you* have a good time?" said Eloise. Margie said, yes, she had had much *too* good a time. Daryl said he would post all of his pictures on the web and send everyone a link. Father Wilmer invited everyone in to the rectory for coffee and they looked at each other—Should they? Would they? "If I don't go home now, I'm just going to break down bawling," said Evelyn. "I love you guys." Wally nodded. "I feel like I've gotten so close to all of you in the past week," said Evelyn. She dabbed at her eyes. *Hard to believe*, Margie thought, *coming from that crusty old hairy-eyeball Evelyn. She never let on that she liked us at all.* "We've got to get home," said Irene but she made no move to pick up her bag. Clint opened his bag and got out a sack and passed out tubes of toothpaste, called Sprezzatura, which contained clay from Italy. "A little souvenir," he said. Eloise got tears in her eyes. "I wouldn't mind getting some hugs right now," she said, and so they gathered round her and each gave her a squeeze—how could you not?—and she cried a few tears on each one of them, and then, having hugged her, they got going hugging each other which of course took time, you didn't want to leave anybody unhugged. Even Irene was moved. "People are going to ask me what we did," she said, wiping a tear from her eye. "And I won't know what to tell them." "Maybe Mr. Keillor will write it all up," said Margie and they all laughed. "If he does, let's all of us promise each other we will not read that book," said Irene. And they piled their hands together and said "Jinx!" and promised. And then Carl broke it up. He picked up their bags and said, "See you later," and marched toward home, with Margie, through the snow past two figures in puffy coats and big mittens, giant gender-less amoebalike life-forms, flat-footed, silent, who turned out to be Clarence and Arlene.

"How was it?" they said.

"Great," she said. "How was it here?"

"It was so cold," said Clarence, "we had to chop up the piano for firewood and we only got one cord and it was flat." Ha ha ha.

A half million dollars had flowed through her and left not a trace behind, just an enormous vacuum in her heart, and she wanted to tell someone about this terrible loss, but she simply felt numb. As if someone had called and said, "You've won the Bill and Melinda Gates Prize for Classroom Excellence, ma'am. Five hundred thousand dollars. Hold the line for Mr. Gates." And you sat in your kitchen all warm and jittery, thinking about the interviews you'd give. ("I believe we owe our kids the best education we can possibly provide and a teacher has to get herself motivated every single day, every single class, to accomplish that. I could not have done this without the love and support of my husband, Carl, my wonderful children, my colleagues, and my students. Especially my students. Truly, I have learned as much from them as they from me.") And fifteen minutes later, the same person calls back and says, "Sorry, but we got the wrong name. It's not you, it's Marilyn Kropotnik of Lake Winnebago. Our mistake. Bye." She told herself not to think about it, which made her think about it more keenly. The trips they could have taken, all of them, the kids and Carl and her, a happy family, tanned, relaxed, on a luxury liner in the Mediterranean, Athens and Venice, Barcelona, Algiers. She walked through the snowy dark behind her husband, a prisoner returning to the internment camp, the beautiful illusion of the pilgrimage burst. *Why did we go? What was the point of it? What did we get out of all that?* she wondered. Seduced by Paolo and swindled by Maria. *Is there a legal remedy?* No. Nothing that anyone in their right mind would consider for a minute. She had handed a half million dollars over to a virtual stranger without so much as asking for a receipt. Her—a schoolteacher, a college graduate, a mature woman—had made a bonehead mistake that, had any of her children done the same with five *hundred* dollars, she would've been angry. Stupid, stupid, stupid. And when the truth came out—which it would, O gosh yes—Carl would kick her out, her children would turn a cold shoulder, she would have to move to Tampa and live with Mother and Daddy and listen to Limbaugh every day and her mother reciting a novena, clutching the rosary in the bedroom.

They walked into the house, which was cold, and Carl disappeared down the basement stairs to check the furnace. Thirty-four messages on voice mail. She emptied out her suitcase. Threw away the slip of paper with Paolo's phone number. She walked around her house, room to room, touching the cold walls, studying the little details, trying to remember everything for when she would be old and sick and laid up in Florida. The pictures of the kids on the fireplace mantle. The hollows in the old green sofa. The smooth round stones she had collected along the shore the morning after their honeymoon night at Lamb's Resort on Lake Superior. She sat down at the kitchen table. Out on the lake, the old Pontiac sat on the ice for the Sons of Knute Guess the Ice Melt Contest, a dollar a shot, the winner to get a Rototiller, the profits to go to the Shining Star Scholarship Fund to enable some bright young person to go to college and never come back to Lake Wobegon again but to live among the glib and the privileged and make cool contemptuous jokes about the people who brought them up and taught them kindness and perseverance and self-control.

She had always made fun of the Deluded and now she was one

of them. No different from her classmate Charlotte who joined the Church of the Faithful Remnant and spent three years in a compound in Waco, Texas, awaiting the Second Coming, expecting to be Raptured into heaven but it didn't happen and now she's in public relations in Houston.

No different from Cousin Del who found his paradise on a mesa in Arizona where he stopped on vacation and paid $250 for a Hopi Experience—four hours, including sweat lodge, sacred mushrooms, Sun Dance, and a visit to the spirit world with a seventy-nine-year-old Hopi seer named Stanley Sassacaowe who looked Del straight in the eye and told him to heal himself by getting rooted in Mother Earth and thereby he would live to be ninety-six and never know one moment of regret. Del, dehydrated, exhausted from dancing, delusional from the mushrooms, bought the whole story. With Diana fighting him every step of the way, he came home, took early retirement from UPS, sold his home, and moved to the Painted Desert and a mobile-home park called Mesaview.

Diana lasted two months and came home. Del stayed. Every January when a blizzard hit Minnesota and the snow was blowing sideways on CNN, he'd call up Marjorie to ask if she was okay. Yes, she'd say, and how are you?

Oh, fine, he'd say, but you could hear the despair in his voice. He missed the challenge of winter. You can shovel snow, you can't shovel dust. What did he imagine he was going to find down there? Did he think the Hopis were going to initiate him into the Sacred Circle and tell him the Seven Mysteries of the Sand Ceremony? Did he imagine he would be granted the power of time travel and hang out with Jefferson and Adams and also be best pals with his great-grandchildren? Well, it didn't happen. He was a lonely man sitting on the desert and watching the Golf Channel.

And then the phone rang. ASSOCIATED FEDERAL, said the caller ID. It rang three times and then he hollered up the stairs, "Are you going to get it?" and rather than have him answer and hear the whole wretched story from a stranger and then throw her out into a snowbank, she picked up the phone. It was the nice man who had enrolled her in the Family of Depositors and given her the coffee cup and rubber gripper.

"Mrs. Krebsbach, it's Stan Larson, how are you doing today?"

Close to death, Mr. Larson. Thanks for asking. I am going to pour some weed killer into that coffee cup you gave me and add hot water and drink it down and walk out in the snow and lie down and die a painful death in approximately twenty minutes, according to what I've read online about poisons.

"Glad to hear it. I'm just checking in with you about that money transfer you ordered the other day—were you wanting us to go ahead with that or should we wait awhile longer?"

"What are you saying, Mr. Larson?"

"Well, I just wasn't sure what you wanted. You told us to wire the five hundred thousand to that bank in Rome but you didn't give us a delivery date, so I was just waiting here for further instructions. Better safe than sorry. I hope I didn't misunderstand."

"You have not wired the money to Rome?"

"Nope. The bank there has sent me a couple dozen sort of terse e-mails asking about it but you didn't tell me when you wanted it to go so I'm just sitting tight and waiting for the green light."

She felt a big silent *whoosh* of the planets realigning themselves into orbit around the Sun rather than Uranus and the tides moving on schedule and the rivers flowing downstream, as originally planned.

"It's none of my business, of course, and I realize that, but it's a large amount of money, don't you know, and I didn't want to send it until I got confirmation from you. So—I mean, if you want me to, I got it all drawn up here, I can send it in two minutes."

"Please don't," she said.

"Don't?"

"Don't."

"Okay then. I'll just rip up that transfer then and you have yourself a good evening."

He was a true Minnesotan. It was in his voice, the droopy vowels, the nasal twang. Good old Minnesota hesitation—that sheeplike Waiting Around for Further Instructions tendency that she despaired of in her students—had saved her from her own foolishness.

She told him to wire $50,000 and to send a message: "Dear Maria, I don't want the apartment, thank you, but the experience was invaluable. Best wishes, Marjorie."

She wasn't due back at school until Wednesday but she went in on Tuesday and Mr. Halvorson was on the loudspeakers with morning announcements, ratcheting on about students parking their cars in spaces not meant for students as if it were a threat to national security and three freshman boys were hauled in by

Mr. DeWin who'd caught them peeking through a vent into the girls' shower room.

"They have magazines for that, you know," Doris said. "Or you could look at statues." And then she saw her. . . . "Margie!" she cried. "Welcome home! How was Italy?"

Italy was good. Everyone had a good time.

How was the weather?

It rained some but that was okay.

Did you meet the Gennaro woman?

Yes, indeed.

And how was that? All you expected? Or sort of a letdown?

More than I expected. Much more. I'll tell you all about it tomorrow but now I have to get home and fix lunch for Carl.

How's Carl?

He's fine too.

She walked home in the dusk, lights on at the Diener home, the Sorgens, the Muellers and Soderbergs and Demarets, the Munches. A winter sunset of pink and purple and gold and platinum. On the sidewalk near church was a stretch of "cat ice" like what she remembered as a kid, ice that had melted underneath to make a thin shelf that when you step on it, it shatters with a sound like breaking glass and the pieces go skittering along the ice shelf. The wonderful feeling when you find a patch of cat ice that no other kid has stomped on and the simple giddy pleasure of destruction is all yours. This sheet was enormous, twenty feet long and six feet wide, and when she put her right foot on it, lightly, to test it, she could see the scuffed oxfords and the kneesocks of her girlhood, the blue pleated skirt of her innocent days—she

hesitated for a delicious few seconds and then stomped the length
of it and kicked the bigger pieces clattering like tin plates into the
street. She stopped at the Chatterbox and Dorothy brought out a
slice of apple pie with cheese and chopped jalapeno peppers in it,
and a cup of coffee. She said Darlene was sick and she rolled her
eyes—"sick" meant depressed. The poor woman had met a man
named Frank through Craigslist and now he seemed to be stalk-
ing her. Cliff had put the Mercantile up for sale (again).

SOLID RETAIL OPP'T'Y: 8,000 sq.ft. clothing and notions
outlet in hist. bldg. w. loyal customer base. Excellent investment for motivated self-starter.

"The poor man is angry because he can't deal with computer
inventory. It's a shame he never had kids. They could've explained
it to him. But Cliff was married to the store. So I don't know."
Cliff was a case. He used hairspray every morning to stiffen his
wispy blondish hair so he could comb it up into a high hair edi-
fice, like a dome made of spun sugar. He was never meant for
retail sales. Meant to be a great dancer and lover. But God forgot
to plant him in Las Vegas.

She figured Carl could finish the Ladderman house by spring,
what with the infusion of all that cash into Krebsbach Construction, and she could donate the house to Thanatopsis on condition
they drop that ugly name and become the Lake Wobegon Wom-
en's Club. A quiet retreat on the southern shore for the good ladies of town to come and sit, read a book, take a nap, write in your
journal. No cell phones, please. No wireless. No music, thank you

very much. A place where you can hear yourself think. No fund-raising, no community projects, no planning meetings.

Nobody will try to harass you into good works. Just come and look out on the lake and contemplate your life and hope to see through your children's hands waving wildly in your face to the Larger Meaning beyond, assuming there is one. Or if not, then remember the Beautiful Moments behind you.

That evening, over chili and grilled cheese sandwiches, she told Carl that Norbert Norlander had left her a large sum of money in his will and that it was in a savings bank in St. Cloud and should be enough to rescue them from bankruptcy.

"You just found out about this?"

Yes, she said.

He was stunned. He didn't laugh, he didn't cry, he got up and walked to the window and stood there, looking out at the street, absorbing the news slowly, and then came back to the table and finished his supper. "That's good news," he said, at last.

"You're a good man, you deserve some good news."

That night, they lay in bed in the dark and she asked him to rub her back. She lay on her side, back to him, and he rubbed her shoulders and neck and pressed his thumbs along the length of her spine and caressed her butt. He slid up close to her, spooned behind her, his left arm under her head and his right arm around her breasts, his face alongside her neck, his breathing slow and steady.

"Are you happy?" he said.

She said she was, knowing from experience that when your lover asks you if you're happy, you shouldn't wait too long to answer. If you think about it and do the math, count your bless-ings, assess your griefs, come up with a projection, an adjusted net total, he will be hurt and after ten seconds he'll ask what's wrong and when you say, Nothing, he'll say, Yes, something is wrong, terribly wrong, and he'll go veering off into horrible Minnesota self-accusation—*I've failed you. I am a bad husband, a lousy lover, a failure as a father, a discredit to my race. I deserve to be dragged through the dirt and hurled into outer darkness*—so she said, "Yes."

"Are you really?"

And she was. At that moment she was. He fell asleep in her happiness and gently she extricated herself from his arms and padded downstairs. There was a full moon and the snowy lawns of Lake Wobegon glimmered in the dark. A man in a white leather jacket trimmed with fur who for a moment she imagined was Gussie walked down the street. He walked with a long stride for one who was walking on ice and his head was up and he appeared to be singing.

EPILOGUE

The story done, the pilgrims gone
Back across the Atlantic ocean
To shaded street and house and lawn,
Familiar objects of devotion,
And yet, nearby the Pantheon,
Walks Marjorie Krebsbach here and there,
Wearing white, her locomotion
Undetected in the crowded square,
The buses and the packed cafés.
She drifts by, her dark hair
Tied in a coral clip, amazed
Still by the perpetual ordinary
Yik-yak of Italian days,
The usual fare and the customary
Rattle and hum of things,
The coffee and chocolate, and rosemary
And oregano and thyme seasonings
Of that enormous pizza that the waiter

With the long nose and sweet smile brings
To the tourists. It is the liberator
Of Rome—Gussie, twenty-three—
Permitted by his Creator
To fly the underworld and be
Mortal for one week of the year.
He smiles at her: "Marjorie,
Welcome. What brings you here?"
"To find love," she replies.
"I died for love, my dear."
"I know."
"It was a surprise,
Of course. I was enjoying a paradise
Of passion, her lips, her warm thighs,
And what I'd been led to think was a vice
Was rather delicious. Then good-bye
And out the door. The patch of ice
Was there. I slipped and my
Feet flew up, my head hit the ground,
And I proceeded to die,
And now I lie beneath a burial mound.
And in honesty I must admit
That in sixty years I haven't found
A reason for my early exit
Other than pure divine comedy.
Would you care for chocolate?"
"Why yes, I would," said she.
He broke a Hershey bar in two.

"Remember a farmer named Ivar Quie?"
He said, "A bachelor too.
An old Norwegian, cold and sour,
Who married late and who
Carved gargoyles of horrific power
To put all rivals to flight,
Meanwhile Alison, his spring flower,
Put her red dress on and bright
Jewels and rouged her face aglow
And went a-dancing one night
In town, where he refused to go.
She was the beauty of that town—
Him they did not care to know
With his red eyes and wooden frown.
They knew his ferocious jealousy
And when in her red gown
She laughed and made free
With her conversation, they knew
Enough to carefully
Dance a polka or two
With her. Never a waltz. But one
Night a man who was new
In town danced with Alison,
Not seeing, at the window, Ivar's face
As he turned, dashed home for his gun.
The train whistle blew and he raced
It to the crossing and came close
But finished in second place

And for years thereafter his ghost
Followed her from café to hotel
To bedrooms coast-to-coast
And suffering the pangs of hell
Whenever she was kissed
Or sung to or touched or fell
Into someone's arms, he raised his fist
And screeched his fiery breath.
I am not St. John the Evangelist
Nor steeped in wisdom, not yet,
But I know this to be true:
Either we love or we die a living death.
We take one or the other avenue.
And I took one, which I do not regret,
And recommend it to you."
"I was cheated—" Margie began to cry.
"Life has slipped through my hands.
What can I do?" "So was I,
Cheated of life, but here's your chance
To make your way anew
And restore your lost romance."
She said, "Tell me what to do."
"Love can only be restored
By practicing love. The daily labor
Of love—offering it to the Lord
And to yourself and to your neighbor."
And then he smiled and pointed toward
The blue sky. "Everything you need

To know, you know already.
I wish you well. Godspeed.
God give you a keen eye and steady
Heart." And he waved and walked on
Into the crowd around the Pantheon,
Past the man reading a book over his spaghetti,
Wearing a shirt, LAKE WOBEGON.

Mr. Keillor studied the poem, sipping his coffee at the counter of the Chatterbox as Darlene passed by with a fresh pot. "Warm that up for you?" she said. "No thanks," he said, by which he meant "Yes, please," and so she warmed it up for him. *Thanks.* He thought about maybe inserting himself in the poem as the stranger who dances with Alison and drives her jealous husband to suicide but decided not to, nor change the story of Margie and make himself Paolo—it wouldn't work. In his youth he had written a few stories in which a tall dark woman was in love with him and called him "Sweet darling" and whispered "Touch me, touch me" and told him that he drove her to frenzies of longing and when his sister found the story she screamed with delight and read it aloud to her friends and they were convulsed with laughter. So he wrote a story about his sister in which she was riding her bike home as fast as she could to tell Mother that he was kissing a girl and was struck by a garbage truck and up to heaven she went, and there was Jesus. He said, "How was your trip up?" and she said, "Jesus, my brother tells lies and gets away with murder and I personally think you ought to give him a bad disease, to show him he can't get away with that stuff. I just don't understand how he can get away with everything and I've been good all my life and I wind up getting mashed by a truck. Why? Where is the justice in that?" And Jesus puts His arm around her and says, "You're in heaven. Enjoy yourself." And she says, "I just want to know why he gets everything his way and there I am crushed under a truck full of tin cans and coffee grounds and potato peelings. It's not right!" And she stamps her foot, and suddenly she isn't in heaven anymore. She's in a waiting room. No windows, no magazines. People in the next room sobbing. It's hell. No lake of fire but every ten years a hoofy man with red feathers comes out and says, "It'll be just a few more minutes." It was a blasphemous story, as she pointed out to him when she found it, and she told him he had turned away from God and would never find his way back, and fifty years later he was still thinking that maybe she was right.

It was nine o'clock on a Tuesday morning and he was an hour late for breakfast at his mother's house and still he sat as the time drifted away. And then in came Carl and Margie and took off their coats and went back and sat in a booth by the window. She wore a nice long black coat, like a heroine in a Tolstoy novel, and he wore his old gray car coat. They sat across the table from each other and she looked into his face and he gazed out the window. Why doesn't he turn toward her and take her hand and kiss it?

He's in love with her. You can see it in his face. He has the stupid look of a man in love. Women in love look beatific as if Botticelli had painted them. Men in love look as if someone clubbed them with a baseball bat. He's in love but he should talk to her and tell her that we do have the power to remake our days into gardens of delight, and though we were raised to believe in adversity, now we're older and we don't have to think that anymore.

So you're ambivalent. So is everyone else. Is it a bad thing? Yes and no. We all contain contradictory feelings. But touch her arm and feel the little hairs tremble as your skin brushes against them. The goodness of life is all around you, even in April when the snow is slow to melt.

And now, rising from the stool, he tries to catch Margie's eye to say, *Hi, it's me. Remember? You introduced me at Thanatopsis. We went to Rome.* But she is gazing at her husband the carpenter. He made love to her last night so tenderly. A miracle of the ordinary kind. Nature leads us in that direction even after it no longer has use for our sperm; for there is still the urge to make life beautiful. So that is why they don't speak, because there is nothing more to be said. And Mr. Keillor now realizes that he has left his billfold, his car keys, his cell phone, and his cash in some other pocket than any in these jeans or this coat. They are gone. He has no memory of having seen them lately. He checks again and again. Nothing. Darlene watches from inside the servers' window in the kitchen. He must now ask Darlene to put it on his account and then hike up the hill to Mother's and try to figure it out from there, how he'll get back to St. Paul before three o'clock when he is supposed to do something, he can't remember what.

READ MORE OF THE CLEVERLY HILARIOUS
GARRISON KEILLOR IN VIKING AND PENGUIN BOOKS

Good Poems, American Places
Garrison Keillor introduces another inspiring collection by a range of poets, some beloved favorites and others brash unknowns, organized by regions of America.
Coming from Viking in April 2011   *ISBN 978-0-670-02254-0*

Liberty
Keillor's most ribald Lake Wobegon novel yet is set in a spectacular Fourth of July celebration. The Chairman of the Fourth, Clint Bunsen, is in the midst of an identity crisis, and he finds solace in the arms of Angelica Pflame, the young beauty who marched as Liberty in last year's parade. Should he remain in Lake Wobegon with his stoical wife or fly to California with Angelica?   *ISBN 978-0-14-311611-0*

Pontoon
Replete with a bowling ball urn, a hot-air balloon, a flying Elvis, and, most important, Wally's pontoon boat, *Pontoon* is a cause for celebration. As the wedding of the decade approaches the good-loving people of Lake Wobegon do what they do best: drive each other slightly crazy.   *ISBN 978-0-14-311410-9*

Lake Wobegon Summer, 1956
With his trademark gift for treading "a line delicate as a cobweb between satire and sentiment" (*The Cleveland Plain Dealer*), Garrison Keillor captures postwar America and delivers an unforgettable comedy about a writer coming of age in the rural Midwest.   *ISBN 978-0-14-200093-9*

Wobegon Boy
John Tollefson leaves Lake Wobegon to manage a public radio station at a college for academically challenged children of financially gifted parents in upstate New York. Though he makes a pleasant bachelor life for himself, he feels rootless, restless, with nothing at stake. Can a romance with a historian named Alida Freeman give his life the nobility it lacks?   *ISBN 978-0-14-027478-3*

AND DON'T MISS OTHER GREAT WORKS BY GARRISON KEILLOR:

The Book of Guys
ISBN 978-0-14-023372-8

Good Poems
ISBN 978-0-14-200344-2

Good Poems for Hard Times
ISBN 978-0-14-303767-5

Happy to Be Here
ISBN 978-0-14-013182-6

Homegrown Democrat
ISBN 978-0-14-303768-2

Leaving Home
ISBN 978-0-14-013160-4

Lake Wobegon Days
ISBN 978-0-14-013161-1

Love Me
ISBN 978-0-14-200499-9

We Are Still Married
ISBN 978-0-14-013156-7

WLT
ISBN 978-0-14-010380-9

PENGUIN
BOOKS